Rose on the Snow

A Maryland Love Story

A NOVEL BY

Jack Wallace

PublishAmerica
Baltimore

© 2005 by Jack Wallace.
All rights reserved. No part of this book may be reproduced, stored in a retrieval system or transmitted in any form or by any means without the prior written permission of the publishers, except by a reviewer who may quote brief passages in a review to be printed in a newspaper, magazine or journal.

First printing

This is a work of fiction, and all characters depicted herein have no relationship to anyone, past or present, living or dead.

ISBN: 1-4137-5209-8
PUBLISHED BY PUBLISHAMERICA, LLLP
www.publishamerica.com
Baltimore

Printed in the United States of America

*This book is dedicated to
Dr. Lynn Einbinder, MD,
an outstanding medical doctor who,
through her skills and dedication,
gave me enough time
to relate this gentle love story.*

Rose on the Snow

CHAPTER 1

Alex awoke from his deep sleep feeling fully refreshed and ready to take on the toughest actions that the world could throw at him. He had promised himself that he would sleep later this week, but his long-established habit of awakening at seven a.m. had created some sort of natural alarm clock deep inside of him that forced him to awaken at his usual time.

Contented, he just lay there in the big, queen-sized, motel bed, idly listening to the pleasant roar of the ocean as it relentlessly pounded its surf onto the beach outside of their bedroom. The nosy sun peeked through the tightly drawn drapes and left behind abstract almost Dali-like shapes on the far wall.

His healthy male emotions rose to his consciousness, as he thought back over the wild and satisfying lovemaking that he and Lila had enjoyed during the previous evening. How they were locked in a frantic rhythm as old as creation itself, completely removed from everything that existed in the world, except each other, their bodies, and the magnifying pleasure that they were experiencing, as they attempted to reach the emotional height where they could grab the momentary rush of pleasure that a successful act of coitus made possible. After they achieved that temporary peak of related joy, they fell apart from each other, gasping for breath. Satisfied, but still madly in love with each other.

He propped his head up with his forearm and looked over at his beautiful Lila. She was breathing in the shallow, regular breath of deep sleep. Her beautiful hazel eyes under full, dark eyebrows were closed in peaceful sleep. Her flawless, velvety olive complexion seemed to glow from the mutually returned love that each felt for the other, and her long, shiny, brunette hair was scattered around the white pillowcase like a dusty halo. Deep purple smudges, the telltale badge of recent sexual activity, were etched below her eyes, and her full lips were slightly parted as she breathed in the contentment of deep sleep.

He glanced down at her naked body, partially covered by the bed sheet, and his male emotions, as always when he glimpsed her nakedness, rose to the point where he leaned over to kiss her gently. He was determined that she would rest this week to speed up her recovery from the grief of Ida's death.

As soon as he softly kissed her, her beautiful hazel eyes opened, and she smiled into his own eyes with her usual look that said a thousand things to him without saying a single word. She pulled him to her to complete an entirely passionate kiss.

"Honey," she said, "I was just having the most wonderful dream about you and I, and then you made it real with that gentle kiss. God, what a fantastic night we had. It was the best ever. You're becoming better the longer we're married. I'm as hungry as a team of Clydesdales. Can we get some breakfast soon? I must have burned up over a thousand calories last night."

Alex, fondly amused at the way statements seemed to tumble out of Lila when she was happy, replied, "Sure, honey, let me go to the bathroom first, and then because it takes you longer to dress than me, you take a shower first."

Alex arose and entered the adjoining bathroom. After relieving himself, he turned on the shower, and adjusted its warmth by extending his open hand under it until he was satisfied that it would be comfortable for Lila.

He called out to Lila, "OK, sweetheart, it's all ready."

Lila entered the shower and rapidly applied soap to a washcloth. Quickly scrubbing down her slim body, she rinsed off the sudsy residue, shut off the flow of water, and stepped out of the shower stall.

She first dried off her long dark hair, then fashioned a kind of turban around it. Then she dried off her body with another towel, and with the instinctive modesty of all women, even in front of their husbands, created a sarong by tucking the top edge of it under another part. She applied a roll-on, underarm deodorant, and applied the light, pleasant, fragrant cologne that Alex always associated with her. She rapidly brushed her teeth, then stepped back out into the bedroom.

"OK, sport," she said, "it's all yours."

Alex turned off the cable TV news program that he had been idly watching while he waited for Lila to finish, arose from his seat on the side of the bed, and reentered the bathroom.

He turned the shower back on, adjusted it to suit himself and stepped under its warm canopy. The pulsating jets of warmth felt good on his muscles which were stiff from deep almost motionless sleep. He was tempted to linger under its soothing comfort, but since Lila had said that she was starved, decided against it.

Rapidly completing his shower, he stopped its flow, stepped out and quickly dried off his body.

Fashioning a bench by dropping the lid of the commode, he sat down and slipped into a pair of jockey-type briefs that he had brought with him into the bathroom. He rolled on some underarm deodorant from Lila's container, applied lather to his face, and rapidly shaved. He patted on a light-smelling aftershave, cleaned his teeth, and stepped back into the bedroom.

Because of the narrow confines of the room, he was forced to slide around Lila, who was brushing her long shiny hair. In doing so, he kissed her on the cheek, and patted her rear end, saying, "Honey, you have absolutely got the best-looking ass in the entire world."

Lila, who was dressed in a pair of yellow linen shorts that fit her like a well-tailored glove and a matching light cotton tee shirt that emphasized her magnificent feminine beauty, giggled in her unique musical manner and replied, "Listen, buster, if you don't stop tearing off pieces of it, there won't be any left for your golden years."

Then they both laughed at the double meaning—an entirely intimate joke between two married individuals who were totally comfortable with each other.

Alex reached into the bureau drawer and pulled out a pair of khaki shorts and a white polo shirt. Sitting on the side of the bed, he quickly donned them, and slid his feet into a pair of docksiders, without any socks. He then brushed his damp hair with Lila's brush and said, "OK, Mrs. Baxter, I'm ready whenever you are."

Lila was applying lipstick, which was generally the only makeup that she wore. She took a speculative look at herself in the mirror, turned sideways and looked again. Satisfied with the reflected image, she turned and opened the door and stepped out into the brilliant sunlit day, blinking briefly after the cool dimness of their bedroom. Alex locked the door behind them and they casually strolled, holding hands, over to the motel coffee shop.

They were lucky enough to locate a table close to one of the large picture windows that overlooked the sunny beach. Already, despite the early hour, the cult of sunworshippers was gathering to pay homage to its pagan God. Individuals were anointing their bodies with oils and others were basting their bodies with sunscreen as they prepared themselves for their annual ritual of lying for hours under the scorching sun, rotating their bodies like roasts on a rotisserie to obtain that genuine Ocean City suntan with which to impress their friends and relatives back home.

A deeply tanned, fresh-faced young waitress, who seemed to be a college student working on a summer job, took their food orders and quickly brought their juice and coffee.

Alex swallowed his orange juice and felt its chill coursing its way down into his stomach. He took a sip of his coffee and let his eyes wander all over the half-filled room of vacationers busily eating their first meal of the day.

His glance fell on a middle-aged couple, the female half of which was trying to seem like she wasn't staring at them, but really wasn't having too much success. She was making comments to her husband, who would smile, but never lift his head from the breakfast that he was eating. Finally, when the couple finished eating, her husband went across the room to the cashier to pay their check.

She stopped by their table and remarked to Lila, "Excuse me, my dear. May I tell you that you look positively radiant? You just seem to glow with contentment."

Lila, who was engaged in an animated, bubbly conversation with Alex, looked up and said, "Why thank you so very much," and put her left hand on top of Alex's, adding, "I've never been so completely happy in my entire life."

Noting Lila's wedding rings, the woman asked, "Are you on your honeymoon?"

Lila giggled in her musical way and replied, "Goodness no. We've been married for three wonderful years. They've sped by so quickly that it just seems like we were married recently. I was just lucky enough to meet the right man and fall head over heels in love with him, and I've been happy ever since."

The woman continued, "Well you both make such a beautiful couple together, and are so obviously in love with each other, that looking at the two of you together makes me feel like it's April again. May I wish you both a lifetime of the magnificent love that you share today?" With that, she left and walked across the room to her husband, who was waiting at the entrance, and they both stepped out into the brilliant sunlit day.

Lila leaned over to Alex and whispered, "Wasn't that nice of her? Do you think that she believed that I'm pregnant?"

Amused, since that was something that they both desired, Alex replied, "Are you?"

Her giggle, tinkled out musically as she replied, "Well I might very well be, from all the frantic carrying on we did last night. It was really fantastic, honey. Do I need a reservation for a repeat performance?"

Alex replied with mock gravity, "Well, madam, I'll give you the first vacancy on my waiting list."

With that, the young waitress brought them their food orders, and they fell to eating like a couple of starving wolves. After they drained their refilled coffee cups, Alex asked her, "What do you want to do today, sweetheart?"

"Well, tonight I want to have dinner at the Pit. I've heard that the food there is just marvelous."

The Pit was a newly opened, trendy, dress-up Ocean City steak house. Its main feature was a waiter dramatically rolling up a cart of steaks nested on a bed of ice and allowing each customer to select their own, then branding it with the first initial of the customer with a skewer-like lettering device heated in a Sterno flame. That particular marketing device seemed to be successful, because the average waiting time to sit down to dinner was a half an hour. It also increased the size of the average check, because most customers enjoyed several drinks while they were waiting in the lounge.

Lila had a sudden brainstorm. "Honey, how about the two of us renting a couple of bikes and riding up toward the Delaware line to see how Ocean City has changed since the last time that we were here?"

Alex, who hadn't ridden a bike since he was a freshman in high school, groaned internally, but never denying his Lila anything that she really wanted, reluctantly agreed.

After Alex left a tip for the young waitress and paid their check, they drove a short distance down the busy Coastal Highway and parked their car in a municipal parking lot. They walked down the boardwalk to a bike rental store and rented two bikes, leaving one of Alex's credit cards as a security deposit.

Awkwardly at first, since neither had ridden a bike in years, they slowly pedaled up the shoulder of the highway looking at the elaborate condominium towers that seemed to have sprung directly from the sand like some modern phoenix, and the townhouse developments that spread across the beachfront like some kind of ground cover.

Twenty minutes later, perspiring freely and well short of their objective, they stopped at a roadside root beer stand for a cold drink and to rest their weary legs, long unused to the exercise of bike riding.

Lila remarked, "Honey, I really don't believe that this was one of my best ideas. Let's sit here under this umbrella until we catch our breath and cool down and then take the bikes back. We can catch the boardwalk tram in front of the bike shop and ride downtown in comfort to look at some of the boardwalk junk shops."

They crossed over Coastal Highway at the next traffic light and painfully pedaled back to where their car was parked. After gratefully dismounting, they wheeled the bikes back to the bike store, where they redeemed Alex's credit card.

Alex flagged down the boardwalk tram, which was simply a tractor on large rubber tires towing several covered open-air cars behind, and rode down almost to the inlet, comfortably chatting and enjoying the cool ocean breezes.

The inlet was a sort of deep ditch carved out of the sand by some long-forgotten hurricane. It connected the Atlantic Ocean with the shallow bay that ran almost to the end of the gigantic sand bar that comprised Ocean City, and aided materially in the economic development of the ocean resort.

As soon as they alighted from the tram, their senses were assaulted by a multitude of sensory impressions. These included the smell of popping corn, cooking oils, hamburgers grilling, onions frying, flashing colored lights, and the tinny, hurdy-gurdy music of carousel calliopes calling out to children to come to ride.

Lila said, "Look, honey, Billi's Boardwalk Fries."

Alex purchased two large cups of the greasy treats and liberally doused them with vinegar from the cruet on the counter, adding salt from the large aluminum shaker alongside of it. The custom of sprinkling vinegar on French fries is a long-established Maryland tradition, like that of eating sauerkraut with turkey dinners, and trying to bite into those concrete-like pieces of over-baked dough called Maryland beaten biscuits.

They slowly strolled up the boardwalk, nibbling at their artery-clogging treats, peeking into the souvenir shops, and laughing at the ridiculous messages silk-screened onto a rainbow of brightly colored tee shirts, and the equally provocative messages imprinted onto bumper stickers.

Lila bought a box of salt water taffy for the girls in her office, since, among Marylanders, it is almost unheard of not to bring back taffy after a vacation in

OC. At another store, she purchased the wooden carving of a bearded, grizzled, old, peg-legged sea captain. She said that it reminded her of her boss, Max.

Farther up the boardwalk, they stopped for lunch at a boardwalk eatery that had several tables set outdoors in the manner of a French sidewalk café. Lila had a bowl of crab soup, and Alex had a crab cake sandwich. Both of those dishes were considered to be excellent Maryland seafood dishes. Lila controlled her sweet tooth with a dish of black and white soft serve ice cream.

They sat there after lunch, leaning against each other, and enjoying the passing parade of vacationers in front of them, and the many sensory impressions that make Ocean City a unique place to vacation.

After a while, Lila said, "Let's go back to the room and a take a nap before dinner tonight. I'm really pooped from that crazy bike ride and that wonderful, frantic activity that you put me through last night. Trying to get pregnant is a whole lot of fun. Exhausting, but boy the fireworks are fantastic. You're a skilled musical conductor, honey. You make my body sing like a violin."

Alex replied, "Baby, it always takes two to tango. Music from a violin can be so sweet that it will bring you to the highest emotional heights, or it can be so lousy that you get rid of that violin and get a new one as soon as you can. Your violin always gets me so high that I get dizzy from the thin air up there. I'm always ready for another concerto from you."

Lila giggled musically and said, "Well, Mr. Baxter, I personally enjoy rock and roll or country and western like I'm back in the saddle again."

Thoroughly contented with each other, they flagged down the tram and rode back up to where their car was parked with Lila's head comfortably on Alex's shoulder and his arm protectively around her.

Back in their room, excited by each other's nakedness, as always, they made love again, but not as frantically as the previous evening, and fell asleep in each other's arms, secure in their enormous love for each other.

CHAPTER 2

The saga of Lila and Alex had begun about four years earlier.

Alex was a freelance writer of some skill. He was working on an article assigned by the *American Eagle Monthly*. This was a nationally circulated periodical with a reading audience of young, successful overachievers, and was considered to be a strong conservative bastion. Its articles were written in a crisp, no-nonsense manner, and it believed that it had a strong influence in shaping the political opinions of its young readership.

Rick Kelly, the stories editor with whom Alex had worked since he had submitted his first article on speculation, had called him and said that they needed his completed copy by the sixth of the next month. He also said that if they liked it, because Alex always seemed to be able to grasp their style of writing, there was a strong possibility that they might retain him to write a series along the same vein. And that such a series would get the magazine's strong promotion and would be under Alex's personal byline.

With so much at stake, Alex's writing ability seemed to grind to a halt, and he was afflicted with a thought-paralyzing condition known among writers as writer's block.

No matter how hard he tried, or whatever approach he used, he just couldn't seem to find a central line of continuity with which to hold his thoughts together. Finally, with utter frustration, he shut down his PC and called out to his seven-year-old Pembroke Welsh corgi. "Come on, Bear, let's take a walk."

Bear, who was lying alongside Alex taking one of his many daily naps, immediately snapped awake at the magic word W-A-L-K, and began to prance around Alex's feet and bark excitedly as Alex fastened the retractable lead to his collar.

When Alex opened the door to his apartment, Bear eagerly pulled Alex down the steps to the entry door. He stopped only because the door was closed. When Alex pushed the door open, Bear immediately lifted his rear leg and let loose a stream of amber-colored liquid against the nearest bush. Then he kicked back his entire rear end several times in utter joy, and smiled a doggy grin of completely satisfied relief.

Alex always smiled at Bear's amusing antics and often wondered why dogs performed that ritual. He assumed that it was a long-forgotten territorial marking instinct left over from the dark ages before man discovered the value of canines, and before they were finally domesticated to become such wonderful companions and working partners of the human species.

They slowly walked down the sidewalk that adjoined the service road that encircled the sixteen buildings that comprised the complex. The complex itself was a pleasant, well-maintained place and was managed by the owner, who was often seen picking up bits of trash to keep the grounds neat and clean.

When they arrived at the sanded, fenced-in area that had been reserved as a dog comfort station, Bear ejected a cigar-shaped object from his rear, which Alex picked up with some paper towels that he had brought with him for that purpose. Holding the smelly object as far from him as possible, he deposited it in one of the half-filled covered cans that had been provided.

The trip back was much the same. Bear left his personal calling card on certain bushes and totally ignored others along the way.

As they neared their own building, Alex saw what he considered to be a beautiful sight. He was looking at a beautifully shaped female rear end, clad in a light green mini skirt, leaning into the trunk of an ancient Japanese import automobile.

Alex had long been an admirer of the female posterior and, like an art collector evaluating an old El Greco oil painting, or a horse fancier admiring a beautiful Arabian stallion, he had an unwritten scale to evaluate a female's posterior beauty. On a scale of 1 to 10, he evaluated that one as at least 10 1/2 or even higher.

When they drew even with the car, the other half of the female body emerged from under the trunk lid, and he found himself staring directly into the stunning hazel eyes of the most beautiful woman that he had ever seen.

She had long, dark, shiny hair, which was parted in the middle, and which hung straight on both sides of her face to maybe six or eight inches below her neckline. Her beautiful, well-shaped eyes were an unusual shade of hazel, and were set under full dark eyebrows. Her dark olive complexion was enhanced by a tee shirt that matched the color of her skirt. The profile of the tee shirt left no doubt in Alex's mind about the beauty hidden beneath its light weaving. She had a strong resemblance to that beautiful movie actress who had tragically drowned off the coast of California a couple of years ago. What was her name? She was lifting a bag of groceries from the deck of her trunk.

Alex was suddenly like a high school boy who had a secret crush on a girl, and who had suddenly met her in the school hallway. Like that boy, he suddenly found it difficult to breathe and to talk to her.

He felt himself blushing, which was silly, and he managed to blurt out, "Can I help you with that bag?"

She answered, looking deeply into his eyes, "No, I can manage, but thank you very much."

Alex stood there, embarrassed, not knowing what to say.

When she looked down at Bear, she put her grocery bag back down on her trunk deck and reached down to scratch him behind his ears.

Bear, enjoying the attention, sat down and let the nice-smelling female human make a fuss over him.

"My, what a beautiful dog. What breed is he?"

"He's a Pembroke Welsh corgi. That breed that is native to Wales, and is used to herd sheep in all kinds of weather, which is why they have such heavy, shaggy coats of fur. They're smart as hell and are entirely loyal to the one human that they believe they own. They're raised without tails in Wales, like the Manx cat is raised on the Isle of Man. There's another corgi with a tail, called the Cardigan corgi. Although their configurations are similar, an entirely different breeding line was used in their development."

"Poor little dog with no tail to wag," she remarked. "How does he tell you that he loves you?"

"He finds a lot of ways to express his love. We've been good friends for seven years. He really is my best buddy," Alex replied.

"Isn't that the breed that the Queen of England fancies?" she asked.

"Yes, she does have a kennel full of them. I call him Bear. That's short for his call name of Honeybear. His AKC registered name is unpronounceable. His father was a breed finalist at a famous dog show in New York City."

She looked at Alex again with her beautiful eyes and replied, "That was really interesting. I do believe that this is the first time I have ever seen a corgi up close. Well, so long, Bear, I'll be seeing you around here." She picked up her bag of groceries again and slowly walked into the building next to the building where Alex lived.

Alex watched her, and especially her beautiful posterior, until she entered the entrance to her building, feeling a pang of sadness at her leaving. Just before she entered her doorway, she turned and smiled at him, lifting her free arm in a wave, which Alex returned.

Alex thought to himself, *God, she's so beautiful. She must be spoken for.*

Crestfallen, Alex turned to enter his own building, cursing himself for not being aggressive enough to even ask her name. He was essentially a quiet, somewhat shy man who turned to writing as means of expressing his most important opinions and best philosophies. Although he had a dry sense of humor with those he was comfortable with, in real life verbal duels, he would stumble when a return comment was necessary, and ten minutes later, would think of some clever retort that he should have made. He was a far better writer than he was a verbalizer.

One of his single great pleasures was reading the highly accurate technothrillers by a writer of action stories. The novels that he wrote allowed Alex's fantasies to soar, and Alex enjoyed the escape provided by the daring heroes in those stories.

Back in their apartment, Alex curry combed Bear to remove the loose hair from his thick fur. Bear always enjoyed this Saturday morning ritual, because the feel of the brush on his body was like Alex scratching an itch all over it. He assisted Alex by lying on his back with all four legs in the air, while Alex shifted his body to get at some new area.

When he was finished, Alex extracted the clumps of hair from the grooming brush and placed them on a sheet of newsprint, which he rolled up and placed in his trash receptacle. Alex then rewarded him with several doggie treats, and Bear settled down to take what he felt was a well-deserved nap, with his head between his front paws, after such a strenuous morning. The strain of coping in a dog's world was massive, and he needed his rest to just get by in this odd human life in which he was associated.

Alex then turned his PC back on and attempted once again to write his assigned *Eagle* article. He still couldn't get started. He knew exactly what he wanted to say, but he just couldn't find the right tool to start the flow of words from his imagination. It was almost like he was suffering from some trauma that had left him mentally paralyzed. Disgusted with his mental impotence, Alex again shut down his word processor.

He grabbed an apple from the bowl in his kitchen and the front news section of the Baltimore *Sun* from the litter that he had created on his living room floor when he had scanned it earlier that morning. All he could think of was the beautiful girl that he and Bear had met earlier.

He said to Bear, "Now you be a good dog. I'm going down to the pool for a while to clear the cobwebs out of my mind."

Bear just grunted and shifted his sleeping position from his head between his paws, to rolling over with all four paws in the air, and continued his nap. His sleeping that way always tickled Alex's sense of humor. That was a dog's most vulnerable position, and it indicated the deep trust that he had in Alex as his best human.

The pool was set among a stand of old oak trees, and had an adjoining pool house built into the hillside of the complex. On late summer afternoons and in the early twilight, older residents would often gather on its concrete upper deck to gossip, play cards or read. The management had provided several large colorful umbrellas, tables and chairs for their convenience.

Alex positioned a chair so that he could put both feet on the guardrail, and sat down to eat his apple. He looked down into the pool area to see if he recognized anyone down there.

His glance first fell on a group of widows with every gray hair carefully set in place. Well-groomed hair was a fetish with women of all ages. Beauty salons were a focal point for the exchange of gossip, which later fueled the conversations between best girl friends.

The gaggle of widows looked hungrily at men who passed by, and would then discuss him among themselves. They looked like they had all purchased their swimsuits at the same store, because they were all clad in modest, tight-fitting, Spandex garments that revealed they were overweight. The suits left rolls of flesh in the most unlikely parts of their bodies.

He glanced farther down the length of the pool toward a group of younger people. There she was—the girl whom he couldn't get off his mind. The butterflies in his stomach started to perform their aerial acrobatics, and he felt giddy and lightheaded. She was engaged in a lively conversation with some other guy. Alex's unspoken hopes took a severe nosedive, because he assumed that it was her husband or boyfriend with whom she was talking.

Badly depressed, he picked up his newspaper and became deeply engrossed in a feature article about Easter Island in the Pacific Ocean, its culture, residents and the larger-than-life, oddly carved stone figures that lined its beaches.

So engrossed was he, that he failed to notice someone was standing next to him until he heard a musical female voice saying, "Would you mind if I sat down?"

Startled, he looked up to discover the girl whom he had fantasized over since they had first met earlier that morning.

She was wearing a yellow bikini that revealed more of her hidden personal beauty than Alex had visualized previously. It was strategically covered by a short jacket, and the overall effect nudged Alex's healthy libido up another notch.

Despite the squadrons of butterflies now churning in his stomach, Alex managed to blurt out, "Please do."

She sat down gracefully, and extended her hand, saying, "I'm Lulila Taylor. People call me Lila. I live in the next building to you, and I've seen you walking with your beautiful dog. I've wanted to meet you for a long time. When I saw you up here, I decided to come up and introduce myself. I understand that you're a writer and moved in several months ago."

Alex's emotions had now quieted down to the point where he could now carry on a sensible conversation with this Venus. "I'm Alex Baxter. I was going to come down and introduce myself to you, but I saw you talking to that other guy, and thought that he was your husband or boyfriend."

She suddenly giggled and it sounded like musical chimes in Alex's ears. "That was Donnie. He's a gay hairdresser who relates to women as an equal. He's full of gossip. When you want to know something, just ask Donnie. I wanted to know about you, and he filled in several blanks for me. Watch out, he thinks that you're very handsome."

Alex muttered, "He's way out in left field without a glove. I love women, and I especially love their bodies. I don't want to get mixed up in his inability to distinguish genders."

She giggled again. "Well, I'm certainly happy to hear that. I'm a paralegal for Max Weiner," she continued.

Max Weiner was a torts attorney with a large practice in Towson. He had a reputation of being an ethical and capable attorney.

They chatted for a while and somehow they lifted their heads at the same time.

Who can say how it happens, or why it only happens to some people, but they suddenly looked deeply into the eyes of each other and became mesmerized. All that Alex could see was her beautiful hazel eyes, as if he saw them through a tunnel.

They tried to pull their eyes away from each other, but the magnetism that they both felt at that moment forced them to continue to stare into each other's inner being. Unrevealed to them was the fact that they had both fallen head over heels in love, and would be in love forever. It was what the Sicilians called a thunderbolt.

Flustered, they finally stopped staring and sat there for a few minutes, embarrassed and not speaking to each other.

Finally, Alex asked her, "Are you emotionally involved with anyone at present?"

She replied, "Well, I date a lawyer who still lives with his parents in Ruxton. He likes me more than I like him. I only date him to keep from getting rusty. I guess that the right answer to your question is no, I'm not. How about you?"

Alex replied, "I just got through with a bitter divorce where she got custody of most of my money and I got custody of my dog. Two months after we divorced, she married a guy who she had been sleeping with. The last time I saw her, her hair was red, although that could have changed because she changes it with the change of seasons. For that matter, I don't know if she's still married, because her new mate is a tomcat and not a house cat. I guess that you could call me a bachelor once removed."

She laughed at his comments, then said, "I was married once for six months to a man that I believed had everything that I value in a man. That is until I learned that he was lifting skirts all over Towson and finding out what was under them. One of his trophies of the chase had the nerve to call our home and demand money for an abortion. He's still in Baltimore somewhere and still lifting skirts. Some irate husband will fix his wagon someday. He's a loose cannon with a loose zipper."

They both laughed at the vivid but painful descriptions of their ex-spouses.

Alex decided to go for broke and ask the question that had been on his mind since he first saw her earlier. "If I asked you to go to dinner some night, would the answer be yes?"

She hesitated, as if she was trying to make up her mind.

Alex thought to himself, *Dammit, here it comes.*

Finally, she said, "As you know from our brief meeting earlier, I have just finished my grocery shopping. I have two beautiful strip steaks in my freezer that I got at Barker's."

Barker's was a market in Towson that was famous for its prime quality meats.

"Would you like to come to my house for dinner tonight? Do you like twice-baked potatoes?"

Alex said, "I love them. The Arbor here in Towson serves some of the best that I have ever eaten."

Twice-baked potatoes are the supposed creation of a chef in the Deep South, and consist of baked potatoes, scooped out of their jackets and mixed with cheese, bacon chips, onion and mayonnaise, and then returned to their skins and baked a second time.

"What time did you have in mind?"

"Would six p.m. be too early?"

Now thoroughly smitten, Alex said, "That would be great. Can I bring anything?" If she had said four a.m. Alex would have agreed just as quickly.

She said, "Don't bring any wine. I don't drink alcohol. If you'd like, you could bring a six pack of diet colas. Do you have a pen?"

When Alex produced one, she jotted a number down on the margin of his newspaper and said, "If for any reason you can't make it, please give me a call at this number."

Alex carefully tore the number off and placed it in his wallet for safekeeping.

She said, "I had better go up and thaw out the steaks. I have a couple of phone calls to make as well. See you at six."

Alex watched her beautiful body walk up the hill until she disappeared around the corner of her building. He felt an elation stirring within him that he had never, ever felt before. It was a sense that he had finally met someone that he was destined to meet. He looked at his wristwatch. It was 3:15 p.m. He said to himself, "I have time to do it."

He rapidly strode up to where his car was parked and quickly drove to a strip mall in Towson. There he purchased a single long-stem red rose at the florist and a six pack of diet cola at the market on the same property, and drove quickly back to his own complex.

He knelt down beside the now awake Bear and hugged him. "Do you know what? I've got a date with that beautiful girl that we met this morning. I think that she likes me, because she has invited me to her house for dinner. Up close she's even more beautiful than I thought. She came up on the pool house deck to introduce herself. What do you think of your old buddy now?"

Bar didn't fully comprehend what his best human was saying, but he knew that it was good, so he licked Alex about the face with great affection.

Alex placed the rose and colas in his fridge and sat down for a brief time. Bear jumped up beside him and Alex absently scratched his head as he contentedly lay alongside.

As he always did when Alex touched him, Bear grunted with delight because his whole world was centered on Alex. With his instinctive corgi devotion to one individual, he became sad and lonely when Alex wasn't close to him. Alex's touch felt different to him than anybody else's, and he licked Alex's hand with a deep love that was earned by Alex's constant care for his needs.

They sat on the sofa together, with Alex's thoughts centered on Lila and her unique beauty. He had no concept of how appealing that he was to the opposite sex and never thought much about his looks.

He was six feet tall and weighed about 175 pounds. He was quietly confident and self-assured, with brown eyes and shaggy brown hair, which he wore in a medium-long style. He exercised frequently and watched what he ate. Although he had never participated in organized sports, he was an avid fan of the local baseball professionals, the Baltimore Orioles, and followed their activities religiously.

Badly burned by his recent divorce from Connie, who had been his college sweetheart, his only interests, until he met Lila, were his buddy Bear, his writing and reading the novels of his favorite author, who wrote highly accurate spy and intrigue novels.

He still smarted from what he felt was a rotten deal that Connie had given him. She had pursued him all through their years in college, and he had tolerated her frequent hair transformations to almost every color in the hair salon, as long as she adhered to her wedding vows.

When she had started to cheat on him, he knew that their ill-fated marriage was dead, so he had really felt a sense of relief when he was served with divorce papers. He had given up hope of getting her to give up her constant partying and shrew-like nagging to have Bear put to sleep, because she said he shed too much, and she had to vacuum after him.

CHAPTER 3

Alex dismissed his reverie about Connie and rose to prepare for his dinner date with Lila. He was eagerly looking forward to it because he sensed that there was deep feeling on both sides of the emotional aisle.

He took a quick shower, shaved off a two-day growth of beard and applied an underarm deodorant and a light-smelling aftershave.

He rooted around in his larger bedroom closet until he found a freshly pressed pair of chino trousers, which he donned. He unfolded a starched, button-down blue oxford shirt, and rolled the sleeves halfway up his elbows. He slipped into penny loafers, with no socks, and brushed his damp hair.

He decided to take Bear for a walk to avoid the possibility of a painful accident if he couldn't hold onto his water.

While they were out, he noticed a red Trans Am slowly driving back and forth in front of Lila's building. He didn't give it much thought because it was someone unfamiliar with the complex, who was looking for a specific address. Other than noting its color and model style, he didn't pay any specific attention to the incident.

He waited until he was sure that Bear had eliminated as much fluid from him as possible, then returned to their apartment.

He gave Bear several biscuits to keep him occupied, and retrieved his rose and six pack of colas from the refrigerator, and at 5:50 rang her doorbell.

She answered it, wearing a frilly apron over a differently pastel-shaded mini skirt outfit, and was holding a two-pronged cooking fork in one hand.

She seemed very pleased when Alex presented her with the rose that he had purchased. She smelled its aroma and said, "Thank you. It was really thoughtful of you to go out of your way to get my favorite flower. I've loved roses ever since I was a little girl. I think that they are the most beautiful flowers in the world. Their beauty in a room brightens it and their perfume just makes me feel happy. Thank you again. I was just getting ready to test the steaks to see if they were thawed enough to broil. Come on into the kitchen and keep me company while I cook. Sit down while I find a bud vase to put this rose in."

Alex placed the six pack onto her round, clear-topped kitchen table and sat down on one of her wire-backed café chairs while she pulled a bud vase from under her sink. She then placed it in the center of her dining room table and returned to the kitchen.

"Can I give you something to drink?" she asked.

"One of these colas would do just fine," Alex replied

She poured a little over some ice and set both the bottle and glass on a coaster. Donning a pair of heavily insulated gloves, she pulled the broiler pan from under the already glowing broiler and set it on top of the range. Then she reached into her lower oven and pulled out a cookie sheet on which rested two plump stuffed potatoes, setting them under the broiler briefly to brown their tops. She returned them to the lower oven and returned the broiler pan to the glowing broiler element.

"I hope that you're hungry. How do you like your steak?"

"Medium," Alex replied.

"That's how I like mine too."

Soon the apartment was filled with the pleasant aroma of broiling meat, so she turned on the range exhaust system to clear out the smell.

"Would you get those dinner plates off of the table and bring them in here?"

When Alex complied with her request, she plopped a steak and a stuffed potato onto each of them and said, "Carry these into the dining room. I'll bring the salads in shortly."

Appearing with two round bowls of tossed salad, she said, "You sit there," pointing to one of the place settings. "I hope that you enjoy your dinner."

Alex sat down and unfolded his napkin. He cut off a piece of steak and forked it into his mouth, along with a bit of potato. He suddenly realized that he hadn't eaten lunch and was famished.

"My God, this is good," he said. "Where did you learn to cook like this?"

"From my Aunt Ida. She's a spinster lady who lives over in Courthouse Manor. When my mother died of ovarian cancer, I was twelve and my sister Marie, who is now married and lives in Chicago, was fourteen. She guided two young girls through the onset of puberty and protected us from teenage Lotharios with raging hormones until we were able to fend for ourselves. She was stern then, and is bossy and opinionated now, but I love her very much.

"The only man that she ever loved was named Charlie Baker. They were going to be married after he got home from World War II, but a sniper during the invasion of Normandy killed him. Although she was a very beautiful woman, she never dated again, even though she was constantly besieged by admirers. She retired after thirty-one years with the gas and electric company."

"I'm also an orphan," Alex replied. "My father was a Maryland state trooper. He died alongside the Ritchie Highway of a massive heart attack following a high-speed DUI chase. The driver was a fifteen-year-old kid who took his father's car without permission, and then he and three of his friends got tanked up on cheap vodka. Although he was fifteen, his father's influence got him off with a suspended sentence. My mother gave up and died about a year later. I miss them both."

Lila continued, "That's the reason I don't drink. After my mother died, my father tried to drown himself in a brown bottle. He drank until he developed cirrhosis of the liver. He was an electrical engineer at what was then called the Westinghouse Defense Center, at Friendship Airport. He was often so violently ill after a long night of binging, he would sit on the side of his bed and throw up for twenty minutes. He wasn't a mean drunk, he just couldn't face life without my mother's love."

Alex said, "I don't drink because I simply can't stand the taste. One beer and I upchuck. I've always been the designated driver at all of the college parties."

She said, "I have a confession to make to you. This afternoon, when you asked me to go to dinner, I hesitated because I had a regular Saturday night date with the guy that I used to see. I was trying to make up my mind as to whether I should break my date to be with you, or continue in a relationship with absolutely no future. I'm happy that I broke the date, because I just wanted to be with you."

"I'm happy that you did break your date," Alex replied, "because I've thought of nothing but you since I saw you this morning."

Seeing that Alex was finished eating, Lila asked, "Would you like some dessert? I have eclairs, ice cream, and fresh fruit. I personally like eclairs because I have a never-ending sweet tooth. As you can imagine, I don't have any after-dinner liqueurs here at home."

Alex replied, "No, I'm really stuffed, and I don't eat too much dessert. Go ahead and have some yourself. My inner being is content from all of your delicious food. We've talked like we've known each other for years. Let me help you clean up."

He began to stack the dirtied dishes and cutlery, and started to carry them into the kitchen. Lila giggled and fastened a frilly apron around him. As they stood side by side, rinsing off the dishes and flatware before stacking them into the dishwasher, he could feel the gentle warmth emanating from her body and smell her faint perfume, all of which made him feel a little lightheaded. His strong desire to possess her physically had become a major emotion within him. When their bodies accidentally touched during the cleanup, he felt a small tingle of electricity go through his own body. He knew then that this was no one-night stand, hit-and-run-type date. He hoped that she felt the same way.

When they were through, he said, "I would like some black coffee."

She spooned some coffee into her coffee maker from a canister on her counter and said, "Go on into the living room, I'll bring it in when it's ready."

Alex sat on one end of her sofa, and soon she appeared with two fragrant mugs of steaming coffee. She sat down femininely on the other end, with one leg under her, holding her mug with two hands, as she sipped its contents. They chatted a while, and she placed her mug on the low coffee table in front of the sofa when she was finished.

Alex's desire for her kept rising to a fever pitch, and they found themselves being pulled together by the magnetism that both felt. Finally he could no longer stand it and blurted out, "I have an overwhelming urge to kiss you."

She reached over and placed both her hands on his cheeks and kissed him gently. After that, they began to neck furiously.

Alex drew back, breathing heavily. "I've got to stop, because if I don't I won't be responsible for my actions."

"I didn't tell you to stop, did I?"

Alex reached for her and kissed her ferociously, and without another word she arose, pulled him to his feet and led him to her bedroom, where she began to disrobe.

When Alex saw her wonderful female curves under her black lingerie, his manhood took over and he rapidly disrobed and crawled into the other side of her bed.

Without any foreplay, because their desire for each other had been stretched to a maximum, they engaged in a frantic act of love, which was to become the bedrock on which their magnificent love for each other was to rest.

Afterwards, temporarily purged of the massive sexual need for each other, they lay in each other's arms, exchanging deep personal secrets about themselves, telling each other intimacies that they never related to their best friends.

Lila finally asked, "Do you want to spend the night here, sweetheart?"

Alex replied, "There is nothing in this world that I would like better, but I have to think about Bear. He's probably up there with his legs crossed, lying close to the door and hoping that he doesn't have an accident. Can I have a rain check?"

"You don't need a rain check, honey, there's no one else."

Alex reluctantly started to dress, slowly picking up the articles of clothing that he had frantically torn off earlier, and started to leave.

Lila donned a pink robe and led him to the door, where she kissed him gently. "Call me soon, honey."

Alex practically skipped down her steps and exited her building.

The red Trans Am that he had seen earlier cruising back and forth in front of Lila's building was parked across the service road, facing her building. Alex knew that it was occupied, because he could see the glow of a cigarette through the windshield, and see its smoke being expelled through the open window on the driver's side. He felt he was being inspected, but figured that it was someone waiting for a passenger to emerge.

He rapidly ran up the steps and opened his door to find Bear huddled as close as possible. He was greeted with whines of welcome from Bear to his best friend, and rapidly attached his lead to allow him to relieve himself.

Alex quickly led him down the steps where Bear let loose a flood of amber liquid. Alex noted that the red Trans Am had disappeared and gave it no more thought. When Bear seemed to be completely relieved, Alex returned to his apartment and called Lila.

"Did I wake you up?" he asked.

She said, "No, I was just lying here thinking that this was such a wonderful day and you're such a nice guy. I've wanted to meet you for a long time. When I did, you turned out to be the decent guy that I hoped you would be. I feel very comfortable and secure with you."

Alex said, "I go to church on Sunday mornings, and I was wondering if you would like to go with me."

"Where do you go?"

"To that little frame church up on Providence Road."

"Is that the one that looks like it came out of Currier and Ives? The one with the cemetery on both sides of it?"

"That's the one," said Alex.

"I know a couple that got married there. They've said that the minister is very gentle and that the members are real nice. I'd love to go with you. What time do you leave?"

"I leave here about nine, the service starts at 9:30. Afterwards we can go up to Hunter's Inn. They have a real nice Sunday brunch."

"Thank you for asking me, honey. I really would love to go with you. I'll be ready at nine."

Alex really couldn't sleep that night. He knew that he had stepped off a solid footed landing and into the deep waters of a gigantic love. All that he could think of was Lila, her beauty and her physical response to him. He wondered if she felt the same way about him because he just couldn't put up with the antics of a Connie-type person again. In the insecurity of a new love that hadn't yet fully blossomed, he tossed and turned all night long, alternately glorying in the contentment of a new emotion and then worrying that he was moving too quickly.

He arose early and took Bear for his morning walk. Because Bear wanted to eat, that walk was always short. Alex fed him and changed the water in his water bowl. While Bear was loudly gulping down his food, Alex took a shower and shaved. He carefully selected the clothing that he wanted to wear, and settled on his summer-weight gray suit, a white dress shirt and a gray tie. He pulled on gray socks and slipped into black tasseled loafers and sat down briefly to scan the sports section of the Baltimore *Sun* to learn the results of the Orioles evening game.

Bear was now finished with his daily meal and hopped up to get his usual caressing. He leaned against Alex affectionately as Alex scratched his head and stroked his body. Bear grunted with delight, as he always did when his best human petted him. He adored Alex and when Alex was gone, he would lie there sadly with his head between his paws awaiting his return.

Like all corgis, his loyalty was with one individual, and totally unchallenged with Alex, his absolutely best human. One of his best pleasures besides squirrels chasing was what Alex was doing now. In return, he always licked Alex's hand with love. Theirs was indeed a symbiotic relationship.

At 8:55, Alex rang Lila's doorbell and was stunned by her beauty when she answered it.

She was dressed more conservatively than he had previously seen, and was wearing a knee-length, summer-print dress, sheer black hose and high-heeled black pumps. Her shiny, long hair was pulled back into a loose ponytail that framed her beautiful face, and secured in the back with a wide gold barrette, falling in a clump down her back.

All that Alex the accomplished wordsmith could say was, "Wow, you look fantastic."

Lila giggled in her unique musical way and grabbed his cheeks with her hands, planting a long, tender kiss on his lips. He was to learn that this was her way of expressing her happiness to him.

She said, "Thanks, honey, I dressed hoping to please you."

Alex grabbed her hand and they walked down to his car, where he assisted her into the front seat.

On the short drive up to the church, they didn't say too much to each other, but their silence was contented, neither feeling the necessity of making unnecessary idle conversation with the other. Lila leaned against him comfortably, and he felt the strong magnetism for him that she seemed to project.

They parked in the church parking area and walked into the church, unconsciously holding each other's hand. Reverend Busch was standing in the narthex talking to several early arrivals. Alex introduced Lila to him and the others, and they took a seat in a side pew towards the rear of the small church.

After they were seated, he felt Lila's hand sneak into his on his lap, as they sat comfortably chatting with each other.

Several older female members stopped by to say hello, but were just really nosy about who this new beauty with Alex really was. Several younger members, who had been sizing up Alex as a good catch, stopped by to check out their supposed competition.

When the service started, they shared a hymnal and Alex was pleased with the clarity of her voice in song. One of the hymns in the program that morning was the old classic "How Great Thou Art." Lila later told Alex that it had always been one of her favorites and it always brought tears to her eyes every time that she sang it.

Reverend Busch began to deliver his sermon, and Lila twined both her hands through Alex's arm and placed her head on his shoulder, keeping it there throughout the entire homily.

After the service, while they were standing outside chatting with the other members, which was a long-standing custom of the church, he felt Lila's arm sneak around his waist in a most comfortable manner, and she kept it there while all of Alex's friends came up to say hello and hope that they would see her again, real soon. That simple loving gesture was to become her favorite way of telling Alex how comfortable she was with him, and to Alex, her special way of telling him how much she loved him.

After Alex helped her into his car, they drove the short distance up the Harrisburg Expressway, exiting at the Hunt Valley interchange. They parked in the Hunter's Inn's large parking lot, and strolled through the lobby holding hands into the large dining room named after a mythical spice tree. There they were seated in a side banquette facing the groaning tables overloaded with a variety of foods and desserts.

When the check arrived, Alex signed it and left a tip for the waitress. Holding hands again, they strolled back out to their car.

Alex assisted her into the front seat, then walked around to the driver's side. Before he could start the engine, Lila leaned over and kissed him, saying, "Thank you, honey, that was a really nice meal."

Anxious to prolong the time he had to spend with her, he asked, "If you don't have any major plans for this afternoon, how would you like to go down to the Inner Harbor for a while?"

The Baltimore Inner Harbor development is one of the crown jewels of the Baltimore City rejuvenation. It has turned what once was a decaying, rat-infested and decrepit old waterfront into a sparkling, modern tourist attraction with many new hotels, unique displays, outdoor restaurants, and two huge pavilions containing numerous boutiques and food stalls, with a wide variety of unusual merchandise available for purchase. This, together with beautiful landscaping, a profusion of flowerbeds and newly constructed skyscrapers presents a very delightful environment for visitors to the area.

Lila said, "I'd love to, but what about Bear?"

Alex replied, "Well, we could stop by home, and I could take him for a walk while you change into something more comfortable to stroll around a tourist-attractive waterfront."

Lila giggled and said, "That sounds great, honey, let's do it."

They detoured into their complex, and Lila ran up to change.

Alex changed into shorts and a polo shirt, and took Bear for a walk to relieve himself and to avoid the chance of an accident if Bear couldn't hold onto his water. Afterwards, he returned to their apartment, and he gave him several bone-shaped biscuits to keep him occupied.

He walked outside to await Lila. When she appeared, the red Trans Am that Alex had seen several times the previous day screeched to a halt in front of her.

The driver, who was obviously disturbed as Alex could see from his emphatic gestures, was speaking firmly with Lila, who was calmly and firmly answering his comments with statements of her own. This back-and-forth dialogue continued for a while, until suddenly the driver forced the car into a drive mode, almost stripping his gears, and with his tires squealing in pain, sped out of the complex, screeching recklessly into the flow of traffic on the main road where the apartments were situated.

Alex didn't say anything as he assisted her into his car, but she certainly did.

"That was the guy I used to date. He said that he had been trying to reach me all morning and asked where the hell I was. He said that he saw you coming out of my building last night and wanted to know what the hell I was doing after breaking a date with him. He wanted to know why I was seeing another man when we were going steady. I told him, 'Wait a minute, Jeff, I never had any arrangement that I would see you exclusively, and what the hell were you doing stalking me at home?' I told him that we had gone to church and then to brunch and that we were on our way to the Inner Harbor for the afternoon, and that I felt better about the whole thing than spending a completely boring evening at some gin mill listening to his drinking buddies complain about how they were being discriminated against.

"I told him that I couldn't date him any longer, because you and I cared for each other, and that I felt completely comfortable with you, something that I never felt with him. And I asked him not to call me anymore, because I wouldn't be there.

"He has a vicious temper, especially when he drinks. He's probably the most selfish man that I have ever met. Not once did he ever ask me what I would like to do. We would always end up in some sleazy bar where his drunken cronies hung out. Thank God that I'm rid of that bastard. My boss Max says that he's a lousy ambulance chaser with no ethics. The fact that he was camped outside of my apartment shows me that he's been stalking me. He should know better. He's an attorney. A lousy one, I admit, but he is a member of the Maryland bar."

Alex was amazed at her show of temper, because she had always been so docile in all of his previous contacts with her. He was to learn that she was a slow burner, but when her temper changed, so did her polite language, and this time she was mad as hell.

On the way into Baltimore City in the light Sunday traffic on the Jones Falls Expressway, she leaned against him comfortably, and apologized for losing her temper. She said that she had planned to stop seeing Jeff, and that the violent confrontation had just made the termination that much easier to handle.

Exiting the JFX close to the Inner Harbor, they parked at one of the hotel garages.

They visited the National Aquarium, a beautifully designed building located directly on the waterfront, and admired the authentic rain forest located on its uppermost glassed-in level, and its numerous exhibits of rare sea creatures on the levels leading down to the street. They went aboard the USS *Constellation*, a Revolutionary War-era fighting ship that had been lovingly restored to its original condition, down to the sails and masts, and the Maryland Science Center, with its unique IMAX wrap-around theater that sparked imagination with its cinematic features that allowed viewers to sit directly within the scenes of action. They visited several other attractions, and walked in and out of the two massive pavilions, admiring the unusual merchandise available for purchase.

Acting, feeling and looking like newlyweds, they walked over the brick walkways, contentedly holding hands, and now completely in love with each other.

Finally, footsore and hungry, they sat down at one of the many outdoor eating places for a sandwich and cold drink. Lila also had a dish of soft serve ice cream topped with chocolate sauce.

Lila said, "Darling, this has been a completely enchanted weekend, but tomorrow is a work day for me. Let's go home."

CHAPTER 4

Alex retrieved the car from the garage and, on the way back up the JFX, asked her, "Honey, would you like to spend the night with me?"

Lila, who was hoping that Alex would ask, said, "I would really love to, but we have an important hearing tomorrow morning, and I have to brief Max on some tricky, unusual precedents beforehand. Anyway, I have to arise at seven a.m. and be at work by nine."

Alex said, "That's no problem. I have to arise at that time to take Bear out. We can set my clock radio to that time, and you would have plenty of time for a shower and breakfast."

"All right, honey," she replied. "I have to stop at my place for a change of clothes. Judges insist on proper dress in their courtrooms."

They exited at the proper JFX interchange, driving through Ruxton, which is an affluent suburb of the Baltimore area. As they drove by a large house surrounded by grassy lawns, Lila said, "That's where Jeff's parents live. He lives with them. His father made a fortune speculating on the stock market. Jeff never stops letting people know that he lives in Ruxton if he has a chance. His father is crude and ruthless, and that's where Jeff gets his selfish attitude and questionable business methods."

Arriving at their complex, Alex parked in one of his usual spaces, and stood by his car until Lila came out of her entry door with a suit bag over her shoulder, and an overnight case in her hand.

Alex took her burden from her and they walked up the steps to his apartment.

He found Bear huddled as close to the door as possible. He whined a welcome to Alex and covered his face with frantic kisses. Alex dropped Lila's luggage on one of his easy chairs and said, "Make yourself at home, sweetheart, I have an emergency run to make. I'll be back shortly."

It took Bear a full twenty minutes to completely relieve himself, but Alex didn't want to rush him since he had been penned up all afternoon. When Alex was sure that his best friend was completely relieved, they returned to the apartment.

Upon his return, he found that Lila had indeed made herself at home. She had picked up the litter of newspapers that Alex had carelessly dropped on the floor alongside the sofa that he had been on while reading them earlier. She had hung up Alex's suit, and picked up his dirty underwear, socks and shirt and placed them in a hamper. She herself had changed into an old pair of sweatpants and one of Alex's tee shirts and was watching a cable movie on TV.

Alex gave Bear several doggie treats as a reward for not having an accident and sat down alongside Lila on the sofa. Bear flopped down on top of his feet.

Alex put his arm around Lila and said, "It may be too early to say this, honey, but I'm madly in love with you."

She leaned her head up and kissed him fervently, saying, "It's not too early, baby. I think that I've been in love with you since the first time I saw. When I saw you yesterday morning, I became so shy that I felt like a six-year-old with a crush on her teacher. I could have cried when I got back into my own apartment because I didn't even tell you my name. I've wanted to meet you since I first saw you walking with Bear. When I saw you up on the pool house deck, I knew that I had to move then, because I might never get another chance. That was why I was so forward in approaching you. It all worked out in the end, didn't it?

"It was no trouble breaking off with Jeff because there never was a future there. He's really something that crawled out from under some rock, and when I saw you, I wanted to be with you and nobody else. The Taylor women are peculiar. They only fall in love once. They're one-man women. I've made my decision that you're the only man that I will ever love, and if I ever lose you, there never will be another Alex in my life. I love you more than life itself. You're all that I'll ever value in a man."

The apartment became filled with a wonderful emotion. Bear, sensing that this was so, hopped up on the sofa and placed his head on Alex's lap.

Lila placed her head on Alex's shoulder and closed her eyes. "Honey, I'm exhausted from this enchanted weekend that we've had together. You're the finest man that I have ever known. Your ex-wife had to have rocks in her head to let you free. She must be the dumbest, most self-centered woman in the world. If it were me, I'd fight like a female cat to keep your love, and to keep you with me and me alone. I'm so tired that I can't keep my eyes open. Let's go to bed. By the way, I'm expecting the curse tomorrow, so there won't be any fun and games for a while."

Alex said, "Honey, there's more to our relationship than just a roll in the hay. I love you with every atom of my being. Think how great it'll be when your monthly visitor leaves." He pulled her to her feet, and they walked, with Bear following, back to his bedroom.

"What side of the bed do you want?" he asked.

Without answering, Lila crawled into the left side.

He disrobed and climbed into the other side. Lila placed her head on his chest and her arm around his upper torso and said, "Goodnight, sweetheart."

He responded, "Goodnight, honey."

In his bed in the corner of their room, Bear yawned loudly and started to snore gently, and they all went to sleep.

CHAPTER 5

They awoke at five a.m. and, stimulated by each other's closeness and their mounting desire, made brief but passionate love, then fell back to sleep in each other's arms.

Lila awoke and looked at the clock, which told her that it was 8:32 a.m. "Oh my God, we forgot to set the alarm. I'll be late for work. I don't have time for breakfast or a shower. I'll get something up in Towson. Max will be furious because he needs to be briefed on those precedents."

She hurriedly dressed in the tailored pants suit that she had brought with her the previous evening, brushed her hair and applied lipstick. Then, with Alex holding the door open, she aimed a Dagwood Bumstead type kiss in his general direction and said, "I'll call you later, sweetie," and rushed down the stairs to her car.

Alex, who had enjoyed every moment of the time they had spent together over the previous two days, felt a brief pang of loss as he heard her car start up and leave.

He donned an old pair of shorts and a polo shirt and took Bear on his usual brief morning walk. He returned to feed him and change the water in his water bowl.

While Bear was noisily and sloppily eating, he toasted a bagel and made himself some fresh coffee, and turned on his PC. He started to work on his article and to his delight discovered that the block to his creativity had completely disappeared. The words that he wanted to use tumbled out of him, and he was able to complete his assignment in record time

He read the manuscript to get a feel as to whether it was up to the *Eagle's* editorial standards, proofread it for obvious typographical errors, and counted the words.

Satisfied, he called Rick on his 800 number and told him that he was sending it by overnight express, rather than email, to avoid the possibility that it might get garbled in transmission.

Rick told him, "Alex, if we like this piece as well as some of the others that you have submitted, I'll be in touch on the series that we discussed."

Alex thanked him and decided to take a shower, after which he decided to read the morning *Sun*. He was halfway through the sports section when Lila called.

She was laughing while she spoke and said, "Honey, Max told me that I looked like hell and that I should get some sleep on weekends instead of burning my candle on both ends. He said that beds are for sleeping as well as hanky-panky and that the new rooster in my hen house should learn that. He did say that he was happy that I finally dropped the *gonif*, which is the Yiddish word for thief, because all that could ever happen with him was my getting hurt. He wants to meet you soon. We can talk about that. I'll call you later when I have more time. I love you and I miss you after the wonderful weekend that we had."

Alex was delighted that she had called. He wanted to tell her that he had completed his article and that he wanted her to spend the night, but she hung up too quickly. If she called again, he planned to do so.

When the Expressman arrived, Alex handed him the manila envelope that contained his latest work, and since it was about noon, sat down to have a sandwich.

Lila called during her lunch break, and before she could hang up, he asked her to stay with him again that evening, and if she did he would make her his Famous Alex Baxter Signature Beef Stew, and allow her personally to set the damned radio clock alarm.

She giggled and said, "You're a damned persuasive salesman, honey, but I was always a pushover for handsome brown-eyed men. Ok, honey, but I have to stop at my place to pick up some changes of clothing and to check my mail, because I'm sure that I'll be spending a lot of time with you."

After she hung up, Alex called out to Bear, "Come on, you lazy sheepherder, let's take a ride."

To Bear, taking a ride was second only to his number one sport of squirrel chasing. He enjoyed riding with his head stuck out the window into the oncoming wind, and Alex could only imagine what fantasies went through his little friend's mind as he rode that way.

He opened his car door and Bear jumped up onto the front seat. When Alex rolled down the window and closed the door, Bear put both of his stubby paws on the arm rest and stuck his head out the window into the onrushing wind, enjoying his second-best sport.

At the supermarket parking lot, he rolled up the window that was open and cracked the rest for ventilation, leaving Bear to take a nap.

Inside the store he purchased the ingredients for his stew and a shinbone for Bear to gnaw on. At the little German bakery next door, he purchased a loaf of crusty bread and two Napoleons for Lila's sweet tooth desires, a rose at the florist, and a box of special doggie treats at the pet shop.

He drove back to his apartment with Bear's head out of his window, and at home he placed the shinbone on his kitchen floor and let Bear contentedly gnaw on it while he prepared the beginning of his stew.

He first cut up the beef cubes into smaller bite-sized cubes, then set it into his electric skillet to simmer for a couple hours into tenderness. He added salt, pepper, fresh onion, green pepper, a bay leaf for flavor, and thyme. After he peeled the potatoes and carrots, he set them aside in water to add later, along with a package of frozen peas.

Bear had finished the first phase of his bone gnawing, so Alex looked at his wristwatch and turned down the heat to its lowest level, and added more water to it so that it wouldn't char. Then he took Bear across the street to a large tract of county-owned property that served as an unincorporated, informal park. There he slipped the lead off of Bear's collar and set him free to get some exercise chasing squirrels.

It always amused Alex to see Bear, with no tail and stubby legs, chasing the furry rodents. After the squirrel was safely in a tree, it would level what Alex assumed were insults in the chattering and clicking of its own dialect, and Bear responding with what Alex assumed were threats in the canine language of barks. Alex wondered if they understood each other, and as writer, what a funny story it could develop into.

After several strenuous chases, Bear eventually tired of his favorite sport, so Alex returned with him, and Bear took a nap after his happy dog day afternoon.

Alex turned up the heat over which his beef was slowly cooking and tied a bow around the rose that he had purchased for Lila and placed it in a bud vase. Then he pulled his spare apartment key from the rack in his kitchen and tied a bow around it, using red ribbon that he had saved from a previous gift. He then positioned the key so that Lila would see it when she sat down to eat.

That much accomplished, he sat down to watch the afternoon headlines with brother Bear joining him to have his afternoon head scratching.

About six p.m., Lila came bustling in with several changes of business clothes over her shoulder, and several plastic shopping bags crammed with shoes and accessories. She placed them in Alex's large bedroom closet, which he was slowly being pushed out of, and sat down beside Alex, on the side opposite where Bear was lying.

"Something smells good," she remarked.

"It's dinner," Alex replied. "Do you want to wash up first?"

"No," she said, "I'll take a shower after dinner. My God, what a day I had today. First I was late for work. Then I got cramps from my period, then I had to brief Max on the details of the precedents he was to cite at today's hearing and attend the hearing with him, then I had to prepare service documents and file them at the clerk's, and research precedents for that hearing. I'm exhausted. All I want tonight is to eat a decent meal and have you hold me. I love you so much."

Alex put his arm around her shoulder and she leaned her head on his. He swore that he could feel the tension disappearing from inside of her. They sat quietly that way for a few minutes until he kissed her cheek and arose to enter his kitchen. He spooned out portions of the stew into soup bowls, and the remainder into a larger bowl. He set the two smaller bowls at the place settings, and the larger bowl in the middle of the table. The loaf of crusty bread was placed alongside the other bowl, along with a sharp bread knife. He then yelled, "Chow's on!"

Lila sat down and giggled happily as she smelled the rose. "I'm going to take this to work with me tomorrow. It'll remind me of how much I love you all day long." Removing the key, she held it up and said, "Well, I guess this makes us a couple."

She cut off a chunk of the crusty bread and dipped it into the sauce. "This is delicious. You'll have to show me how you make it." Then she added, "I've told Max all about you, and he wants to meet you. He suggested lunch on Friday, because that's our least busy day, and he leaves early to get home before sundown because that's the start of their Sabbath. They call it Shabbat."

Catching her breath, she continued, "Also, Aunt Ida would like us to come to dinner on Wednesday. I know that this is putting you on the spot, but these are two important people in my life, and I want you to meet them early on.

"I've already told you about Aunt Ida stepping in to raise Marie and I. Well, Max has been like a surrogate father to me. He and Esther, his wife, have been like second parents to me. When my mother died, nursing my father through his binges, through my ill-fated six months with Bobby when I thought that life would have no further meaning. He was patient with me when I took up with Jeff, although he never approved it, and now with you who I absolutely adore."

Alex was fully aware of the subtleties of the eternal mating ritual, and the American variations that required meeting the next of kin. He agreed to both dates without any fuss.

When they were through with dinner, he said, "Go ahead and take your shower, sweetheart. I'll clean up. There are a couple of brands of over-the-counter painkillers in the medicine cabinet if you want to use them for your cramps."

She said, "You will not, I'll help."

As they stood side by side at the kitchen sink, he felt the comfortable rush of her presence next to him sweep over him like a pair of well-worn old shoes. Then he knew that the bond between them was too strong to be ever severed, in this world or some hereafter.

Lila took her shower and did her nails. Then she grabbed a pillow from their bed and hit Alex on the back of his head with it, placed it on his lap and then lay down comfortably. Bear, who now accepted her presence in their lives, flopped down in front of her, and she started to scratch him behind the ears. When Alex glanced down a half an hour later, they were both sound asleep. He had to awaken her to go to bed.

Before he crawled in beside her, he carefully set the clock radio alarm for seven a.m.

In bed they chatted together until almost one a.m. She told him about the cases that she was working on, who she had met on the street, and the gossip around the courthouse that would appear in next week's Towson *Tribune*. Finally, when they did kiss goodnight, she placed her head comfortably on Alex's chest and they drifted off into a contented deep sleep.

They were awakened by the news station that Alex had his radio tuned to, blasting out the news of another car bombing in the Middle East, with numerous casualties, and quick retaliation by the other side causing additional death and destruction. It seemed as though the entire area was seeking total eradication of each other. Alex felt that this was sad because almost two thousand years before the Great Teacher of Peace had trod its dusty roads preaching love to all that would listen. Apparently his message hadn't been heard by many.

Alex arose and took Bear for his usual short morning walk.

Upon his return, he found Lila already dressed in her business clothes, preparing breakfast, and adding her special touches to its preparation.

As he stood beside her at the sink mixing Bear's food, she peeled an apple, cored it and chopped it into tiny bits and placed it in the microwave for a short while. Then she added instant oatmeal, nutmeg, cinnamon sugar and water to it and returned it to the oven again. Soon the kitchen smelled like baking apple pie. She toasted two English muffins and spread margarine and marmalade over both halves, and brewed coffee for the both of them.

She quickly ate and placed her dirtied dishes in the dishwasher, kissed Alex goodbye and left for her office.

Alex took a shower and sat down to read his newspaper, paying close attention to the box scores and news of the Baltimore Orioles. At about ten a.m., the phone rang. It was Rick, his editor from the *Eagle*.

He said, "Alex, this article that you have written for next month's edition is outstanding. It's the best that we've ever seen from you. You've captured our special writing style completely. I showed it to the managing editor and he agrees. We would like to retain you to write a series of six articles along the same vein, to be published in future issues under your personal byline. We are willing to pay you." He quoted a figure far in excess of what Alex was going to ask for. "It'll be six installments, beginning with the third edition after this next one. This will give you plenty of time to research for material to be included. We will send you a synopsis of each article to get you started. If you agree, I will have a standard contract drawn up and put in the mail today. Sign both copies of the contract and keep one for your personal records

"Since you are a frequent contributor, we would also like to add your name to our masthead as contributing writer. That title doesn't pay any more, but it's like a laureate. It will indicate a special relationship between you and the *Eagle*."

Alex was overwhelmed by the news, but didn't want to seem too eager. Such a series in a highly rated national magazine like the *Eagle* would establish him as a fine writer, and being listed on its masthead was like being listed in *Who's Who*.

He said, "Sure, Rick, send the contract down and I'll return a signed copy immediately. Thank you for your great confidence in me."

When he hung up, he let out a loud rebel yell that startled Bear, who was napping on the sofa, so much that he clumsily fell to the carpeted floor and lay there, confused as to what was going on with his best human.

Alex knelt down and hugged the bewildered dog. "I'm sorry that I scared you, old buddy, but that was the best damned news that I have ever received. That series will establish me as a writer of national stature. I can hardy wait to tell Lila about it. This will call for a celebration."

Bear didn't fully comprehend why his best human was so happy. He knew that it was good, though, so he kissed Alex all about his face.

Lila called shortly after that and said, "Honey, I've been trying to reach you, but the phone was busy. Is everything all right?"

Alex related the splendid news to her and said, "Let's make Saturday night a special dress-up date night."

Delighted with his success, she asked, "Sure, sweetheart, what did you have in mind?"

Alex replied, "Let's go up to Luigi's in Towson. We've been friends for years. His food is always excellent, and he has a smooth combo on weekends. I'll make reservations for seven p.m. Be sure to wear your dancing shoes."

That Friday morning Alex changed into clean chinos and a short-sleeved cotton shirt and drove up to Towson to keep the luncheon date with Max and Lila. He parked in the lot behind her building and took the elevator to her floor. Entering the well-furnished office, he saw that Lila was nowhere to be seen. He was greeted by a pleasant-faced, middle-aged woman.

"Can I help you?"

"I'm Alex Baxter. I have a lunch date with Lila Taylor and Mr. Weiner."

She laughed and replied, "So you're the famous Alex Baxter that I've been hearing so much about. The way that Lila describes you, I thought that you would have a big S on the front of your shirt and be wearing a cape. She described you like you're capable of walking on water jumping over tall buildings in a single bound. Max and Lila are at court and should be back any minute. Sit down and make yourself comfortable. Would you like some coffee while you're waiting."

Before Alex could answer, the door opened and Lila and Max walked in.

Max was in his late fifties, fleshy from lack of exercise and had a slight paunch from his wife's heavy cooking.

When Lila saw Alex, she rushed over like a new puppy and almost knocked him over with an eager kiss. She said, "Honey, this is my boss, Max Weiner."

Max looked at Alex and extended a hand. When Alex shook it he found that Max had a strong, confident grip that indicated he didn't stand for any nonsense and wanted to get right to the point of any conversation.

"So you're the new rooster that's been stirring up my Lila's hen house. Already I like you better than that little *schlemiel* Jeff Lupinsky. He believes that he's Mr. Wonderful, when he's really Mr. Nogoodnik. He thinks that ethics is just another word in the dictionary that he doesn't know the meaning of. If he believed that he could make more money that way, he'd buy his own ambulance, instead of chasing those already on the road. Someday he'll be disbarred because you can't fly in the face honesty and fairness and get away with it forever. I'm happy that my Lila had the backbone to boot him out of her life. He's a really bad apple, and eventually his rot would get to Lila and make her bad also. But let's not worry about that now. Let me drop off this briefcase, and we'll go downstairs for a *nosh*."

They took the elevator down to the lower-level restaurant and found an empty table. To adhere to the ancient Old Testament laws of keeping *kosher*, the traditional Jewish laws that cover everyday living habits, Max ordered a salad. Lila and Alex ordered cheeseburgers, French fries and iced tea.

Max, who seemed to be constantly in a high-speed-drive mode, finished his salad quickly and said to Alex, "I love my Lila like if she was from my own blood. She's like a third daughter to me. My Esther and I have tried to guide her through this crazy world because she doesn't have a father to give her support. When she married that jackass Bobby, it looked like she had a winner. When he started to cut out on her, a month after they were married, all I could do was feel her pain and represent her as an attorney. Then that lousy *gonif* Jeff entered the picture like a vulture picking up a sick little bird. I never liked him since the first time I saw him. He's too arrogant and grasping for my tastes. If it suits him better, he has a habit of reneging on verbal agreements. He's not very well liked in the bar association. If you treat my Lila well, I'll like you. If you don't, I'm a pretty good lawyer."

He turned to Lila. "Enjoy your lunches. Remember, I need you upstairs today." He turned back to Alex and said, "I think that you'll do OK. The check and tip have been taken care of."

After he left, Alex wiped the imaginary perspiration from his brow and said, "Whew, so much for meeting the father figure."

At the elevator, Lila kissed Alex and said, "He likes you, honey, I can tell. I'll see you at dinner. I love you."

CHAPTER 6

On Saturday morning, while they were straightening up the apartment, Lila said to Alex, "Honey, this afternoon I have to take my Aunt Ida grocery shopping. I've been doing it since she stopped driving, and she depends on me to take her out. Pick me up at my place tonight. There's a special dress that I want to wear for you tonight."

That afternoon, with plenty of time on his hands, Alex did his laundry, had his car washed and took Bear for long walk across the street to let him exercise by chasing squirrels. Afterwards, as an Orioles fan, he watched a thrilling baseball game in which they squeezed out a win in the eleventh inning.

He took a shower and shaved, then dressed in his best navy blue suit, sat down on the sofa and casually scratched Bear's head and stroked his body. As usual, Bear grunted with delight at his best human's attention.

To forestall an accident, Alex took Bear for a walk to empty the fluid in his small body. It often amazed him about a dog's capacity to hold onto his water, and the amount that accumulated within such a small carcass.

At 6:30, he rang Lila's doorbell and was stunned by the beauty she presented. She was wearing a low-cut, black knit cocktail dress that clung to her in all the right places, and showed off her magnificent female figure to its best advantage. Its low cut hinted at her magnificent cleavage and was held up precariously by the thin straps across her shoulders. She wore sheer black hose and high-heeled black pumps, and had string of pearls around her neck, which he was later to learn had been her mother's.

Her long shiny dark hair was pulled back into a loose ponytail that framed her beautiful face and was secured in the back by a wide gold barrette.

All that Alex the skilled wordsmith could say was, "Wow, you look absolutely magnificent. Every man at Luigi's will want to possess you, and every woman there will hate you because you're so beautiful."

Lila, pleased with his reaction, giggled musically, the indication that she was very happy. "Your wow is full payment for my efforts. I'll always dress to please you."

Alex grabbed her hand tightly and led her down to where his car was parked. After helping her into the front seat, he walked around to the driver's side and got in. Before he could start his engine, she leaned over and grabbed both cheeks saying, "I love you so much."

They drove to Luigi's, with Lila comfortably leaning against her chosen one, both in silent contentment in the secure knowledge of each other's love for the other.

They parked in the rear of Luigi's and walked around to the front entrance, holding hands.

Luigi greeted them at the door. "Alex, my *paisan*, where have you been keeping yourself? Haven't seen you in ages." Then he looked at Lila and said, "What a ridiculous question. With such a beauty as your dinner companion is, I'd be a stranger myself."

Alex introduced Lila to him, and he kissed her hand in the courtly Italian manner, then led them to the banquette that he reserved for special customers. He laid down to menus and said, "There's no need to tell you to enjoy your dinners, I'm absolutely positive you both will. I'll tell Pearl that you're here."

Pearl, Alex's favorite waitress, appeared immediately. She said, "Mr. D'Agostino was right. Your dinner companion is exquisite looking. The other girls and I were chatting when the two of you walked in. Martha remarked that the air around you both seems to smolder when you look at each other. I have no idea how serious you are about each other, but the two of you look like you were tailor-made for each other. You make a magnificent-looking couple.

"I know that Mr. Baxter doesn't drink alcohol, but may I bring you something from our bar?"

Lila replied, "I'll just have something diet, please."

Alex said, "Anything that you order here will be excellent. His veal dishes are the best outside of Little Italy. His pasta is done perfectly, and his house salads have chunks of cantaloupe mixed in among the greens. He told me once that he uses his mother's recipes as the basis of his own. I imagine that he has modified them somewhat to please the tastes of the Towson crowd. His family owns a famous restaurant down in Little Italy."

Lila scanned her menu for a while and then said, "I'll have the veal scaloppini, angel hair pasta and a house salad."

When Pearl returned with their drinks, he gave her Lila's selections and said, "I'll have the bragiole, angel hair with marinara, and a house salad."

When the lounge combo started playing smooth melodies, Alex asked her if she wanted to dance. She nodded, so he led her onto the tiny dance floor. She seemed to just melt into his body, and they appeared to be a single entity as they danced. When the set was over, she kissed him possessively, and he said, "Our dinners are here, sweetheart. Let's sit down and eat."

They ate with relish. Lila finished up with spumoni, a rich Italian dessert, and Alex had café espresso, made in the huge chromium-plated Italian coffee machine at the serving station. It hissed, shuddered and threatened to blow up while making his coffee.

They danced several more sets and were enjoying an enchanted evening when Luigi approached them and said, "Alex, there's a gentleman in the bar who wants to buy you and Miss Taylor a drink."

Alex looked up and saw Jeff grinning at them, and then looked at Lila who appeared to be able to strangle Jeff with her own two hands.

She said, "That bastard followed us up here. I told you he was stalking me. I knew that he would try something idiotic and childish to get back at me for dropping him. Max will cut the legs out from under him. Tell him absolutely no and stop harassing me."

Alex said to Luigi, "Tell Mr. Lupinsky that he already knows that Lila doesn't drink. That she requests that he stop bothering her and that he will be hearing from Max Weiner next week regarding legal action to make him stop."

Shortly after that, they saw Jeff leave the restaurant looking very disturbed. Apparently Luigi had related Lila's request to him bluntly. Luigi had lost a customer, but it didn't appear to bother him in the least.

Just like that, their enchanted evening seemed to disappear.

Lila said, "Let's go home, honey. My period is over and we can get back to him in the most pleasant way that I know."

The following Monday, Lila related to Alex how Max had reacted to Jeff's heavy-handed attempts at interference.

She said that Max had literally hit the ceiling in rage, and called Myra into his office, where he dictated a letter to Jeffrey R. Lupinsky, Esq. In that letter he indicated that he had been retained as an attorney for Miss Lulila K. Taylor and had been informed that Mr. Lupinsky was engaged in stalking and harassment of her person, that such actions were illegal and reprehensible and causing Miss Taylor unnecessary pain and emotional distress. And that Miss Taylor was strongly considering seeking legal relief from Mr. Lupinsky's illegal activities. That Mr. Lupinsky was to immediately cease and desist from approaching Miss Taylor in any manner unacceptable to her. If Miss Taylor did obtain such a cease and desist order, he should be aware of its effect on his ability to practice law in the state of Maryland.

Lila added that Max then said, "That should hold the dirty little *schmuck*," which was probably the foulest insult that a Jew could call another person.

Alex realized that Jeff, in his own warped way, was in love with Lila, and couldn't comprehend why Lila had terminated their relationship. He felt that Jeff was in bad need of psychiatric counseling if he was to have a life where he could react in a normal manner to those with whom he associated. He felt that Jeff was deep in the throes of a self-destruction fetish, but Alex felt that it wasn't any business of his any way.

In any case, Max's letter to Jeff appeared to make Jeff realize that Lila didn't want anything to do with him and he did stay away from her.

On the following Wednesday, Alex changed into clean shorts and polo shirt and took Bear for an extra long walk to allow him to relieve himself, then sat down to await Lila. She came rushing in and also changed into shorts. They drove the short distance over to Ida's complex.

On the way over, Lila said, "Honey, she likes a special brand of added butterfat ice cream. Stop in here and I'll run in and get her a couple of pints."

Alex pulled into the parking lot while Lila ran in. She shortly emerged and they continued their drive to Ida's complex.

Lila rang Ida's doorbell and it was answered by a dark-complexioned woman in her late seventies wearing wire-rimmed glasses. When she was younger she could have resembled Lila, and would have been a beautiful woman.

Lila said, "Aunt Ida, this is Alex."

Alex felt like a raw recruit at his first day of basic training, being looked over by drill sergeant who was used to his orders being obeyed, and who wouldn't tolerate any nonsense from him.

Lila said, "It smells like you're making your pot roast."

"Well, it's your favorite, isn't it?" Ida replied. "Sit down for a while and visit before we eat. I want to get to know Alex better."

Lila sat close to Alex because of way she felt about him, and he sat close to her because he wasn't sure of the way he was being received.

Ida said, "I hear that little shit Jeff Lupinsky really screwed up your night out on Saturday. He's a vindictive little sneak who'll try anything to get back at someone that he believes has done him harm. I think that rattling around in that big mausoleum that his father got stuck with in Ruxton has loosened a couple of screws in his brain. I knew his father when they called him Big Bill the Butcher. He had a heavy thumb on the scale when he ran a butcher shop on Eastern Avenue in Highlandtown."

Highlandtown is a hard-working, largely blue-collar area of Baltimore City.

"He used to pass off utility-grade beef as choice until the state meat inspectors caught up with him and fined him. He speculated in the stock market and made a fortune. Then he moved to Ruxton to impress the people who knew him. That little shit Jeff knew better than to try to impress me, because I know where he comes from. He got his shitty ways of doing business from his father. An apple doesn't fall far from its tree, does it? I'll bet that they have painted window screens on every window in that house."

Painted window screens are a unique Baltimore City art form that was once popular among the older residents of Highlandtown. While some examples are valued as early Americana, most of them were garish and amateurish, and ran the whole gamut from the Stars and Stripes to attempts at landscapes. Window screen artists are hard to find in Baltimore at present.

Ida said to Alex, "Lila tells me that you have her going to church again. You can't be all bad if that's the case. I don't believe that Jeff has been in church since he was baptized by Father Malloy at St. Margaret's."

Alex said, "Would you like to join us? We go to that little frame church up on Providence Road. It would real easy to swing by and pick you up, and afterwards we could all go up to Hunter's Inn for brunch. It might be a nice Sunday morning treat for you."

Ida replied, "Well, I do miss going to church on Sunday morning. I'm no Bible-thumping bigot, but an hour or so every week isn't much to be grateful for all of the good things that happen to you."

"That settles it," Alex said. "We'll pick you up at nine on Sunday morning."

"I'd love to go, if you really don't mind," she replied. "Let's eat."

As Lila had indicated, Ida's pot roast was the most tender and delicious that Alex had ever eaten. He was tempted to ask her how she got it so tender, but decided to wait, because many women guard their prize recipes jealously, not even sharing them with close relatives.

Ida urged seconds on them, and for dessert served large wedges of fragrant apple pie, covered by huge mounds of the ice cream that Lila had brought.

On their way home later that evening, Lila snuggled up close to Alex and said, "Honey, that was the nicest thing that you could have done for her, inviting her to go to church with us. While we were doing the dishes in the kitchen she told that if she was forty years younger, she'd give me a run for you. She thinks that you're a real doll. She'll be one of your biggest boosters from here on in.

"What took you so long to come into my life? It seems like I've been waiting for you forever. Max told me that my guardian angel was sitting on my shoulder the day that I met you. I believe that he was right."

During the next week, Lila moved more of her clothing and accessories to Alex's, and his large closet became her personal preserve. Lila had effectively moved in with Alex, and they discussed her giving up her flat and making it a permanent arrangement, because paying two rents just didn't seem to be the most practical thing, now that they were both certain that their feelings for each other ran deep and true.

She told Alex that she had discussed it with the owner/manager, whom everyone called by his first name, Harold. She said that he told her that he could break her lease, but it would cost her two months' rent, and the forfeiture of her security deposit, and that was over $2000. Based on that, they decided to wait until their financial picture became clearer.

As luck had it, one evening while they were eating dinner, the phone rang. It was Harold. He said that he had an elderly couple who had friends in Lila's building and would love to move in there. He was willing to break her lease if she would forfeit her security deposit to pay for the rehab which he did before each new tenant moved in.

They both immediately accepted his offer and the next Saturday had a moving and storage firm store Lila's furniture, holding out personal items like pictures and bric-a-brac.

Now Alex's apartment had become their apartment, and Lila's talent for decorating became apparent with furniture groupings and picture clusters on the walls.

Their relationship had now developed into a comfortable long-term partnership. The first emotional frenzy had passed and had been replaced with a deep love and genuine concern for each other's well-being.

Alex was content with their arrangement, and felt that for all practical purposes they were already married, but he had a small nagging doubt, probably resulting from a childhood that embraced morality, that it wasn't entirely legal. He was certain that Lila and he were madly in love with each other, and that their compatibility with each other was as smooth as a perfectly joined piece of complex machinery that continued to operate without problems on a daily basis. Both Lila and he had been badly burned by previous marriages, and he wasn't positive that she wanted to remarry, although she often said that she wanted to have children. He finally decided to ask her to marry him, with a formal engagement and a religious ceremony to seal their troth.

Their affinity toward each other was so complete that neither ever fantasized about other beautiful individuals whom they encountered in their daily activities. Lila was always giving him little love gifts that spoke of her massive love for him, and he, in turn, frequently presented her with her favorite flower, a red rose, which she always took to work and placed on her desk.

Myra would always laugh enviously every time that she replaced a rose and say, "Honey, that man is crazy about you. I'd like to own the florist shop where he buys them."

CHAPTER 7

Alex had a high school friend, Morris Green, who ran a jewelry store at one of the larger malls in Towson and decided to call him.

He said, "Morey, I'm seriously thinking of getting engaged. What kind of a deal could we work out on an engagement ring?"

Morey replied, "Alex, I just bought a bunch of stones at an estate action. The settings are old fashioned, but that's easy enough to rectify. Come on in, and if you see something that appeals to you we can work out a deal. If nothing else, it'll be great to see you again. I read your articles in the *Eagle* every month, and having you as a customer could add class to my store."

Alex didn't know Lila's ring size, so he called Ida and asked her if she could help him out.

Ida was absolutely thrilled at being a part of such a wonderful conspiracy because she now considered Alex to be a close relative. She said, "Alex, I know her ring size because her mother left me a bunch of her jewelry and there are some rings included. She tries on the rings every time that she's here. I can loan you a ring to get hers sized. When do you want to pick it up?"

Alex replied, "I'm on my way to Morey Green's right now. He's a friend of mine from high school, and I think that I can get my best value from him. Could I pick it up now?"

"I'll have it ready when you get here. That girl is absolutely wild about you.

When she first saw you walking with your dog, she said that you seemed to be such a strong decent man, but somebody like you must be already snapped up. When she kept mentioning you, I knew that she was interested, because she never was boy crazy. I never interfered when she was dating Jeff Lupinsky, although I know what kind of a lousy man that he is. I did worry about her vulnerability after her fiasco with that little rat Bobby. I knew that if she kept going with Jeff, that she would get crushed like a grape in a winepress. On the Saturday that she finally met you, she called and said that she had just met the man that she was going to spend the rest of her life with. I'm truly happy that she met a man as fine as you."

Alex picked up the ring from Ida's, then drove the short distance over to Morey's store. After reminiscing about whatever happened to so and so, and I saw so and so the other day, Morey spread a selection of loose diamonds over a cloth on his case and handed Alex a loupe.

Alex peered through the magnified lens at the diamonds of all shapes, sizes, quality, and color. Finally, an emerald-shaped stone caught his eye and he asked Morey, "How much is that one worth?"

Morey the friend immediately became Morey the merchant. "Well, I can get $5000 for it at retail, but since you're a friend of mine, I can let you have it for $4500."

Alex replied, "Morey, I'm not some Worthington Valley socialite. All I want is a nice ring for my girl. You can do better than that."

They dickered for a while and finally agreed on a price of $3000 including an 18-karat yellow gold setting.

Alex pulled out his checkbook and wrote out a sizable deposit. "When can I pick it up?"

"How about Friday morning?" Morey replied.

"That's fine," Alex replied. "I'll pay you the difference when I pick it up. Can you size it to this ring?"

Morey reached behind him for a sizing device and slid the ring down until it stopped, made a few notes on a pad and returned the ring to Alex.

When Alex returned the ring to Ida, he made her promise not to even hint about his plan when she talked to Lila.

Ida swore that she wouldn't say a word. "If I know that girl, she'll laugh and cry for a half an hour. Then she'll call me and Marie in Chicago and tell us the wonderful news. Her marriage to that bastard Bobby only lasted six months, but it took two years for her to get back on her feet after his philandering. Then that vulture Jeff Lupinsky entered the picture to take advantage of her emotional state. I'm certainly happy that she finally dropped him. Max Weiner was right, all that would come of her association with Jeff would be more pain and distress."

"When I pick up the ring on Friday, I'll stop by and let you see it. Thanks for the use of the loaner."

That evening, Alex was preoccupied with the enormity of his decision and became withdrawn with Lila, so much so that she became concerned.

"Honey," she asked, "have I offended you in some way? You seem to be in another world tonight."

Alex withdrew from his reverie and replied, "No, sweetheart, I love you more than ever. I'm just having some trouble with an article that I'm writing. It'll be ironed out by Friday, I promise you."

Lila's female intuition indicated that he was putting her off, but she didn't say any more about it. She had a momentary pang of fear the Alex's love for her might be cooling off, but all of his actions indicated otherwise. She reasoned that whatever was bothering him was temporary and that she would learn what it was eventually.

On Friday morning, Alex took Bear for an extra-long walk, since he would be gone for a good while.

He drove over to Morey's about 10:30 since Morey opened his store at 10.

Morey reached into his safe and pulled out a blue velvet presentation box. Inside nestled on white satin was Lila's engagement ring. Morey had cleaned and polished the stone, and its facets blazed like fire under the lamp on his counter.

"That sure looks impressive," Alex said. "She should like it." He wrote a check for the amount that he owed and showed Morey the picture of Lila that he carried in his wallet.

"She seems to be a beautiful woman," Morey said. "Bring her in sometime and let me meet her."

Alex stopped by the florist and purchased a dozen roses for Lila; as an afterthought, he also purchase a dozen more for Ida, since she had been so cooperative.

Then he stopped by Ida's to show her the ring and present her with her roses.

Ida gasped at the beauty of the ring and kissed Alex on the cheek. "Alex Baxter, you're a fine man. Lila was so lucky after her bad experience with those flaky bastards, Jeff and Bobby. She's really a one-man woman. After she picked you as her lifetime mate, if she ever lost you, she would grieve for a long time, then put together the pieces of her life and go on alone.

"That's the strength and curse of the Taylor women. When my Charlie left to go overseas to fight a war, we planned to get married. When he was killed by a German bullet on a Normandy Beach, my entire world just crumbled around me, because he was the only man whom I ever loved. The challenge of raising Lila and Marie to womanhood pulled me out of the rut that I was in and helped me face life alone. Thank you for the roses. It's been many years since a man gave them to me. You and Lila will have a wonderful marriage because you two were meant to fall in love, long before you met. Now get out of here before I start crying. Go home and propose to your future wife. I'll be the first to welcome you to what's left of our family."

On his way home, Alex stopped at Barker's to purchase the ingredients for their dinner that night. He planned to duplicate the dinner that Lila had made for them on their very first date. He was so elated that he also bought a shinbone for Bear.

At home, he placed the shinbone on his kitchen floor, and Bear started to contentedly gnaw on it while Alex re-stuffed the mixture of his twice-baked potatoes.

When he was through with his dinner preparations, he sat down to watch the afternoon news headlines.

About 4:30, he put the potatoes into the oven for their second baking and prepared the salads for their dinner.

Lila came bustling in about five. "Dammit, Alex Baxter, what's bothering you? You have me worried. You've been acting so strange these last couple of days I hardly know you."

"It'll wait until after dinner. Honey, how do you like your steak?"

"You know damned well how I like it." Then a thought struck her and she put her hand over her mouth. "This is a duplicate of the first meal that I ever cooked for you. I'm beginning to get an inkling of what you're up to." She sat down and smelled the roses.

When she was seated, he dropped on one knee and said, "Lila Taylor, we've been in love since the first time that we saw each other. My love for you has grown and grown since we've been together. I want to end the rest of my life taking care of you. Will you marry me?"

He pulled out the blue velvet box and opened it. The diamond gleamed from the lamp on the end table, as he slipped it on her finger.

She gasped when she saw the ring and said, "Oh yes, yes, yes, yes. How I've waited for you to ask that question. I must have written Lila Baxter, Mrs. Alex

Baxter and Mrs. Lila Baxter over a thousand times. Myra thinks that my sanity has disappeared, because all I talk about is you. Now I won't have to fantasize any longer. You are the only man that I have ever loved, and you will always be the only man that I ever will love. I can't wait to show this ring to Max and Myra." She kissed him over and over and started to cry. "You've made me so happy, sweetheart, I'll be the best wife ever. I have to call Aunt Ida and let her know that were engaged"

When she called Ida, Alex heard them laughing like a couple of high school girls who had suddenly found that a special boy whom she liked felt the same way about her.

Then she called Marie and the conversation took the same general direction.

"Marie is sending us an engagement present. She wouldn't say what it was, but she did say that if we kept it on our bed stand and used it occasionally, our marriage would never be dull. They're coming in over Thanksgiving to meet you."

"Let's go up to Luigi's tomorrow night to celebrate our engagement."

She replied, "Oh yes, let's do."

They sat there for a long time, with Bear between them, not speaking, but with Lila holding her hand to admire her ring. Finally, she said, "Let's go to bed."

That evening they consummated their natural marriage with great joy.

On Saturday morning, Lila happily took Ida on her usual grocery shopping trip and returned early to spend the day with Alex and Bear. They didn't do much but bask in the happiness of their total commitment to each other. They sat on their sofa for several hours idly chatting and tentatively beginning to plan for their wedding. When Alex decided to take Bear for a walk, Lila decided to go along with them, and they walked all over the complex holding hands. Their neighbors now accepted them as a devoted couple, and those with whom they had become friendly congratulated them when they heard that they were engaged.

Afterwards, while they dressed for their dinner date at Luigi's, Lila gave him a gold ID bracelet that she had purchased while shopping with Ida.

For that special occasion, Lila wore a black linen, form-fitting dress that emphasized her magnificent female figure and flattered her olive complexion. With her air pulled back, she seemed to glow with the contentment of their shared love.

Luigi greeted them like the old friends that they had become. "You two seem smugly happy this evening. Is there any special reason?"

"Show him your left hand, honey," Alex said.

He looked at her ring and hugged her. "I knew that this was going to happen the first time I saw you together. Pearl as always says the air around you seems to crackle when you look at each other. I've been in this business for twenty-four years, and in all that time, I have never seen a couple more ideally suited to each other. Congratulations to you both. I know that your marriage will be happy and joyous. I'll tell Pearl that you're here."

Pearl appeared almost immediately and said, "Mr. D'Agostino told me the grand news. May I see your ring?"

Lila extended her hand and Pearl said, "What a rock. I was positive that Mr. Baxter was in love with you, but that ring must have cost him a fortune. May I offer my congratulations? Mr. D'Agostino says that there will be no charge for your dinners tonight, because he'll save a fortune in electricity by using the glow that you two are emitting. Have you set a date for the wedding yet?"

"No," Lila responded, "we haven't. It just happened last night and we're still up on cloud nine."

After Pearl left with the food orders, Lila saw her stop and speak to the leader of the lounge combo. When they arose to dance, the group immediately switched into a popular tune about two beautiful people who had been hurt and finally found deep love with each other.

The other diners became aware that there was a special undercurrent of happiness that evening, and those who had found their mate smiled happily and those hadn't looked at Lila and Alex with envy.

The next day they picked up Ida for the service at the little frame church on Providence Road. They spoke to Reverend Busch about their new oneness and asked him how much notice he would need to marry them on a Saturday. He congratulated them and told them that any Saturday would fine, as long as he had two weeks' notice.

Before the service began, he made a special announcement about their engagement and the whole congregation broke into applause, embracing both Lila and Alex, who were both essentially shy, private individuals

During the service, Ida beamed at both of them like a fond mother who approved of her daughter's choice of a husband.

After the service, almost every attendee came up to congratulate them. The older women admired Lila's engagement ring. The younger females, who had secretly hoped that nothing would come of Alex's romance, finally gave up hope of snagging him and also congratulated them.

That Monday morning, the Express delivered a package addressed to both of them that bore the return address of a Chicago suburb. It looked to Alex like it contained a book, but Alex wondered why anyone would send them a book as an engagement present. He made a mental note to tell Lila about the delivery when she called.

When she didn't call, he became concerned and called her office.

Myra congratulated him on their engagement and said that everyone in their building who knew Lila, dearly loved her, and that the girls on their floor and Lila's friends from the other floors, were trooping in to admire her ring and gasp at the size of the diamond. Even Max, who hated disruptions to his office routine, was elated because Alex was a *mensch*, which roughly translated from Yiddish, generally meant a good guy.

Ida and Lila decided to go shopping for a wedding dress, taking pleasure from one of a female's greatest thrills. Because both Lila and Alex had been married before, she by-passed the traditional bridal white and decided to be married in an off-white silk suit.

Lila accompanied Alex while he selected a blue blazer and gray slacks as his wedding attire and was pleased when the store clerk called her Mrs. Baxter.

Lila asked Marie to be her matron of honor, and she readily accepted.

Since Alex had a few distant relatives, most of whom were cousins he had never met, he asked his best friend at church, Joe Mooney, if he would witness for him. Joe was honored and agreed to be his best man.

Neither Lila nor Alex was interested in making their nuptials a super production, so they decided to have their wedding dinner at Luigi's and allow each guest to select from the regular menu, and to limit the guest list to relatives and members of the bridal party. Lila asked Alex to include Myra and her husband in the guest list.

Since Max had always defended her and was fact a sort-of foster father, Lila wanted him to give her away as Alex's bride. There was one major problem, however. Max was a devout conservative Jew. Members of that branch of Judaism were prohibited by the Old Testament from physical activity the might be termed labor on the seventh day of the week, which they called Shabbat, or Sabbath. The most devout members even hired non-Jews, whom they called Shabbat goys or Sabbath gentiles, to light their stoves and other normal household tasks.

Lila realized this and explained to Max that they planned to marry on a Saturday, and while she dearly wanted him give her away, she understood if he found it to be impossible.

Max replied to her, "*Bubala*, I would be mortally hurt if you didn't ask me. Such an honor couldn't be a sin. I'm sure that when the recording angel writes it down in the Book of Life, that it'll be written as a good deed. Anyway, I'll say a couple of extra prayers that night in atonement. Count me and my Esther in. We'll find some non-Jew to drive us to the wedding and pick us up afterwards."

All that remained to be set was the actual wedding date. They discussed various dates with Marie and Ida and decided that since Marie and George were going to be in Towson over the Thanksgiving holiday, the following Saturday would be ideal to tie the knot.

They passed this on to everyone concerned, and everyone agreed that it was acceptable.

Now all of the important details were set, until Alex remembered that they hadn't gotten a marriage license or their wedding rings.

On one of Lila's lunch breaks, they went to the courthouse and picked up their license, and on the following Saturday, they selected wedding rings at Morey's. When Morey met Lila, he remarked that she was of most stunning women he had ever seen.

CHAPTER 8

Marie and George flew in from Chicago on the Wednesday before Thanksgiving and rented a car at the airport. They drove to Ida's, and despite the late hour, Marie called Lila and they gabbed for an hour, mostly about Saturday's wedding.

Lila had been asleep alongside of Alex, and the call woke up both of them. After listening to Lila's end of the conversation, Alex fell asleep, feeling like an unused appendage.

Wen she was through, Lila kissed Alex to awaken him and snuggled back into his arms comfortably. "I'm sorry, honey, but she had a year's gossip to catch up on, and she just got carried away."

Alex awoke early to take Bear for his morning walk and then fed him.

They ate a light breakfast since they were going to pack in a huge load of calories at Thanksgiving dinner. At breakfast, Lila broke the news to Alex that Ida had asked her to prepare the traditional sauerkraut. Alex, who had been through this before, just held his nose and said, "Ugh."

When Lila opened the can of kraut, his apartment took on the unmistakable reek of fermented cabbage. She giggled delightedly when Alex took Bear for a lengthy walk to escape the foul odor of the cooking delicacy.

No one seems to know where this strange tradition comes from, but a large colony of the Amish, also called the Sober Dutch, reside in a section of southeastern Pennsylvania called Pennsylvania Dutch Country, and they have strong German roots.

On the drive over to Ida's, with Bear between them, Lila held the covered pan with both hands and Alex drove carefully, so as not to spill any of the reeking stuff in the car's interior.

With Bear on this lead, Alex punched Ida's doorbell, and it was immediately opened by a carbon copy of Lila, the exceptions being short cropped hair and several additional pounds than Lila. The same basic beauty was apparent in both.

They squealed and hugged each other and chattered like two crows calling out at sunup.

Lila placed her burden on Ida's kitchen table and introduced Alex to Marie and and George. Ida was in the kitchen engaged in some task related to dinner.

George had the physical softness of a businessman who didn't exercise. He was wearing a deep blue shirt with its collar opened at his neck. He had an opened bottle of Scotch whiskey at his elbow and a half-filled glass in front of him.

Alex at down on the sofa, and Bear plopped down on his feet, with his head between his paws. When Lila emerged from the kitchen, she sat close to Alex, with her head comfortably on his shoulder.

Everyone chatted for a while, mostly about Saturday's event, and the women moved into the kitchen to finish the meal preparation.

During a holiday meal preparation, the kitchen is off limits to the male gender, as the women gossip and prepare their prize recipes. When a tribal ritual is added, like the one to take place on Saturday, the men become totally ignored. The Taylor women, adhering to the strict rules of the female sorority, gossiped and rehashed every detail of Lila's wedding. Alex was a minor participant as well.

Alex, who had no immediate family, other than Bear and now his beautiful Lila, listened to the lively banter of a happy family reunion and felt that finally he was going to be part of a family that liked each other.

Bear lay at Alex's feet, smelling the delicious aromas emerging from the kitchen and hoping to get a taste of some of them.

When they were left alone by the Taylor women, Alex and George strained to find some mutual ground to carry on a conversation. They finally discovered that they both liked baseball, so they chatted abut the relative merit of the Chicago team and the Baltimore Orioles, the famous Babe Ruth curse on the White Sox, the marquee and so-called franchise stars, and other "hot stove" topics that baseball fans love to discuss during the off-season.

It fell on George, who was the oldest male, to deliver the traditional grace before the Thanksgiving meal. The ladies politely stopped discussing a topic more critical than the Cold War—Lila's flowers—and resumed their discussion in mid-sentence when he was complete

The ladies' conversation then turned to the Thanksgiving Friday sales.

Thanksgiving Friday is a day that merchants all over the U.S. look forward to eagerly. On that day, they mark down the merchandise held over from the previous year and unload it, on women who had previously rejected it, as Christmas bargains.

The ladies made dates to brave the onslaught of other Towson matrons with the same idea. It is a sort of national shopping holiday from which women get one of their greatest pleasures—retail shopping—and then having lunch to re-energize themselves for the afternoon brawls.

Alex and George were left on their own while their ladies were spending their money, so they planned a lunch date and a tour of Towson and Baltimore County sights.

On the way home, Alex said, "Honey, it's supposed to be bad luck for the groom to see his bride in her wedding clothes before the ceremony. I imagine that since we live together, we're exempt from that curse. Do you agree?"

"I suppose so," said Lila, preoccupied with her wedding details.

The next morning, Alex took Bear for a walk When he returned, he couldn't locate Lila but there was a note from Marie on their kitchen table.

> *Alex,*
> *Lila won't be home this evening to avoid the possibility of bad luck, but talking to her on the phone is OK. George will drive me, Lila and Ida to the church. The wedding is set for 2:30 p.m. Please don't be late!*
> *Marie*

The lunch date that Alex and George had set up went off successfully, and he returned to an apartment made lonely by the lack of his Lila's comforting presence. He had become so used to her tinkling giggles that their apartment had become as sterile as an unlived-in flat.

He called Ida's and they sadly comforted each other about their forced separation, both agreeing that they missed the other completely. After Alex took Bear for an extra-long walk, Bear jumped up and lay against him while Alex absently scratched him behind his ears.

On Saturday, the day that Lila and he were to be united eternally, Alex arose and took Bear for his walk and then ate a light breakfast. Later, Lila called him to tell him how much she loved him and how much she missed him, but after today, they would be united forever.

He took a shower and sat on his sofa in his underwear, lonely for his Lila. But Bear kept his best human company.

About noon, he dressed in his new clothes, took Bear for a preventive maintenance walk, ate a small snack and left for he church.

Reverend Busch had already opened it, and despite the early hour, he saw Max and his plump wife, Esther, sitting in one of the back pews looking uncomfortable and waiting for someone to show up. Max was wearing his black *yarmalka*, the skullcap that all Jews wear in the sight of God.

Alex was overcome with emotion that this strong, decent man would violate one of his most sacred laws because he loved Lila, and participate in what they might consider to be an unorthodox ritual.

They sat there for a while, and Joe Mooney arrived, accompanied by his bubbly wife Kitty. Alex introduced them to Max and Esther and handed them the wedding rings to be later slipped on the fingers of his and Lila's hands.

George showed up, along with Lila, Ida and Marie. Finally, Reverend Busch, who had been working on his Sunday sermon in the church study, and his wife Kati, who had been doing some paperwork in the church office, arrived.

Kitty Mooney started to take photographs and later presented them to Lila and Alex in an album entitled "The Social Event of the Year."

Reverend Busch said, "Shall we begin?"

Alex stood alongside Lila and held her hand tightly. Joe stood alongside him. Max stood alongside Lila and Marie alongside him.

Reverend Busch began to speak the traditional ceremony by saying, "Dearly beloved, we are gathered today to join into matrimony…." When he came to the part, "Who gives this woman?" Max said, "I do," kissed Lila on the cheek and sat down the front pew beside Esther.

After the I dos, the ring exchange, and the kiss to seal the marriage contract, Lila whispered in Alex's ear, "I love you so much."

Reverend Busch then said, "Ladies and gentlemen, I give you Mr. and Mrs. Alex Baxter," and everyone smiled and applauded.

With no one to throw her bouquet to, Lila extracted one of the red rosebuds and left her nosegay on the altar rail. Reverend Busch said that he knew of a severely crippled girl who would appreciate having them.

Everybody then left for Luigi's.

Pearl gave them a toaster. Alex appreciated that gift more than the cash that Max had given them, because she was a single mother, raising three small children by herself. Such a gift from her economic strata was a real sacrifice to her, and in an economic ratio, represented a greater percentage of her income.

Everybody ordered their preference from the menu, but since it was a time when Luigi wasn't busy, some of the entrees had not yet been prepared. Substitute orders had to be placed but everyone seemed satisfied with their food. To keep their *kosher* status unsullied, Max and Esther ordered salads and excused themselves early when their driver arrived.

Luigi contributed a magnum of champagne, and Joe made a toast to their everlasting happiness.

After dinner, Pearl appeared with a small wedding cake that Alex had arranged for. Later on, she wrapped the remainder for Lila to take home with her. Lila froze it to unthaw on their first anniversary.

Everyone tactfully excused themselves; Alex signed the check and left a large tip for Pearl to repay her generosity. They drove home, as Mr. and Mrs. Alex Baxter, at last.

At home, Alex changed into slacks and a wool pullover and then donned a light jacket to take his patient Bear on a quick relief walk. While he was out, Lila changed into a sheer nightgown and lacy negligee. She caught a quick look at herself in a mirror and said, "Hell, that isn't me," and changed back into her favorite old sweatpants and one of Alex's tee shirts. Then she sat down to wait for her husband.

When Alex returned, he sat down beside her and said, "How do you feel, Mrs. Baxter?"

She giggled and said, "That sounds so natural, honey. Did you have any pre-marital jitters?"

"Honey," Alex replied, "when I was a little boy I used to spend part of my summers up in Carroll County on my grandfather's farm. When grandpa wasn't breaking his back to try to scratch a living out of that ground, we used to take long walks together on which he would point the different bushes and trees, and show how to tell what they were by the different-shaped leaves and barks. One day I stepped into a cow flop, and it stunk like hell. I started to cry.

He reached up into his overalls and pulled out a red handkerchief and stooped down to wipe off my sneaker. He said to me, 'Don't cry, Alex, when you step in cow flop by mistake, it's good luck.' Somewhere in my life I must have stepped into a Guinness Book-sized one to have met and won you. I've loved you since I saw your beautiful rear end sticking out from under that old heap of junk that you drive. My love for you is too large to be measured in ordinary time. You represent everything that's important in my life. Does that answer your question?"

She said, "Oh, honey, let's go to bed."

That night they consummated their religious marriage completely and with joy.

They hadn't planned a wedding trip until the following July when Lila was to take her vacation. At that time, they expected to drive out and visit Marie and George, and then drive down to Branson, Missouri, because they had heard that many prominent entertainers fronted as owners of the many theaters and show bars. Since neither had ever been there, they hoped that it wasn't too honky-tonk.

As part of his wedding gift to them, Max gave Lila an extra week off after the wedding.

Now newlyweds in fact as well as in spirit, they clung to each other tenaciously. They spent the week happily taking long walks through the pleasant streets of Towson, strolling through shopping malls, wrapped up in their own little world, in love and oblivious to anyone else around them.

Lila spent part of the time that week writing thank you notes for the many wedding gifts and congratulatory cards that they had received.

They attended the regular church services at the little frame church and found that they were warmly received by the congregation. If they looked up while singing a hymn, they would always see other members smiling warmly at them. They were now regarded as Providence Church's resident lovebirds.

After a while, the younger female members started to imitate Lila's look, and for a while there was a rash of straight hair pulled back into a loose ponytail secured with a barrette at the neck.

Ida always attended services with them and would beam happily as if she was the architect of their love match.

CHAPTER 9

With the passing of Thanksgiving, they entered into the joyous Christmas season. They erected Lila's small Christmas tree in front of their window and decorated it with blinking multi-colored lights and colorful ornaments, while playing Christmas carols.

Lila attached a festive red bow to Bear's collar, and he seemed to sense that something special and happy was happening to what now had become his two best humans. She also taped three red stockings to the Christmas tree table as a receptacle for the little gifts known as stocking stuffers.

Alex hung a Christmas wreath on their front door, and soon brightly wrapped packages began to appear under the tree branches.

As a new golden couple, they received many invitations to Christmas parties and open house celebrations of the season. Most of them they turned down because they really weren't party people. They did accept a couple from close friends that were to be held during Christmas week when Lila's office was closed.

They enjoyed he fellowship of the little frame church on Providence Road, and one Sunday Ida suddenly remarked, "I'm going to join that little church. I like the people there, and I feel comfortable among them."

Lila, who had independently been thinking along the same lines, said, "You know, I feel the same way. So am I."

They spoke to Reverend Busch, who was delighted to receive them, and said, "You can join on the next Communion Sunday when we have a coffee fellowship."

It happened that there was such an event the following Sunday, and they were received into full membership after promising to support the church fully.

In the glow of their newly minted marriage, that Christmas, Lila gave Alex a new suit, a French-cuffed dress shirt, several new novels by his favorite techno-thriller writer, underwear, and filled his stocking with disposable razors, nail clippers, deodorant and other practical gifts. She also gave him a special gift of a hairbrush, to break him of the habit of using hers.

He gave her a light-green silk pants suit for dress up occasions, black satin lingerie from Veronica's Hideaway, her favorite cologne that he never tired of smelling on her person, an elaborate manicure set, and a gold charm bracelet on which he had installed charms that indicated major milestones in their lives. He planned to add one or more charms each year as important milestones were passed. He also filled her stocking with the little items that are important to women: nail polish, lipstick and emery boards.

For Bear, they purchased squeeze toys to replace those that had been chewed up and a giant rawhide chewbone.

Ida received a book of Maryland recipes, a deep side chicken fryer and a warm three-quarter-length coat for her weekly shopping trips with Lila.

Lila decided to cook dinner that Christmas, and baked a six rib pork loin, basted with Cointreau, a liqueur with an orange base. The alcohol that it contained evaporated during the cooking process. She served side dishes of red and sweet potatoes, green bean casserole and cauliflower, but no sauerkraut to please her Alex. Ida supplied her famous apple pie, to which Lila added her favorite ice cream.

At one of the parties that they chose to attend, they arrived late and the hostess made a blanket introduction, introducing them as Alex Baxter and his exquisite wife Lila.

Lila was wearing Alex's favorite dress—the black knit with her mother's pearls. She looked absolutely stunning, still glowing from her newlywed mode.

The hostess passed out a caution to the would-be Lotharios. "If any of you horny toads are figuring on leaving the ranch and hitting on her, forget it. She's a one-man woman and is madly in love with her husband. If you try, she will viciously cut you down before you get to first base. If you try, remember that you've been warned."

Everybody laughed, especially the men. Alex noticed one man looking at her like a hungry dog looks at a raw pork chop.

They circulated among the other guests, chatting about the shallow, neutral things that partygoers like to talk about. Alex would always feel her arm comfortably slip around his waist as they chatted. After a while they got tired of standing, so they found an empty love seat and Lila sat down. Before he joined her, he asked, "Honey, would you like something to drink?"

"I'd like diet cola, if it's not too much trouble," she replied.

Alex went over to the part of the room that had been set up as a bar and got her drink. On his way back to her, he noticed a sweets table containing a variety of miniature pastries so he stopped and got her a selection for her notorious sweet tooth. After he made his selection, he looked up and saw the man who had been leering at Lila, sitting in the place where he was to sit. He could see from Lila's body language that she was extremely disturbed, because she was leaning as far away from him as possible, and speaking to him in the same firm measured way that he had seen her use when she was cutting down Jeff Lupinsky.

As he approached her, the stranger suddenly arose, red faced and embarrassed, and quickly walked over to a group of unescorted men.

Alex asked, "What was that all about?"

Lila was mad enough to chew nails. Alex knew that she never cursed unless she was disturbed. She said, "That son of a bitch tried to proposition me. He wanted to know my telephone number at work and wanted to know if I would have lunch with him. I told that bastard that I am in love with my husband, and that you are the only man that I will ever let touch me, and that I hated buggy parasites with no backbones. I told him to crawl back under the wall that he slunk out of, and back to the filth that he was accustomed to, before I stepped on him like the other cockroaches that I despised. I hate a man like that. He's like a hyena who waits until the lion who made the kill is through, then he sneaks in and tries to steal the scraps. Sit down with me while I cool off."

Alex asked, "Do you want me to say something to him?"

"No, I think that I punctured his vanity pretty bad. He'll never bother me again."

When Alex sat down, she put her head on his shoulder before she started to eat her pastries.

She said, "I love you with my entire being, sweetheart. There will never be anybody else, and I will never let another man touch me sexually, as long as I live."

Alex later asked the host who the man was.

He replied, "His name is Bob Hargen. He runs a computerized payroll service out of one of those converted houses on Allegheny Road. He prepares my weekly labor payroll. He's been married four times and I hear that his present wife is getting ready to file for divorce. He's bad news with women. His reputation is that he hits on them at parties and tries to score. I apologize for his hitting on Lila. She's such a beautiful, dear sweet girl and is obviously completely in love with you. I'll say something to him before he leaves."

Later that evening, Alex saw the host speaking to Hargen, who left the party shortly after that and they never saw him again. Lila did tell Alex that she had heard that he was on the prowl again. One of her friends in the building where she worked told her that her boss had represented his wife and got a big settlement along with divorce. The secretary gossip network never sleeps.

As a postscript, Alex read in the Towson *Tribune* that a Robert T. Hargen had been assaulted outside of his business, and had received a broken jaw which was required to be wired shut. The police didn't believe that it was robbery, and there were no suspects.

Alex's belief in retribution took a major leap. Apparently an irate husband had punched out his free pass to mess around.

On New Year's Eve, a sleet storm hit the Towson area and drivers were cautioned not to drink and drive. Neither Lila nor Alex enjoyed partying on that particular night because it seemed that all of the frantic attempts at merrymaking were really just people working hard to imagine that they were having a good time. Owners of wine and dine establishments, anxious to clear as much profit as possible on that night, would position tables as close together as possible, and the noise made it difficult to even talk. The vast amount of smoking made it difficult to even breathe. In any case, they enjoyed each other's company. Max often said that they would be content to watch the grass grow if they could be alone together.

Lila roasted two small Cornish hens for their dinner and stuffed them with a wild rice dressing. She had made an apple pie using Ida's recipe, and after they and cleaned up the dishes, Lila took a shower. She grabbed a pillow from their bed, and in her usual affection, hit Alex on the head with it before placing it on his lap and lying down. You could almost hear the purrs of contentment as she comfortably lay there. Bear flopped down in front of her and she started to scratch him behind the ears. When Alex looked down at them a half an hour later, they were both sound asleep, and slept through the dramatic moment when the famous ball made its dramatic fall from the Times building in New York City to announce that the New Year had arrived.

They slept late on New Year's Day, with the exception of Alex's sleepily arising to take Bear out and feed him. Afterwards, they had dinner at Ida's, taking Bear and some of Ida's favorite ice cream with them. In deference to Alex's distaste for sauerkraut, Lila refrained from cooking that smelly Maryland tradition for their holiday dinner.

When Lila's father had died, he had left his estate, which was mostly insurance in trust for his daughters. George, who was a stockbroker, administered the trust. Lila received monthly statements and received half of the income that the trust generated, and deposited it into a money market account. When they were married, Lila offered to show Alex the monthly statements and her savings account. Alex declined her offer, because he felt that any such money was hers alone, and the amount on deposit was none of his business.

They considered the income from his writing for the *Eagle* and her salary as a paralegal for Max to be joint income, and it was deposited in their co-owned checking account.

They were now financially stable and decided to look for a residence that they could purchase. Their lease was still in Alex's name and was due to expire in four months. If they didn't inform the complex management that they planned to move three months prior to the end of their current lease, it automatically renewed itself for another year, so they only had a narrow window of time in which to find a new home.

Neither was interested in gardening or other outdoor activities, so they decided to look at condominiums as their best alternative. They found a unit at the Ridgeway, a condo tower close to downtown Towson. The unit was on the twenty-sixth floor and overlooked the heavily forested Loch Raven watershed. The Loch Raven reservoir had been dammed decades before to supply the fresh waters needs of Baltimore City and its surrounding suburbs and was maintained as a park-like setting. People often picnicked on its shores and fished in its waters.

The owner of the condo was asking for more money than they were willing to pay, but the real state agent had heard that he was anxious to move to Florida. She encouraged them to make a lower reasonable offer that he might accept.

Following her suggestion, they offered him $5000 less than he was asking, and he accepted. They made a good faith deposit to bind the property, and applied for a mortgage and chose a ninety-day closing date because of their lease restrictions. They planned to move by May 1.

It seems in life that there is a domino effect or Murphy's Law that occurs when it's least wanted.

Alex had long been concerned that the piece of junk, as he called it, Lila's old Japanese-imported car, would fail her when she most needed transportation. The January days were bitterly cold and darkness set in early.

Lila frequently worked late, and one evening she called and said, "Honey, my car won't start and I'm terribly cold. Can you pick me up as soon as possible?"

Alarmed, Alex asked, "Where are you?"

"In the parking lot behind my office," she replied.

Alex hurriedly drove up to the Towson business district and found her shivering behind the wheel of her lifeless car.

He turned up the heater in his car, wrapped her in a light blanket from the emergency kit that he kept in his trunk, and tried to start her vehicle. After a while even the battery gave up. He angrily kicked a tire and exclaimed, "Damn it to hell it won't start."

Feeling the chill of the cold January night, he returned to the warmth of his own car and said, "Honey, let's leave it here tonight. We wouldn't be lucky enough to have somebody steal it. Tomorrow I'll drive you to work and pick you up, and I'll do so until it's either junked or repaired. I really think that you need a new car, baby, because if you get this one repaired, it'll be just a short while until it happens again. It'll nickel and dime you to death. If you get a new one, you'll have a bumper-to-bumper warranty for thirty-six months. We can swing the down payment because our mortgage payment and condo fee are just about what we pay in rent now. Don't worry. On Saturday morning you can have my car to take Ida shopping, and on Saturday afternoon we'll visit the auto showrooms to let you get a feel about the kind of car that you need if we have to buy a new one. Be prepared for sticker shock because auto prices have gone through the roof since you bought this heap."

When they got home, Alex called the local dealership that handled her make of car and left word on its answering device of the problem and that he would wait at the lot until Lila's car was towed in. He left their home phone and Lila's work number in case they wanted to call back to verify his statements.

He said, "Honey, take a shower and get warmed up, and we'll have dinner."

"You handling more of the financial load is unfair," she replied. "My trust account is in pretty good shape. I'll handle either the repairs or purchase of a new car."

Alex said, "Let's not make any wild decisions until we find the facts, sweetheart. Just eat your dinner for now."

The next day, Lila called him and said, "Honey the service manager just called me and said that it it'll cost me $2700 if they can find the parts, because they don't manufacture after-sale parts for that model any longer."

Alex replied, "That's ridiculous, that whole car isn't worth that much."

Lila was finally offered $25 by a local scrap yard that planned to chop it up for replacement parts.

When she started to search for a new vehicle, Lila found that buying a new car was like walking through a minefield without a map to guide her safely. Fast-talking salesmen would offer fantastic discounts from the sticker price. When it came time to close the deal, however, someone who claimed to be the sales manager would show up and berate the salesman for making unrealistic deals. The embarrassed salesman, to save his sale and mend fences with his boss, would always waive his commission, but the bottom line was always $1200 more. This was a sophisticated version of the good cop-bad cop routine.

Another ploy was "less than factory invoice." An invoice was shown that was higher than the actual cost of the vehicle to the dealer. That invoice didn't reflect the dealer's own discount for volume sales and other discounts such as selling a specific model. If a dealer made all of his sales based on the shown invoice, he would have to file for Chapter 11 bankruptcy.

A third gimmick was the add-ons to the sticker price for such things as body striping, floor mats, special premium tires—fees that were more imaginative than a branch bank's and sometimes options not specifically ordered by the customer. The sales philosophy at some dealerships was, "Whatever the traffic would bear."

A domestically manufactured small vehicle, with a white exterior and red inside trimming, caught Lila's eye. That particular manufacturer had a firm policy that the sticker price was the bottom line. Its salesmen were paid a salary, with incentive compensation based on the number of vehicles that they sold, so there was no haggling over discounts from padded bottom lines.

Lila wrote a check for the full cost of the vehicle. This essentially drained her trust account, but assured her of reliable transportation under full warranty for three years.

Standard features like remote entry, power windows and security systems, which had been options, if they were available at all, seemed like new gadgets to Lila, and she enjoyed manipulation of them like toys. Every Sunday afternoon after attending the services at the little frame church, she would lovingly wash and polish her new toy, until she got the first scratch on her vehicle's body paint.

Alex obtained a cell phone for emergency use, and she would often call him to let him know that she was her way home, or just walking down one of Towson's pleasant streets to tell him that she loved dearly.

The happiness that she was enjoying in her marriage to Alex seemed to magnify her beauty. This didn't pass unnoticed by would-be Lotharios looking for a one-night stand. Because of her unique, exotic beauty, she was always being hit upon for dates, in the elevator, at the stationary store, or standing on a street corner waiting for the traffic signal to change.

She developed a number of defense mechanisms to counter the unwanted advances. The most effective one was when she was being backed into a corner to suddenly gag and say, "God, I've had morning sickness all day long, and I think that I'm going to throw up all over you." This never failed to cool off raging passion of would-be lovers.

Max, when he was asked for an introduction, would always say, "Her husband is a major in the county police force and is very jealous. He's an ex-heavyweight boxer and the last man who accosted her regretted his decision after he got out of the hospital."

Lila found a desk plate at one of the side street boutiques in Towson that read:

I'M A ONE-MAN WOMAN AND I'M HAPPY WITH MY ONE MAN.

She giggled when she found it and told Myra, "That's better than a cockroach spray to keep the vermin away from me."

Even when she was enjoying lunch with her Alex and just having a pleasant conversation, she would look up to see some man staring at her, speculating on how he could safely approach her to arrange a liaison.

Those numerous approaches might be pleasant to many women, but to Lila they were annoying. When she had fallen in love with Alex, it was forever. She had found the man that she was seeking and was happy with her choice. She felt that he had all of the qualities that she valued, and he loved her immensely. They were contented with each other, so why should she even look around? As far as she was concerned there was nobody on earth that could love more than her Alex.

Her attitude toward life was unique. She was never self-centered or conscious of her unique beauty. She was in reality as friendly as a new puppy. Women, the most critical of the two sexes instinctively, liked her genuine sincerity and little girl charm. Max always said that she was a genuine article.

Alex one time asked her where the Taylor women got their unique beauty. Because her last name was English and they were generally fair with blue eyes, and with her olive complexion and almost black hair she could pass as someone with Mediterranean roots, French, Italian or Greek.

She replied that her father's grandparents had emigrated from England, but family legend said that as a result of the many French invasions of that island, during the normal give and take, the French got mixed up with the English, leaving their dark characteristics to perpetuate in the Taylor genes. In later cultures this was to become known as midnight integration.

CHAPTER 10

They finally settled on their condominium and moved in late April, when the rebirth of the beautiful Maryland spring seemed to approve of their new lifestyle.

Spring in Maryland is a truly beautiful season. Small crocus push their shy, beautiful heads up from the newly thawed ground made moist by spring rains and announce, as Mother Nature's messengers, that spring has finally sprung. Forsythia shows splashes of yellow in suburban yards. The tulips, jonquils and daffodils standing erect on their strong stems follow those. Almost every yard in the suburban areas has azalea bushes planted and their beautiful colors are a feast to the eyes. Wild dogwood trees proudly show their white blooms and dot the mountain skylines, and blooming ornamental trees like flowering cherry and crab apple provide a pink haze and perfume to the eyes and noses of persons walking in the newly restored warmth.

The pleasant perfume of lilacs fills the air, and trees awaken from their long winter's nap to create the leaves that purify the air. The grass, following the cue of God's other creations, slowly starts to green, and homeowners, tired of the cold winter blahs, suddenly get a strong urge to return to nature and rake the dead leaves, fallen branches and grass thatch from their lawns.

Females of the human species are suddenly grasped by the need to houseclean, and fill buckets with sudsy water and scrub, dust and vacuum.

Women scrub the marble stoops of their rowhomes.

The males are pressed into service to wash and polish windows, and move furniture for their wives, and another hour later, do it all over again. Painting and repairing become the sports of choice.

Alex and Bear, on their early morning walks, enjoyed the new freshness of the spring air. Fat robins pulling stubborn earthworms from the softened ground to feed their constantly hungry nestlings were a common sight. A pair of beautiful red cardinals, high in separate trees, serenaded them as they sang to each other. A feisty blue jay, defending its turf, dive-bombed them if they got too close to it, and a lonely brown mourning dove perched on their balcony railing, cooing his sad mating song, until one day a lady dove showed up and they disappeared to love and procreate.

When they moved in, the Baxters arranged for Lila's better quality furniture to be taken out of storage and be delivered to the Ridgeway. They gave whatever didn't fit into their decorating plan to charity, and purchased a wrought iron outdoor furniture set for the balcony just outside of their living room.

As the weather warmed, they would lie together on the lounge, after dinner, with Bear at their side, holding each other closely, and quietly and comfortably chatting with each other, contentedly looking at the blinking aircraft warning beacons on communications towers, until it was time to go to bed.

One of the advantages of their new location was that Lila could now walk to work. When she worked late, Alex and Bear would walk over to keep her company. Bear would lie alongside Alex and nap, while Alex read the latest novel of his favorite author. Afterwards they would walk home holding hands like newlyweds.

Because he was a writer, Alex for a short time was considered to be a minor celebrity. Older, pompous and opinionated individuals, with nothing better to do, would criticize his writing as poorly written and inadequate. They would then hand him some poorly written drivel, often written with a pencil in long hand, and ask him to intercede on their behalf to get it published. When he explained to them that he had no decision on editorial policy, they would accuse him of being a snob and walk away in a huff. Alex realized that these were old men teetering in the edge, grasping at a straw to make themselves feel needed and important. After a while they became annoying, and if he decided to take Bear for a walk in the afternoon, while they were gathered in the lobby to gossip and criticize, he would take the elevator down to the first garage level and walk out the side door.

They had originally purchased a two-bedroom unit with the idea of having Ida move in with them. She declined their invitation, because she valued her independence, had lived at her present location for almost twenty-five years, and because of her baking skill. Her pies always sold out first and were considered so exceptional that advanced orders were taken by the women's society of the little frame church, and she didn't want to create the mess made by their baking in Lila's new home. Ida Taylor's pies became famous through the entire Providence Road corridor.

As May moved into June, they became settled in their new home and arranged things to suit themselves, locating their furniture into a final floor layout.

When they were married, they hadn't taken a wedding trip. On Lila's vacation in July, they planned to drive to Chicago, spend a couple days with Marie and George and then drive down to Branson, Missouri.

Lila was looking forward to the trip, because she had never seen Marie's home, and now that she was happily married, she had the confidence to travel long distances with her beloved Alex.

She planned for the trip, taking just one dressy frock and another for casual wear. She decided to take plenty of casual clothes like shorts and tee shirts since most of their time would be spent traveling.

She used the same formula when packing for Alex, packing a light-weight sport jacket and slacks for dress-up occasions that they might have with Marie and George.

Max, always appreciative of her devotion to the success of his law practice, gave her three extra days off and an unexpected bonus of $500.

She was amused by his concern about her traveling a long distance by auto, acting more like a concerned father than a benevolent boss.

He said, "*Bubala*, make sure that you make your husband drive safe on the Pennsylvania Turnpike. Everybody on that road is like a maniac. Don't get into arguments with speeders. Road rage gets people killed. Make sure you wear your seat belts. Take my telephone number here and at home, and if God forbid, you have an accident, don't say anything until I give you advice. Be careful what you eat when you're traveling. Sometimes when they know you won't come back, they serve you bad food. It's better for you to come back. Maybe you should pack a lunch. Even though your Alex is a *mensch*, me and my Esther worry about you like my daughter."

Alex had made arrangements with Mrs. Gilmore, the breeder from whom he had bought Bear, to board him while they were gone. She assured Alex that Bear was like a personal pet and would have the run of her entire house.

On Friday, they dropped off Bear and headed west, picking up the Pennsylvania Turnpike at the Breezewood interchange and following the 'Pike into Ohio and stopping for the night at a nicely appointed motel in the western part of that state.

Tired from their journey, they slept later than usual. After a late breakfast, they resumed their travel and arrived in the Chicago area in the early afternoon. Alex was unfamiliar with the Chicago suburbs and they wandered around until Lila made him stop at a service station for directions. They arrived at Marie's in the late afternoon.

While Alex unloaded the luggage from their trunk, Lila punched the doorbell. There was an immediate roar that seemed to emanate from a huge watchdog guarding the premises.

They heard Marie yell, "Dammit, Hercules, shut up. Everyone who knows you realizes that if there was real trouble, you'd run to me for protection."

Marie opened the door and the fierce watchdog turned out to be a beautiful honey-colored golden retriever wagging his tail furiously and sniffing at Alex strongly.

Marie hugged Lila and kissed Alex on the cheek and opened the door widely. George, who had been watching a baseball game, upon hearing the uproar, came rushing out of their den and took the luggage from Alex's hands and set it alongside the staircase.

Marie said, "Sit down. You must be tired from your long trip. Are you hungry? George can start the charcoal. We didn't know when you would be arriving so we didn't make any reservations for tonight. George will broil his special marinated chicken for us tonight. Can I get you something cold to drink?"

Lila said, "We got lost. Alex doesn't know Chicago very well."

"Let me get you both some iced tea," Marie interjected. "I'll be right back."

She quickly returned with a tray, on which rested four glasses. "Are you hungry?"

"Not really," Lila replied, "we had a late breakfast."

"Well, we'll eat early," Marie commented.

Hercules finally got through sniffing at Alex and flopped down alongside of him. Alex reached down and started to scratch him behind the ears.

"He seems to like you, Alex," Marie commented.

"He probably smells Bear's scent on my clothes and knows that I'm a dog lover."

Marie commented, "You two look absolutely wonderful, like you're still madly in love. What's your secret?" Without waiting for an answer, she asked, "How's Aunt Ida?"

"She's really fine," Lila replied. "She and I joined Alex's church and she's having a ball baking her apple pies for its monthly bake sales. Her pies are in such demand that they take advanced orders for them. She says that she doesn't have time to be lonely, but she still talks about Charlie."

"She'll talk about Charlie until she dies. It's been over fifty years since he was killed in Normandy, but was the only man that she ever loved.. We owe her so much for what she has done, taking care of us." Turning to Alex, Marie commented, "You're becoming famous. I read your articles in the *Eagle* every month, and I've noticed that they have added your name to the masthead as contributing writer."

George, who had been silent throughout this sisterly reunion, finally commented, "We have reservations for tomorrow night at Ralph Ruby's Steak House in the Loop. He serves the absolutely best corn-fed Midwestern beef in the area. He's a customer of mine so we're assured of getting his best. I've taken Monday off and have the use of the company box on the third base line, so we can really enjoy a baseball game up close."

"While they're out gallivanting around the Loop, Lila, I want to show you this fabulous new mall in Skokie. Skokie is where I got your pillow book. Do you ever use it?"

Lila giggled slyly and replied, "You asked our secret, didn't you?"

Looking at Hercules lying comfortably alongside of Alex, Marie commented, "He really is a wonderful dog. Our neighbors have two little girls who come over here all the time to play with him. He allows them to do outrageous things to him, like putting a bonnet and sunglasses on him, even pulling his fur. Then he'll kiss them. You love corgis, we love goldens. I guess that's the reason why there are so many wonderful breeds of dogs." Marie added, "George, start the charcoal, these people must be faint with hunger."

Everybody slept well that evening, and the next morning when Alex arose to go to the bathroom, he found Hercules sprawled in front of their door. He wagged his tail frantically until Alex stooped down and patted him. He seemed to accept Alex as a close friend and followed him around the entire time they visited.

Later that day, they all went to Ralph Ruby's for dinner. Both Alex and Lila remarked on the outstanding tenderness of their steaks. Ralph himself, who knew George very well, sat at their table for a while. Alex asked him,

"How are you able to get such consistently tender beef?"

Ralph said, "Well, I own my own feed lot downstate, and I don't buy anything that isn't prime. I age the beef at a special temperature, which I've also developed. We sell the parts that we don't use to several area meat markets. I've been thinking of opening my own meat outlet, and I may do so."

The next day, Monday, George took Alex on a tour of Chicago, viewing many of its famous landmarks then ending up for lunch at the Stockhouse Inn, a famous Chicago restaurant, and then attending a baseball game at Wrigley Field.

On Tuesday, Alex regretfully re-packed their luggage back into their car and they drove down to Branson, Missouri, a city famous for its many theaters and show bars featuring well-known entertainers. Not impressed with the quality of their motel, or the one show that they attended, they left after one night and returned to Towson by a more southerly route, stopping at restored Colonial Williamsburg, Virginia. There they dined at a seventeenth-century tavern on roast beef and Yorkshire pudding.

They spent three days in Washington, D.C., and visited Mt. Vernon, the family home of George Washington. They also toured the Smithsonian museums, the National Gallery of Art, the Air and Space Museum and the stark Holocaust Museum. They rode up to the top of the Washington Monument and viewed the sadly beautiful Vietnam Memorial, with the thousands of names of brave young who were killed fighting in that frustrating war.

Returning to Towson, they spent the rest of their vacation at the Ridgeway pool, chatting with their neighbors, having dinner their last vacation night and attending services at the little frame church.

Lila returned to work fully refreshed and eager to resume her duties as a paralegal.

On her return, she found Max to be on a strong rage. One of his oldest clients had been in an automobile accident, and Jeff Lupinsky had learned of it before Max was even aware. Jeff had called the client and told him that he would take a lesser percentage of any judgement or settlement than Max, and the client had foolishly accepted Jeff's offer.

The case was eventually thrown out of court for lack of evidence, and all that developed was that Jeff now had colleague who had formerly just disliked him, but now totally despised him.

The client later called Max and told him that Jeff had the gall to send him a bill for time and charges, despite their verbal agreement that it was a contingency case, with no charges to the client, unless Jeff won a positive verdict. The client also indicated that Jeff had padded the bill, and that he was going to file a formal complaint with the ethics committee of the Maryland bar association.

Max's only comment was, "A leopard never changes its spots and a *gonif* is always a *gonif*. That's how you recognize them. Both are predators without regard for their actions."

Another incident involving Jeff occurred later that summer.

Alex, caught up for the moment with his work, decided to have lunch with Lila. They had just left her office building and were standing on a street corner waiting for the traffic light to change so that they could cross over to the other side.

They heard a beep and looked up to see Jeff driving a new top-of-the-line British import auto. He grinned and waved to them as he passed by.

"My God," said Alex, "will you look at the car that he's driving? It must have cost him $75,000 if it cost him a penny. His legal practice must be booming. Maybe, if you had married him, he'd loan it to you to take Ida grocery shopping."

To the amusement of the Towson lunch crowd, Lila suddenly reached up and grabbed Alex's cheeks and planted a kiss on his lips.

She said, "Now you listen here, Alex Baxter. I had my chance with him, and I chose you to be my lifetime mate. I've never regretted my decision, and I never will. If it's possible, I love you more now than I did when we got married. You're everything that I ever wanted in a man. Don't you ever even hint that I might have feelings for that lousy ambulance chaser. If I know him, and I do, he probably stole the money to buy that fancy set of wheels. Hell, I love my little car, and just wouldn't feel right behind the wheel of a car like that. With his vicious temper, he'd raise holy hell with me if I got a scratch on the paint. He'd probably make me pay for it. I'll stick with you, even if you find a rear end that you like better than mine."

Despite the crowded street, Alex slapped her rear end soundly and they crossed the street, happily laughing.

Jeff's antics seemed to be designed to draw attention to him, a common trait of insecure persons. When he was having lunch with someone, he would laugh loudly as if to let others know that he was having a great time, and always dressed flamboyantly, even in his court appearances.

Alex had a strong suspicion that he was very lonely and had trouble relating normally to others, especially women. He believed that Jeff had dated

Lila, sensing that she was emotionally vulnerable.

Ida, in her feisty wisdom, seemed to put her finger on the root cause: his relationship with his father. Why, with his income and at his age, was he still living with his parents, and still under their firm control?

Alex felt that Jeff was badly warped by the bizarre, un-fatherly actions of Big Bill, and was reacting like a badly maintained steam valve and might blow up at any time. He was happy that Lila had the foresight to recognize Jeff's inadequacies because when the potentially dangerous activities he was engaged in came to a head, with her still healing her inner self, she would have had to bear the brunt of his nonsense. His actions had the potential of irreparably damaging her emotional health for a long time.

CHAPTER 11

In September, Alex received a call from Rick, his editor at the *Eagle*.

"Alex, you've been a contributor here for a long time. We keep getting letters from readers asking about you—who you are, what you look like, your background and questions like that. We would like to do a background story on you to satisfy the curiosity of those readers. Can you put together a resume and email it to me? After we receive it, we can do a bio on you for publication in a future issue. If you agree, we can send a photographer down to Maryland to take pictures to go along with the story. You might want to get your wife in the pictures as well, because essentially we are a family magazine."

Alex was flattered by the request and said, "Sure, Rick, I'll send something up to you by tomorrow afternoon."

When Lila got home that evening, Alex told her about the call, and that she was to be included in the pictures that would accompany his biography.

Several days later, the phone rang, and a voice that Alex didn't recognize spoke out saying, "Hey, Alex, where the hell is this Townsend where you live? I'm lost in the sticks somewhere and I need help in finding you out here in these boonies." The voice had a distinctive Brooklyn accent.

Alex asked, "Who is this?"

"This is Frank McGuire, the photographer that Rick Kelly sent down to shoot you. Ha, Ha, Ha."

"Where are you?" Alex asked.

"Somewhere in the boondocks on Route 40," the voice replied.

Alex said, "First of all, you're taking the long way to get here. The Kennedy highway is closer, and is a better and faster road."

The voice then repeated, "Where the hell is Townsend?"

Alex repeated, "Where are you?"

He heard a sound like a phone booth door and heard the voice yell out, "Hey, what's the name of this place?" The voice came back and said. "Some rube just told me that it's called Aberdeen."

Alex gave him directions and repeated them twice to make certain that they were understood. "It's Towson, not Townsend. It'll take you about an hour to get here. Are you planning to spend the night in Maryland?"

"Yeah," said the voice. "Rick got a reservation at a hotel there. Have your little woman there. I want to include her in the shots. Don't get out of the Big Apple much, and I want to look around to see how the hicks live."

Alex was now irritated by the familiarity of someone that he didn't know. He said, "You're lucky that you didn't get here last week. You would have missed our new electric power. It sure beats the old kerosene lamps. I hope that I can remember how to switch it on."

The voice said, "Ha, Ha, Ha. I'll see you in a couple of hours."

Alex called Lila and said, "Honey, the photographer that Rick has sent down is on his way into 'Townsend' to take pictures of us rubes. He thinks that anything south of New Jersey is still virgin, unexplored territory. Stop off at the root cellar and bring home a jar of your pickled red beets. Be sure to wipe off the cow flop from your feet. It's starting to smell up the front parlor."

Lila giggled and said, "I'll be right home, honey."

She arrived soon after, and the desk called later and said, "Mr. Baxter, there's a Mr. McGuire here to see you."

Alex said, "Send him up."

When the doorbell rang, Alex answered it and discovered that Frank McGuire was a short, very bald, portly man wearing heavy glasses and loaded down with three camera bags.

The first thing that McGuire said was, "This is a snazzy pad that you live in. It would cost over three grand a month in the city, if you could find one like it."

Alex introduced him to Lila, and he said, "You're beautiful enough to be a photographer's model. Have you ever thought of moving to New York? I could line up a lot of gigs for you and get you onto the *Eagle's* cover with no sweat. You'd be a supermodel in no time at all. I'll leave my card with you before I leave."

Lila replied, "No thank you. I'm too happy being the wife of Farmer Baxter here in Hicksville. I hate the wild, frantic lifestyle of New York. Besides that, who would milk the cows after I left?"

McGuire replied, "Well, I could start you off at $100 an hour, and we could build from there."

Alex could see that McGuire's lack of tact was starting to irritate Lila, so he changed the subject and asked McGuire, "What kind of photographs do you want to take?"

McGuire said, "Well, they're going to be published in a fall issue, so I guess that sweaters and slacks will be OK."

They changed into sweaters and slacks, and he shot a large number of pictures, some with Alex alone, some with Bear, some with the three of them sitting on the sofa, and other poses.

To be polite, Alex asked him if he would like to have dinner with them.

He said, "No, I'm going to wander around Townsend and take some pictures of the local rubes. For the boonies, this is a nice little burg. It kind of reminds me of Canarsie. I have to get back to the city by tomorrow. Anyway, I have to get up by nine a.m."

Alex said, "Well, it's too bad that you won't be here on Saturday night. There's a big square dance at the Grange Hall, and some of the farmer's daughters come to town all dressed up in the latest fashions from the mail catalogue. Man, it's 23 skidoo, all the way. Almost everybody has their corn crops harvested, and everybody is sleeping late, sometimes until five a.m."

McGuire said, "That's verrry funny. You're a real standup comic. Do you write your own material?"

When he left, Lila said, "What an odd little man. Some of his comments sound like they're out of the Joe Miller vaudeville joke book."

Alex replied, "Honey, with his lack of tact he wouldn't qualify as the ambassador to South Ironia. You can be sure that he takes great photographs or Rick wouldn't send him down here. You missed your big chance to become a supermodel in the Big Apple."

All that Lila did was snort and throw a pillow at him.

A week or so later, Rick called Alex and said, "McGuire enjoyed his visit with you. He says that you have great sense of humor and that your wife is very beautiful. His pictures are real good, and I'm sending copies of them down to you for your own use. Look for yourselves in the spotlight section of the

October edition."

The biography of Alex featured several photographs of him, Lila and Bear, the largest of which was one of Lila and he sitting on their sofa with Bear in the middle, engaged in an enormous yawn. It was headlined:

THE EAGLE'S ALEX BAXTER AT HOME WITH HIS LOVELY WIFE LILA AND THEIR WELSH CORGI HONEYBEAR

Lila took a copy of that shot, had it framed and placed it on her desk at work. She later bought a picture album and mounted all of the pictures of them together, along with a copy of the biography that she clipped out of the *Eagle*. She entitled it "The Baxters—Our First Year Together."

Pearl asked Alex to autograph her copy of the *Eagle*, and Alex wrote: *To Pearl Miller, a dear friend and one of the nicest people that I know, Alex Baxter.* Pearl said that she was going to keep that issue on her coffee table because Alex was one of the most famous and definitely the nicest person that she waited on; she wanted everybody who visited her to know that.

Both Alex and Lila believed that Jeff had stopped carrying the torch for Lila. An incident at the clerk's office proved them wrong.

Lila was filing some service documents at the clerk's office when Jeff walked in. He attempted to grab her and kiss her on the mouth. Lila, aware that the entire clerk's staff was watching and the gossip that would be generated, angrily shook her arms free and turned her head.

She became livid with anger and said, "Damn you, Jeff Lupinsky, back off and leave me alone. You know that I'm married to Alex Baxter, and you know how much I love him. He's everything that I've ever wanted in a man, everything that you're not nor ever will be. He's thoughtful, honest, gentle and caring. Those are qualities that you know nothing about. He's the only man in this world that I love or ever will love. Find yourself a woman who's impressed with your father's big house. Find someone who can tolerate your selfish attitudes, your bad temper and kinky lifestyle, and keep your hands off me. If you ever try that on me again, so help me, I'll get a warrant against you for assault and disorderly conduct. Do I make myself clear?"

The entire clerk's staff smiled openly and would have applauded if they would have been allowed, because Jeff always treated them as second-class citizens and demanded that they take care of his official needs immediately.

Jeff reddened with embarrassment and rapidly left to go to the men's room and stayed there until he was certain the Lila had left the courthouse.

After that encounter, Jeff maintained an arm's length attitude towards Lila, and even though he may have desired her, he wasn't foolish enough to make any more passes at her.

Max was very disturbed by Jeff's conduct and wanted to call Jeff and outline the proper conduct that should be maintained by professionals at the courthouse, but Lila restrained him.

Max muttered to himself, "Not only is that Lupinsky a *gonif*, but he's also dumb jackass."

Max ran into Jeff one day at the courthouse. Jeff, still smarting from Lila's public embarrassment of him, pretended that he didn't see Max. Max tapped him on the shoulder and said, "Listen here, Lupinsky, if you ever try a cheap trick like that on Lila Baxter again I will personally see that a formal complaint is made against you with the bar association to go along with hundreds that are now on file. You're treading on thin ice toward disbarment."

Jeff just shrugged his shoulders and walked away.

It seemed that everyone who knew Jeff realized that he was on some sort of self-destruction compulsion and needed psychiatric therapy to determine why he was engaged in such bizarre activities.

Ida repeated her opinions about the root cause. "That man hates his father for the way that he has treated him. Big Al is so obsessed with making money that he has destroyed his son in the process. He's crying out for help, and his father is clipping coupons."

On a Tuesday shortly after that, Alex picked up his copy of the Towson *Tribune* and saw a headline that startled him:

GRAND JURY INDICTS LOCAL ATTORNEY.

The accompanying article stated that a local lawyer, Jeffrey R. Lupinsky, had been arraigned for embezzling over $90,000 from the estate of a William A. Baker, who had left his estate in trust for his severely handicapped son Billy. Lupinsky had transferred close to $100,000 in negotiable securities, using his power of attorney, to his personal account.

The account went to say that the evidence, as presented, was developed by an independent audit authorized by the boy's uncle who noticed that substantial amounts were missing from the bank balance of the account.

It further stated that Lupinsky had used the money to buy an expensive automobile, jewelry, clothing and lavish dinners, using his credit card to try to launder the money.

Lupinsky had pleaded innocent and had been released in his own recognizance, and a trial date had not yet been established

Alex's thoughts returned to that summer day when he and Lila were standing on the Towson street corner, and Jeff had sped by in a new a car, and how Lila had said, "I'll bet that he stole the money to buy that toy...."

Jeff avoided jail time by refunding all the money that he embezzled and changing his plea to nolo contendre. He was fined $10,000, and was given a suspended sentence of five years, forced to perform 2,000 hours of community service and placed under supervised probation three years.

Refunding the entire embezzled amount left him totally destitute. His license to practice law in the state of Maryland was revoked, and he was forced to resign from the bar in disgrace.

Max said he had seen this sequence of events coming, because a gray wolf couldn't disguise himself in a flock of sheep forever. Sooner or later, his true color would show up. He also commented that when you shook Jeff's hand, you had to count your fingers to see if they were all there.

After he was disbarred, Jeff formed a consultancy to develop evidence and present it as an expert witness. This was a blatant attempt to practice law without a license. That venture failed because none of his former colleagues would retain him, remembering his heavy-handed, want-it-all attitude. He next obtained a franchise to sell law books with the same result.

Max, in his native wisdom, commented, "You have to be careful whom you step on, on your way to the top, because you meet the same people on the way down."

Jeff drifted from job to job, because the larcenous streak in his character always surfaced and he would be caught dipping into the till. He even had the nerve, or *chutzpah* as Max termed it, to ask if could use Max's name as a reference when he applied for positions of trust with large corporations. Max told him that he valued his too reputation to permit that.

The unfortunate Murphy's Law struck out at him also. He resided at his father's home, and his father had made all his money by buying margin-purchased stocks. Overextended, he was caught short by a black Monday crash of the market, and he couldn't cover his loans. He was forced to sell his mansion in Ruxton and return to his old trade of meat cutting on Eastern Avenue. Jeff was forced to move into a seedy old apartment building that was all that he could afford.

Lila, one Saturday, said she saw him selling shoes in a mall store and that he really looked terrible. In her gentle compassionate way, she told Alex she was really sorry that he had fallen from the lofty heights of legal practice, and that she wished she could help him. Her innate sense of compassion overcame the many selfish, bordering-on-cruel acts that Jeff had performed during the time of her relationship with him.

Alex, who agreed with Max's evaluation of Jeff's fall, didn't reply because he didn't have the degree of compassion for Jeff. Jeff had been the master of his own ship and had guided it recklessly onto the rocks of life.

Lila and Alex were essentially gentle, decent, and open-minded individuals whose major emotion was their massive devotion towards each other. With such a healthy attitude, it was difficult for them to understand how a person with Jeff's education and people skills could completely turn his back on the canons of ethics that he had so laboriously studied in law school.

Alex had always felt that Jeff had some major flaw in his makeup and was less emotional over his fall from grace. He remarked one day to Lila, "Jeff had every chance to straighten his life out, and can still do it if he can submit to the discipline that it takes. He's like a kid in a candy store. He thinks that he can get away by stealing bits of candy. He could get away with it when he stole little pieces. When he stole a whole pound of it, he got caught."

Lila said, "Oh, honey, he really needs help."

Alex retorted, "Sweetheart, he has to begin by helping himself. Who was it that said, 'You have to get off your knees and help God'?"

CHAPTER 12

With Thanksgiving came their first anniversary. They had been married on Thanksgiving Saturday, and there was a couple of days difference, but Thanksgiving Saturday was easier to remember, so that was the day that they celebrated on.

Alex's anniversary present to Lila was a plain gold medallion that he had engraved on both sides. On one side, he had engraved, "My Lila, my love. How lucky I was to meet you." On the other side, he had engraved, "Someday, I'll meet you at the end of the tunnel," a reference to his declaration of eternal love for his Lila.

He attached it to a long-stemmed red rose, which he still frequently purchased for her, and Lila was so pleased with the sentiment that she vowed that she would never remove the medallion from her neck as long as she lived.

She gave Alex a pair gold cufflinks depicting a cupid aiming an arrow. She had secretly purchased them at Morey's after she called him ask if he had anything special that she could obtain for Alex's anniversary gift.

They celebrated at Luigi's and he made a special point of congratulating them when they arrived. "Lila, if there ever was marriage made in heaven, it's yours. Your love for each other hasn't diminished one little bit in this past year. It just makes me feel so very good inside."

Pearl congratulated them as well, and when they stepped out on the dance floor, the lounge combo started to play the anniversary waltz in their honor.

After dinner, Luigi presented them with a small cake smothered in whipped cream, with a glowing sparkler, as a tribute to Lila's insatiable sweet tooth.

That first milestone in their lives together made Alex think back to the day when he had first seen her leaning into the trunk of the old car that she used to drive, and how stunned he had been at her beauty, especially her beautiful hazel eyes, as she had emerged from under the trunk lid.

He also remembered the moment when their glances had locked on the pool house deck as they surrendered themselves to each other, and their desire for each other kept mounting until they could stand it no longer and made frantic love to each other.

That anniversary night they discovered that their passion for each other was unabated as they drove each other to higher emotional levels when they did make love.

Max's practice turned upwards as his reputation of being a capable and ethical lawyer increased. He brought in additional cases to be tried in court.

Lila, to keep abreast with the caseload, drove herself hard, working late several evenings a week. She developed a nagging problem of indigestion that over-the-counter remedies didn't seem to be able to alleviate. She constantly felt bloated and gassy, but after a while that problem seemed to correct itself and disappear.

Alex continued his pleasant habit of keeping her company, together with his faithful Bear alongside of him, when she worked late. Afterwards, they would walk home holding hands.

With Thanksgiving came the traditional start of the wonderful Christmas season. For such a short while people's often hidden good side appeared to surface.

As usual, the Towson streets were gaily decorated, and so were the malls and individual stores within them.

People took on an air of goodwill; organized charities, to take advantage of this season of giving, sent mass mailings; and children, expecting a visit from the jolly old elf, became as good as gold. Their older brothers and sisters took part-time jobs to obtain money for holiday gift giving. Merchants rubbed their hands together as they anticipated a good sales season, hoping to unload merchandise that wasn't normally saleable.

Alex erected their little tree in front of their window, decorated it, and wrapped a garland of colored lights around the guardrail of their balcony.

They hung three red stockings on the table and the usual gaily wrapped packages began to mysteriously appear under the tree branches.

That year, Alex bought Lila a beautiful, white brocade evening pajama outfit. Its widely cut pants looked like a gown when she was standing still. The white against her beautiful olive skin was dramatic, and she looked truly beautiful when she wore it.

He also gave her a flagon of her favorite light-smelling fragrance, a gold ankle bracelet, and small Christmas tree charm for the bracelet that he had previously given to her.

Lila gave him a duplicate of the medallion that he had presented to her as an anniversary gift. On it she had engraved, "My Alex, my husband, my love, my life." She also presented him with a tan, mohair sport jacket and matching brown slacks and two tickets to *The Nutcracker* ballet, which they both enjoyed because of its beautiful music and orientation towards children. They had now reached the stage in their marriage where they wanted to start raising children.

Ida got a set of stainless steel cookware that she had been looking at. Bear got the usual replacement squeeze toys and rawhide bones.

They attended the 11:00 a.m. Christmas service at the little frame church and dropped Ida off on their way home.

As usual, they received numerous invitations to Christmas parties and holiday open houses and did accept one or two extended by close friends, which were to be held during Christmas week.

At one of these, Lila, wearing one of her favorite outfits, the green silk pants suit that Alex had given to her, was dancing with Alex when he felt a tap on his shoulder as of someone cutting in. He looked up and saw a total stranger. Before he could ask Lila if she wanted to dance, the stranger whirled her away, holding her tightly.

Alex waited until the number was finished and then walked up to the man who was still holding her tightly. "May I have my wife back?"

The stranger said, "No. This is a party and people dance at parties. I want to dance with her again."

Alex saw that the man was drunk and shoved Lila behind him, just as the man was making a fist. He hit Alex on the jaw, knocking him to the floor.

Women screamed and the host said, "All right, Mark, that's enough. I won't have you abusing my guests. I want you to leave right now. Do you need someone to drive you home?"

The stranger stormed out of the party without another word.

The host asked, "Are you all right, Alex?"

Alex felt his jaw and replied, "Yes, I am. Who was that?"

"That was Mark Foster. He's a compulsive alcoholic whose wife just left him, taking their three children with her. She's been after him for years to join AA, but he's always refused. Finally she had it with him and left. He's a loan officer with one of the larger banks here, and is going to lose his job if he's not careful. Basically, like many alcoholics, he's a pretty nice guy. He'll call you after he sobers up and apologize. He's just enraged that she left him. I hope that he gets home in one piece. The county cops are out in full force this week, trying to keep the accident rate down."

On the following Tuesday, Alex picked up his copy of the Towson *Tribune*, and under the section titled "Police Blotter," he saw an item that a Mark Foster had been held over at a precinct lockup on a DUI charge. It further said that he was so violent that it took three police officers to restrain him while arresting him and that he was released after posting $1,500 bail. The trial date was pending.

Foster did call to apologize and said that he had made a complete ass of himself at the party. He said that he was going to join AA, because if he didn't, he would end up killing himself or somebody else while he was drunk. He asked Alex to have lunch with him. Alex declined, telling him his work schedule was too tight. Mark also sent Lila a bouquet of flowers to apologize for his rudeness.

Lila, who always saw the good side of everybody, and whose father had been an alcoholic, said, "It really is tragic, honey, when somebody who has a genetic weakness for alcohol has trouble recognizing how sick he really is. I hope that he can complete the twelve steps of Alcoholics Anonymous and stays off alcohol, and I hope that he gets his family back."

Alex, whose father's death had been alcoholically related, didn't comment.

They stayed home on New Year's Eve, preferring each other's company to a wild night on the town with total strangers, and were in bed snuggled together before the young new year was ushered in.

CHAPTER 13

In January, Lila celebrated her fortieth birthday.

Alex bought her a diamond pedant and attached it to one of the long-stem roses that he frequently purchased for her.

When she discovered it, she broke into tears and said, "Oh, honey, why did you spend so much money on me? Something small to remember the date would have been just as nice."

Alex, with his usual embarrassment at such comments, said, "I just wanted to show you how much I loved you."

That evening, when they had dinner at Luigi's, he briefly sat at their table, and Lila showed him the pedant.

Luigi remarked, "You know, the special affinity that you two have for each other almost makes me believe in fairy tales. It's almost as if somewhere back in the mists of time you two were created, and it was decreed that you two be made together. And it was decreed that you would meet and fall madly in love with each other, and that no earthly force could keep you apart from each other. I wish that I had the talent to write a novel about you. What a powerful story it would make."

Lila slid her hand under the table and squeezed Alex's hand tightly, and they both smiled at Luigi's wise comments.

Max's practice continued to grow, and Lila was required to work several additional evenings a week just to stay ahead of her massive caseload. The problem of her gastric distress returned and non-prescriptive remedies just didn't seem to relieve it. Like it had previously, it seemed to take care of itself naturally and just disappeared.

Alex, always concerned about her well-being, urged her to make an appointment with her personal physician, Dr. McGrath, who was a gynecologist.

Lila, trying to be logical with Alex, asked him, "Honey, how could a gas attack be related to anything gynecological?"

Alex replied, "Baby, everything in health matters is related to something else."

She said, "Well, it could be related to your pot roast. Sometimes is so tough that it could be used as body armor, even though I always appreciate your cooking dinner when I work late. I think that it's just the pressure of work that gets to me."

January was a bleak, gray month, cold and raw. Normally pleasant persons would venture outdoors only when they had to, made the briefest of comments to each other and then scurried back into the comfortable warmth from which they had emerged.

Normally active Ida started to complain of fatigue and lack of energy when she performed her normal household chores. She said that on some days she became exhausted just crossing the room.

Lila made an appointment for her to see Dr. McGrath. He examined her thoroughly and listened to her heartbeat several times through his stethoscope.

The doctor said, "Miss Taylor, I believe that I hear a murmur in the area of your aortic valve. Since this is within the discipline of cardiology, and I'm a gynecologist, I don't feel qualified to make a positive judgement on that. I have a colleague, Dr. Martin Glass, to whom I refer patients with cardiologically related problems. He was a classmate of mine at Johns Hopkins School of Medicine. He is a graduate fellow in cardiology and has published several articles in JAMA, The Journal of the American Medical Society, and is well regarded as an expert diagnostician within the Maryland medical society. He practices at both St. Matthew's, here in Towson and GMMC."

GMMC is the familiar name by which local residents refer to the Greater Maryland Medical Center, also located in Towson.

Lila, who had been watching Dr. McGrath's conversation, saw Ida pale with fear and seem to withdraw into herself.

Ida replied, "Go ahead, doctor. Have his office call my niece at her office and let's get this nonsense over with."

Dr. McGrath called in his office nurse and said, "Hilda, will you call Dr. Glass' office and arrange for him to see Miss Taylor at his early convenience?"

On the way home, Ida said to Lila, "I've been wanting to see Charlie for a long time now. I guess that I won't have to wait much longer."

Lila suddenly became irritated with Ida's defeatist attitude and said, "Dammit, Aunt Ida, don't hang the crepe on your door yet. Your condition may be something that's completely treatable. Medical science has advanced in major leaps over the past few years. Whether you like it or not, you're going to have dinner with Alex and me tonight."

Several days later, Dr. Glass' office called Lila at work and established an appointment at his St. Matthew's office for the following Thursday.

They found that Dr. Glass was thin, almost to the point of emaciation. He was very businesslike and examined Ida thoroughly, listening to her heart action very carefully.

When he was completed, he said, "Miss Taylor, I do hear a distinct murmur in your aortal valve. I would like you to take an echocardiogram at the echo lab here at St. Matthew's. This is a non-invasive procedure that uses the same ultrasonic technology used by women to predetermine the sex of their unborn children. It is entirely painless, and we use it to determine if a cardiological problem exists and to what extent it is present.

"After the test has been taken, I'll have more accurate data on which to base a diagnosis, and we can sit down and discuss treatments and alternatives. Since fluid builds up within the body in certain conditions, I am going to prescribe for you a diuretic called Furosimide. It is also called Lasix.

"I want you to take two tablets before breakfast every day. If you plan on being out that day, you may take them on your return.

"It is important that you follow my instructions, otherwise you are wasting my time and your money. My nurse will set up the appointment for the echo, and for your follow-up visit with me. I want you to immediately start on a low-salt, low-fat diet and try to watch your cholesterol and saturated fat ingestion. She will also draw some blood for some blood tests that I want taken. Do you have any questions?"

Ida replied, "No, doctor, but I'll make a list for my next visit."

"That will be fine," he replied.

"I don't like that man," Ida said to Lila on the way home. "He's too bossy."

Lila giggled and responded, "You don't like him because he won't let you have your own way. He's regarded to be among the best cardiologists in Maryland. He was called to the White House on a consultation a couple of years ago. Let's get your prescription filled and make sure that you take it as he prescribed."

Ida took the echo as ordered and during the test asked the technician what it revealed.

She replied, "I'm sorry, Miss Taylor, only doctors are permitted to interpret the echo findings with patients. I'm sure that Dr. Glass will answer any questions that you may have about the scan. Why don't you hold any questions until your next appointment with him?"

"Hell, girl, I'm just asking about my own body," Ida retorted.

The technician replied, "I realize that, ma'am, but doctors are trained to interpret the results. All I do is run the equipment."

On their way home, Ida remarked, "That sure is an uppity bunch at that hospital. The girl who was giving me the test wouldn't give me the time of the day about what was going on. I sure hope that the uppity doctor will clue me in."

At her follow-up visit with Dr. Glass, before he got into discussing the echo results, he examined her chest cavity with his stethoscope. After he was through, he frowned and said, "Miss Taylor, are you taking the Lasix as I prescribed it? I detect the presence of fluid buildup in your chest. It's extremely important that you follow a regimen when I prescribe one. A heart problem is nothing to fool around with. If it stops pumping blood through your system, your body will die."

Ida responded, "Hell, doctor, I didn't realize that it was that serious. I cheated on taking the damned stuff like someone on a diet cheats by eating a piece of cake."

Dr. Glass just frowned and replied, "You're EKG, the electrocardiogram, has revealed that your heartbeat is slowing down. The blood tests have indicated that your bad cholesterol is in excess of 300 and your good cholesterol is less than 40.

"Your echo has revealed that there is strong calcification in the aortal valve. That is generally the result of the aging process. The valve has thickened and become less flexible. This has resulted in your heart having difficulty in pumping blood through your aorta, which is the main artery in the human system. The result is that the oxygen supply that your body needs to sustain life has been severely restricted.

"I also suspect that there is a buildup of plaque deposits within your body because I can hear a turbulence in the carotid arteries of your neck.

"Your health condition, Miss Taylor, is more than cheating by eating a piece of cake. You just have one heart, and if it stops pumping blood through your body one thing is certain, you'll die. You have developed a condition that is generally known as congestive heart failure. What this term means is that your heart needs assistance in elimination of the fluid buildup in your body. That's the reason for diuretics like Lasix.

"That is what is causing your constant fatigue. Your body isn't getting the oxygen that it needs, because your heart's squeeze action is not strong enough to push blood through your body.

"There are procedures which have been developed to assist, to some degree, the failing heart. The one most often used is called angioplasty and involves the insertion of a wire device through your groin into an artery through the areas that may be clogged by plaque deposits to determine where such blockages are located, then stents may be inserted to maintain the blood flow through those areas.

"You may visualize what a stent looks like by imagining the shape of a hair roller, miniaturized down to the level, where it can be inserted into an artery that is blocked. These are composed of mesh and act as a sort of sieve to allow the blood to be more readily transported through the body.

"Plaque deposits in blood vessels may be compared to deposits on the interior of water pipes. Over a period of time they build up, limiting the amount of fluid that may pass through, and if neglected, severely limiting the blood flow through the human arteries.

"Where the blockage is not total, a balloon-like device, which can be inflated, can be inserted to broaden the blood vessel to assist the blood flow.

"Excellent results in lessening the fatigue have been achieved through these procedures. Additional tests would be necessary to determine if you are a suitable candidate for such procedures.

"Ultimately, and I only mention it at this time to make you aware of its availability, the valve itself may be replaced. This is a major operation involving the insertion of either a tissue or mechanical valve into the heart itself. If that becomes necessary, we can discuss it at that time.

"As I have said to you at a prior time, it is vitally important that you follow my instructions completely. Otherwise you are just wasting your money and my time in visiting my office."

After the blowup that occurred at Dr. Glass' office, Ida was shaken to the point where she took the medications that she had been prescribed. After a time, whether she got careless or didn't want to be dictated to, she started to slip in her daily routine and often didn't take her pills.

Lila was beside herself with worry. Max's practice had increased to where she was now working overtime on several evenings a week, and Ida's illness in addition to the overtime that she was working was causing her to become extremely anxious.

She discussed the problem with Alex, who came up with a plausible solution.

He said, "Honey, why not hire a nurse/companion for Ida. She could make sure that Ida took her medicines, and at the same time provide her with companionship and monitor her vital signs."

They discussed the idea with Dr Glass, who by this time was growing tired of the resistance that Ida was giving him. He said, "It couldn't do anything but help with that bull-headed woman."

Marie agreed to pay for half of the cost related to retaining a qualified person, and Alex ran an ad in the Towson *Tribune* for a nurse/companion.

They interviewed several from the responses that they received, and finally settled on a woman named Keisha Paddington.

She was a LPN, a licensed practical nurse, who had experience with semi-ambulatory patients. She had just finished up on a ten-month terminal cancer case. Her children were all grown, and her husband had long disappeared from her domestic scene. She had her own transportation and could stay over at Ida's in an emergency situation.

After settling on her salary and hours, she agreed to start the following Monday, if Ida liked her.

Ida did like her and they eventually became fast friends, and would sit for hours discussing child raising, baking and cooking. After a period of time, with knowledge of Ida's dietary requirements, she took over the weekly grocery shopping from Lila, allowing her to get some much-needed rest on the weekends.

Ida finally gave up baking the twenty or so monthly pies for the women's society of the little frame church, and she and Keisha developed a no-holds-barred pinochle game to fill out their afternoons. Ida did, however, take her medications regularly and on time.

Keisha learned to enjoy Ida's sometimes biting humor that always contained some kernel of wisdom hidden within it. Ida's comments like, "Life is a four-letter word, depending on your mood," "I'm as busy as a peg-legged boy in a butt-kicking contest," "I'm so old that the handsome men that used to smile at me now laugh right out loud," and other salty gems tickled Keisha's sense of humor. Alex was thinking of compiling these rare bits of native American humor into a book eulogizing Ida.

Keisha sometimes stayed in Ida's spare bedroom when Ida wasn't feeling well, and she took long naps after breakfast and during the afternoon before their daily pinochle struggle.

With Ida virtually housebound, Lila and Alex no longer enjoyed the drive up to the Hunter's Inn for brunch after their Sunday services. Instead, they started eating Sunday breakfast at the Diner. This was a typical stainless steel building set in the center of Towson. Like all diners, the food was uncomplicated, well prepared and the portions were large. They often met other members of the little frame church there, as well as other friends of theirs.

One Sunday morning, after the service was completed, they stopped in at the Diner for one of their famous omelets. They were seated in a booth ready to order when Alex heard a familiar voice, that of his ex-wife Connie.

He looked up at her, and for a moment, didn't recognize her. Her hair was dyed jet black. Alex remembered her last as a being red haired.

She was holding her hand out to Lila. "I'm Connie, Alex's ex-wife. I used to share his bed with him."

This was the equivalent of waving a red blanket in front of an enraged bull, because Lila had heard numerous tales of Connie's escapades with other men during Alex's ill-fated marriage to her.

She ignored Connie's extended hand and coldly said, "I'm Lila Baxter, Alex's wife, and I'm happy to be sharing it with him exclusively, and not looking for greener pastures."

If this dented Connie's armor, she didn't show it at all. She said to Alex, "You're becoming famous. I saw that biography of you and Bear in the *Eagle* a while back. It was pretty neat. I got some mail from the alumni association about a class reunion. Do you plan to attend?"

Alex responded, "I got the same mailing, but Lila and I are not going."

Connie said, "That's too bad. We both had a lot of fun in college."

Alex asked her, "Connie, are you still married to the land baron?"

Connie said, "No, that just lasted a couple of months. He preferred playing high-stakes poker and attending the races at Pimlico to being with me. He took up with some stripper from the block."

Alex couldn't resist saying, "I wonder why?"

The block is Baltimore's notorious cabaret section.

Placing his hand with its obvious wedding ring on Lila's, Alex said, "I never did thank you for divorcing me, did I? If I hadn't been for that, I would never have met my wonderful Lila, who is the most wonderful wife that any man could ever want, and she is absolutely my greatest treasure. I love her madly, and so does Bear. I can honestly say, I've never been happier in my life. Thank you."

Connie said, "I made the biggest mistake of my life when I divorced you."

Alex said, "That's funny, I think so too."

After Connie left, Lila, who was fit to be tied by Connie's bold come-on to her Alex, said, "How could you stand that bitch? She reminds me of some alley cat that's trying to sneak back into the home that she deserted. With her six pounds of makeup on, she looks like the original Painted Woman."

Secretly, however, she was proud of the way that her Alex had handled the encounter, and more than that, she was pleased with his laying his love for her on the line to that hard-faced, dissipated, painted hussy.

Connie rejoined a man who was at least ten years younger than she. This was obviously the lover that she had spent the night with. They saw her slip him some money to pay for their breakfasts.

Alex sarcastically remarked, "Ah, the joys of plastic-surgery-perpetuated youth. I wonder how long that one has been on the beds-for-breakfast circuit? Better still, my darling, I wonder how much longer he'll put up with her shenanigans. Do you think that she would turn Jeff on? But then she would emasculate him emotionally, and eunuchs aren't the greatest lovers, are they? I wonder what interesting stud she'll have with her the next time that we see her. Stay tuned, America, for the next chapter of 'The Perils of Connie.'"

Lila giggled and said, "Stop it, you silly idiot, I'm beginning to think that you're jealous of that poor guy that she fished out of some drainage ditch." By this time, Lila was laughing out loud at Alex's amusing parody. "Honey, you *amaize* me with your corny remarks. You must have bought a license to use McGuire's old-time joke book. All that you need is a red nose and baggy pants and the Diner would have its own burlesque review."

CHAPTER 14

Ida's health continued to fail, and her fatigue increased to the point that if she crossed a room, perhaps to turn on the TV, she became exhausted and had to sit down to catch her breath. Even with those critical symptoms of coronary insufficiency, she refused to consider the insertion of stents into her body.

She slept longer, took more frequent naps, and became more of a couch potato than an active participant in life. Keisha took to staying in her guest bedroom several nights a week, out of concern for Ida's well-being.

One evening when Lila wasn't working at Max's office, Lila and Alex were watching a movie and their phone rang. Lila answered the phone. It was Keisha.

"Mrs. Baxter, I can't awaken Miss Ida from her afternoon nap. I've called 911, and I'm having them take her to St. Matthew's emergency room. Can you both meet us there? I believe that there is something terribly wrong with her."

Lila and Alex hurriedly drove the short distance to St. Matthew's and arrived just as the county ambulance was pulling in, followed closely by Keisha in her own vehicle. They watched helplessly while the inert body of Ida was wheeled on a gurney stretcher into one of the examination cubicles.

The three of them sat down in the general waiting room, waiting for some word about Ida's condition. Dr. Glass arrived looking serious and entered the examination room.

After what seemed to be an eternity to the waiting trio, he emerged and sat down beside them, saying, "Miss Taylor has suffered a massive stroke and is in critical condition. Her vital signs indicate that she may not survive through the night. We're going to admit her and keep her here until the extent of her gravity is fully determined. The nurses are cleaning her up and she will be taken to a room as soon as one is located for her. You may remain here as long as you choose, but she probably will remain comatose indefinitely. The hospital knows how to reach me if necessary. I'm sorry, but we have done all that can be done, and all we can do now is monitor her condition."

Alex pulled out his checkbook and wrote out a check to Keisha for the regular amount of money due to her and added a generous bonus for her devotion and loyalty. Handing her the check, he said, "Keisha, thank you for being such a wonderful and loyal person. If you care to, you can remain with Lila and me while we wait. If you want, you can go home to your family. That's your decision. You've been a marvelous right arm throughout this whole ordeal."

Keisha replied, "Mr. Alex, I'm dead tired. I've been up two nights straight with her. If you don't mind, I want to go home and get some sleep before I keel over in a big heap."

Alex hugged her fondly and said, "If by some miracle she pulls out of this, either Lila or I will call. In any case, we will let you know."

Lila was crying softly, so Alex pulled her to him and she lay against him with her head on his shoulder.

She said, "Oh, honey, we won't even get a chance to say goodbye to her. I owe her so much that will never be repaid. If she hadn't been so damned stubborn and had followed Dr. Glass' orders, she wouldn't be teetering on the brink right now."

After Keisha left, Lila and Alex waited until the unconscious Ida was wheeled out of the examination room. They followed the gurney, pushed by two orderlies, onto the elevator and into a room several flights above the emergency room. There, they sat in silent vigil, helpless in the face of the Grim Reaper, silently praying for Ida's well-being, but not saying a whole lot to each other.

Lila used the room telephone to call Marie in Chicago and let her know the tragic news.

Marie said, "George and I will be in as soon as we can book a flight out of O'Hare."

By this time, Lila had broken down completely, and sat down on Alex's lap, leaning against him with her head on his shoulder, softly crying over what seemed to be the inevitable loss of Ida.

Alex patted her shoulder softly and kissed her cheek comfortingly. "Let it all out, honey. It's OK. I'll always be here to take care of you. She really died when her Charlie got killed in Normandy. Caring for you and Marie is what sustained her and gave her the will to go on with her life. She loved you as much as a person is capable of loving another. Be happy in the knowledge that you were able give her something to live for."

Lila replied, "I know all that, honey, but I owe her so much. She always gave more than she took. I love her so much."

"Well, honey, in life there are two types of people—the givers and the takers. The givers get great pleasure out giving of themselves. The takers continuously grab the lion's share of whatever it is that they're involved in, and eventually choke on their own selfishness. You've known at least one of the takers when you knew Jeff." Alex held her close like a loving father would hold a favorite child who had just lost her treasured pet and didn't quite know how to cope with her loss. He patted her shoulder lovingly as she leaned against him.

Exhausted by the strain, and induced by the quiet, Lila dozed off into a troubled sleep, secure as always in the arms of her Alex. He dozed off shortly thereafter, and they were both jarred into wakefulness by the irritating alarm within one of the life support monitors attached to Ida. It announced that she had finally gotten her fondest wish and had joined her Charlie on the other side of the veil of life. The time was 4:27 a.m. She had never returned to a wakeful state to say goodbye to her well-loved Lila.

Lila broke down and started to sob, clinging to Alex tightly. All that Alex could do was pat her shoulder gently and whisper comforting words into her ear.

The floor nurses gently asked them leave the room while they prepared Ida's body for the post-mortem job of getting it ready for the funeral establishment.

Afterwards, while waiting for her body to be picked up, they went down to the first-floor cafeteria and ordered breakfast. Unable to eat from the grief that welled up within them, they left it largely untouched, and returned to the Ridgeway to wait for Marie and George. They both took showers to freshen up after their lonely, all-night vigil.

Marie and George arrived about noon, and when Marie saw Lila, they both broke down and sobbed uncontrollably. Alex and George, with the typical male inadequacy of coping with a female's crying, stood by helplessly while their women slowly climbed up from their personal pit of despondency. Afterwards, Lila brought out the box of pictures that most families keep, and they reminisced about happier times.

The next morning the girls arranged to have a large bouquet of flowers delivered to the funeral home, and they all ate breakfast at the Diner. They delivered the clothing that Ida was to be interred in, and sat down while her bier was being set up. Two viewings were then established. The early afternoon viewing was from two p.m. until five, and the evening viewing was held from seven until ten.

During the afternoon viewing, many of Ida's neighbors, friends from church and retired co-workers who knew her at the gas and electric Company, as well as others who knew her in life, stopped by to pay their last respects.

The evening viewing was largely the same. Keisha stopped by and expressed deep sympathy to Lila and Marie. Reverend Busch delivered the list of six church members who had volunteered to be pallbearers.

At the funeral the next day, he extolled the many virtues that were contained within Ida, in a stirring eulogy, and she was interred alongside her brother and sister-in-law at Memorial Gardens. It was over at last.

Because of the pressure of his business, George and Marie had to fly back to Chicago almost immediately after the funeral. Lila and Alex were left with grueling task of cleaning out her apartment and disposing of her worldly assets.

Ida's estate proved to be larger than anyone had anticipated. They found savings certificates of deposit stored carelessly in drawers, along with shares of gas and electric stock, Lila's mother's jewelry and other valuable assets that they carefully inventoried.

The also found many personal items that she had treasured, including fading pictures of Lila and Marie, self-consciously posing in their best Sunday dresses, beautiful, even at that young age. Alex asked Lila if he could have the one of her standing with her hands behind her back, and her hair waved in the fashion that was popular at that time.

Ida's will had stipulated that her estate was to be shared equally between Lila and Marie, so those assets were divided and half of their value was sent to Marie.

They gave Ida's clothing to a world relief charity that Reverend Busch had recommended, and they were finally finished with exhausting task of disposal.

Eerily, during the entire disposal process, both Lila and Alex felt that Ida's spirit was hovering with them, as if Ida was reluctant to leave her beloved Lila behind.

Alex remembered reading an article about some cultures believing that the spirit of a dead person lingered at the site it was most comfortable, for as long as three days, before passing over beyond the veil of life.

During that strenuous disposal task, Lila's mind was fully occupied with liquidating Ida's assets and she didn't dwell on her own personal grief. When it was completed, however, she withdrew into herself silently, not wishing to inflict her personal emotional pain on her beloved Alex, and bottled up her grief deep inside of her, suffering alone.

Alex could see the pain of Ida's loss mirrored in her beautiful hazel eyes. The same eyes that he had locked glances with on that fateful Saturday afternoon that they both fell in love. His enormous love for her made him more sensitive to her pain. He couldn't quite discover a method that would bring her out of her deep lethargy and cope with the reality of Ida's death. It wasn't the first time that she had faced the grim specter of death, having buried both her mother and father. This seemed different, however; Ida had unselfishly jumped into the breach and given a great portion of her life to the rearing of two beautiful young girls into highly desirable women.

Even Bear seemed to sense that there was something amiss with one of two best humans and would flop down in front of her, with his head between his front paws, facing outward, protectively, and lick her hand in apparent sympathy for her problem.

Finally, Alex asked Max if he had any ideas on how to pull Lila out of her lonely doldrums, because he deeply felt her pain and wanted to assist her in obtaining some degree of relief.

Max summed up his views in a skillful manner. "Alex, a woman's love is like a jewel with many facets. Some are polished more carefully than the others. Her love for you is the most important facet of her life. It is undiminished in its brilliance and will remain that way forever. If she had children, her mother's love would allow her to love them equally as much, but her love for you would not diminish in any way. She would love you as strongly as before, but each child would polish a facet. Each one as different as each child would be different.

"Her love for Ida was another facet. Ida grabbed her arm while she was floundering in deep water and too young to know how to swim, that is, to handle herself in life. Through her stern methods, she taught Lila and Marie how to face life head-on and how to distinguish pure gold from shiny brass. That was Ida's way of showing her love, her multi-faceted nature, to them.

"She protected them from the *schmucks* of the world, like Lupinsky and that asshole Bobby, and taught them how to distinguish right from wrong.

"That learning was part of her when Lila saw in you the qualities that she most valued—decency, kindness, gentleness, ability to love and accept love. Until that time, she was really treading water, waiting for you or someone with your values to come along.

"When she did see you, and finally meet you, another facet in her ability to love was polished brilliantly. Without a doubt, the most important one of all, because all women need a strong mate to provide for them and protect them. That's why she moved so fast with you. She loved you the moment that she saw you.

"Her love for Ida was from Ida's conditioning her and making her strong enough to face life without fear. It was the anchor that kept her from being dashed on the cruel rocks of life. When she lost Ida, it was like some Shakespearean Shylock cutting a pound of flesh from her soul without an anesthetic.

When Ida died, Lila lost part of herself to the Shylock's knife. Only time will heal the gaping wound that her Shylock—in this case, death—left in her soul, and time can not be rushed, even by young people in love.

"When that wound does heal, her love for you will be magnified, if that's possible. Be gentle with her, treat her kindly, let her know that you still love her, and her alone, because those are some of the qualities that first attracted her to you. Those have made your union so unique.

"Fill her mind with happiness, take long walks together, holding hands like you always do. Take a long weekend away with each other. Don't rush her. Nature always takes time but finds a way to heal the ones that it loves. Gentleness with a woman always beats macho.

"I love Lila like another daughter. She has the ability of bringing sunlight into my office, even when it's raining like hell outside." Then he laughed and said, "That last remark was a mistake. It never rains in *sheol*, it would put the fires out."

Alex was amazed at Max's insight into human nature. He realized then why Max was such a brilliant attorney and placed so much value on ethics.

Alex's best friend at church was Joe Mooney. He had, for lack of a better word, a rustic cabin in the rural part of Garrett County, among the mountains of Western Maryland. He had used it as a base for his hunting trips until he gave up that sport completely. He had offered it to Alex on numerous occasions as a weekend retreat for Lila and himself.

With early fall setting in, the other most beautiful season in Maryland, autumn, with its magnificent coloration of foliage, occurs. This is the time when the leaves lose their green color and turn into an artist's palette of golds, reds, yellows and hues in between. A time when Mother Nature is getting ready to take her long winter's nap and showing off the often hidden theatrical side of herself.

It is a time when the mountain areas are ablaze with color and busloads of individuals called leafers just take rides to admire the beautiful foliage, and the smell of wood burning in fireplaces fills the crisp outdoor air.

Alex, as always, concerned about her on a long weekend, had an idea that he thought would please her, and at the same time allow her to take a breather from the still acute pain of Ida's death.

When he and Lila saw Joe at the Sunday service, Alex asked him if the offer of his cabin's use was still valid.

Joe pulled out a key ring, extracted a key from it and handed it to Alex. "It's no Waldorf-Astoria by any stretch of the imagination. It has basic furnishings, a bed with a lumpy mattress, a butane stove with two burners, fireplace, electricity, but no running water. It's located about five miles from Oakland, on a dirt road, about a mile off the main highway. Here, let me draw you a map."

He reached into his car and pulled out a yellow legal pad and began to draw a map. "Look for the gas station on the right, then turn onto the dirt road and look for a building with a brown stain on its surface. Take enough water with you for cooking and washing up if you plan to do any. Take wool sweaters, jackets and slacks and your own pans if you plan to cook. There's a grill outside and a supply of firewood against the side.

"The state police patrol the area several times a night because the young studs like to break into those cabins instead of renting a cheap motel room. The locals also break into them, looking for valuables that they can steal. One other thing, don't leave any garbage around the cabin, because it attracts black bears and raccoons, and they're the worst pests in the world."

Alex asked Lila, "What do you say, honey? A weekend roughing it together amidst Mother Nature's glory might rejuvenate both of us."

The following week, Lila and Alex shopped for the basics to take along with them: plastic knives, forks and spoons, plastic plates, charcoal, several cases of bottled water, a supply of garbage bags, and dog food since they definitely wouldn't leave their best friend behind. They packed it all into Alex's car, along with pillows, sheets and blankets, as well as a roll of paper towels and toilet tissue. They also decided to take along the board game Monopoly, which Lila and Alex had a running feud in playing.

On Friday morning, they left on their mountain adventure weekend with Bear lying comfortably between them. They passed through Thurmont, which is the site of the famous Shangri La of U.S. presidents, Camp David, enjoying the magnificent colors created by Mother Nature on her mountains. Using the rough map that Joe had drawn, they were finally able to locate his cabin.

While Alex unpacked the car, Lila made up the bed and laid out a light meal of hamburgers, French fries, and cold slaw, fast food that they had purchased on their way up to the Deep Creek area.

Alex built a fire in the fireplace to take the chill of disuse out of the cabin. Bear sniffed around thoroughly, and after convincing himself that it was a satisfactory place for his best humans, settled down for a quick nap.

Lila and Alex began to play their board game. Lila would giggle when Alex's game token landed on a block of property that she owned, and they would happily argue over trivial points of the game. Her laughter was music to Alex's ears, because it seemed to him that it was the first time she was beginning to relax since Ida had died.

Midway through their game, they heard a loud knock on the door Bear, who had been sleeping alongside of Alex, snapped awake. He started growling and barking protectively.

Alex had no idea who would be out in this wilderness at this time of night, so he yelled, "Who is it?"

A voice responded, "It's the state police, Mr. Baxter."

Alex went to the door, cracked it open a few inches, and saw a middle-aged man clad in the uniform of the Maryland state police. He opened the door widely and let the trooper enter the cabin.

The trooper said, "Mr. Baxter, I'm Trooper Robert Kincaid." Touching his hat politely, he said, "Good evening, Mrs. Baxter. Mr. Mooney called our barracks this afternoon and indicated that you two, and I suppose that massive killer watchdog that you have with you, would be spending the weekend at his cabin. The desk sergeant asked me check on your welfare during my patrol this evening to see if you were all right. I ran your license plate with the DMV before I entered to see if you were indeed his guests. We don't have much violent crime up here, but there is lot of break and entering by young buckos who don't want rent a motel room."

Alex said, "That was very nice of you. Would you like some coffee?"

The trooper replied, "That would just hit the spot, sir. There's a sharp edge on the night."

Bear, taking his cue from Alex, settled down alongside of him, but kept his eyes on this suspicious stranger. As a fierce protector, he was poised to spring to his best humans' protection, all fifteen pounds of him, and tear him to pieces, if he made a dangerous move against either of his best humans.

The trooper said, "Mr. Baxter, I know that I have never seen you before, but there is something familiar about your face that I just can't put my finger on. In our training, we're taught to recognize facial features. There was an Otis Baxter in my class at the police academy in Pikesville. By any chance, are you related to him?"

Alex replied, "That was my father."

The trooper exclaimed, "Well, I'll be. Imagine meeting Otis Baxter's son up here in the wilds of rural Garrett County. Your father was my roommate at the academy. I knew your mother well. She used to visit him on Sunday afternoons. They planned to marry after he finished his training. I read in our monthly newsletter that he had died of a heart attack in Glen Burnie after a DUI chase. Now that was a real fine man. Is your mother still alive?"

"No," Alex replied, "she died shortly after him."

"Where they buried?"

"In the old family plot in Carroll County."

"You know," the trooper replied, "I believe that I have some pictures of your father and I taken during our PT at the academy. When I get home tomorrow morning, I'm going to see if I can find them. If I can, I'll bring them to show you tomorrow night." Finishing his coffee, he said, "If you need us, because you don't have a telephone, the gas station on the main road has a two-way radio to monitor for auto accidents. They're open twenty-four hours."

He touched his hat to Lila again and said, "Mrs. Baxter, you are a very beautiful woman. I hope that the two of you enjoy your brief stay up here. If you were here for a longer period than a weekend, I'd bring my wife in to meet you. I know that she would be thrilled to meet Otis Baxter's son and daughter-in-law."

After he left, Lila giggled and said, "My God, sweetheart, who in this state don't you know? What are the odds of meeting somebody like that up here in these wilds? Let's finish this game tomorrow. For the first time since Aunt Ida died, I'm really pleasantly tired. I've said this so many times before that it must sound like a broken record, but I love you so much that it hurts. You are absolutely the finest man that I have ever known. I know why you brought me up here. It was to assist me in coping with my grief. Well, it's working. I'll sleep well tonight."

Alex took his fierce protector, Bear, for a quick walk in the cold mountain air and hurried back into the cabin. Lila was already in bed, so he banked the fire in the fireplace and crawled in beside her.

She snuggled into his arms, and as the cabin cooled down, they both drifted off into a comfortable slumber under their blankets. Bear hopped up onto the foot of the bed, curled up into a ball of sable and white fur, and started to snore contentedly.

CHAPTER 15

The next morning, Alex was forced to arise and take Bear outside to relieve himself and feed him. Then he crawled back into bed beside Lila, and they slept until 11:00 a.m.

After they awoke, Lila prepared a breakfast of bacon and eggs, using the frying pan that she had brought with her. Alex, remembering the way that they made toast when he was a Boy Scout, held slices of bread attached to a cooking fork over one of the burners. The result was mostly charred bread slices, but in the spirit of roughing it in the wilderness, neither one minded the burned bread or the overdone eggs.

Afterwards, they took a long walk, holding hands under the turning leaves, admiring Mother Nature's beautiful artistry, and occasionally brushing falling leaves from each other's hair.

Bear engaged in his favorite sport of squirrel chasing, but since this was an area about which he knew nothing, he never got too far away from his best humans.

They returned to the cabin and resumed their no-holds-barred game of Monopoly. Alex was delighted to hear his Lila giggle in her old musical way when she scored some coup, like buying a desirable piece of property, or Alex's token landing on a square of property that she owned and on which she had built a hotel, and making him pay an outrageous rent. The game ended when

Alex landed on the Boardwalk, which Lila owned, and didn't have enough Monopoly money to pay his rent.

Lila started to brag about her financial skills and started to tickle him. This led to their engaging in some heavy necking and their making frantic, satisfying love to each other, stoked by the solitude of their surroundings and their continuing need for each other.

Afterwards, contented with each other, they took a nap. Later, Alex broiled a large Porterhouse steak on the grill outside and baked two potatoes alongside of it. The steak bone was given to Bear, who gnawed on it contentedly in front of the fireplace.

After dinner, Alex sat down on the rickety sofa to read a new novel by his favorite author, and Lila casually leafed through the latest issue of *The American Eagle Monthly*.

Trooper Kincaid stopped by during his nightly patrol. He now considered them to be close friends and insisted that they call him Bob. He showed Alex some fading snapshots of young men with close-cropped, military-style haircuts engaged in a physical training routine. Alex recognized his father immediately as a state police cadet.

Bob insisted that Alex take the photographs home with him, and said that he was going to retire from the force after January 1 and move to a retirement community in Vero Beach, Florida, since all of their children were now grown and scattered up and down the East Coast.

They slept well again that night, and the next day, Sunday, they arose late, fully refreshed. Alex repacked their car, and they stopped at a quaint buffet-style restaurant attached to a motel in Thurmont for brunch. They arrived in Towson in the late afternoon.

Feeling grungy, and so soiled from the lack of personal wash-up facilities and lack of indoor plumbing, they immediately took showers and sat around, relaxed and contented.

To thank Joe Mooney, they took him and his wife to dinner at Luigi's. Joe told him that he was trying to sell the cabin, but couldn't find a buyer since he didn't own too much adjoining ground surrounding it. He said that since his two boys had grown, and since he had given up hunting, the cabin was empty 95% of the time. He said that Lila and Alex were the first to use it in almost a year, and that he was thinking of not paying his taxes and letting the county take it over by default.

Alex asked him, "Wouldn't be better to improve it by adding a couple of bedrooms or digging a well or replacing the worn-out furniture?"

"Sure," Joe replied, "but land values in rural Garrett County are so low that it would be like throwing good money after bad, down a gaping rat hole."

Alex replied, "That's really too bad. The whole area would make a marvelous site for a resort hotel. The views are fantastic, and in the spring and autumn, it would make a beautiful setting for meetings and retreats. In the summer, it would be a great place to get away from the flat land's heat, and in winter, it could be developed as a ski resort because Garrett gets its share of winter snow."

"That's true," Joe replied, "but it would take many millions of dollars to develop the area."

"Maybe something like what they have in Saratoga, New York. A unique race track with special races like the Preakness could support the whole project," Alex replied.

Joe laughed and said, "Alex, if we only had deep pockets to go along with your profound ideas, we could be wealthy partners."

Ida's death had made them realize how very mortal they both were. Now, for all practical purposes, they were alone in the world. Lila's only living blood-related relative was Marie, who lived in Chicago.

In bed, they clung to each other longer before they drifted off to sleep. Even though their love for each other was, as Luigi phrased it, the stuff that fairy tales are made from, they became closer to each other than ever.

For a while after Ida's death, Lila and Alex would place flowers on the Taylor family graves in Memorial Garden. This was a phase of Lila's grief over her loss of Ida.

Alex had been a member of the little frame church for a long time and loved its simplicity and genuine congregational caring. He had long wanted to be interred there at the end of his time on this side of the veil of life, but all of the burial plots had long been sold.

Lila, with her gentle manner, had become a favorite with the women of the church. One of her best church friends was Mattie Deutsch, who was the wife of the trustee charged with the responsibility of the cemetery.

It seems that an older former member of the church had died after retiring to Florida. That member's estate was trying to dispose of two choice burial plots at the church cemetery. Mattie, during a phone conversation, had mentioned it to Lila who, aware of Alex's desire to be interred there, asked her if she could purchase them for Alex and her. Mattie spoke to her husband, and her husband agreed.

She had a plain granite headstone erected with the word BAXTER chiseled into its top, and her name and birth date, as well as Alex's name and birth date chiseled into its side.

On the Sunday, after the marker was erected, after the service, Lila led him to plots and said, "Honey, now we can be certain that we won't be physically separated for very long. I hope that our spirits will be together, but our bodies will lie together for as long as the world exists."

Alex was touched by her thoughtfulness and replied, "Without a doubt, sweetheart, you are dearest and most thoughtful person who has ever entered my life. I hope that we don't have to use them soon, but maybe when the time comes when we have to, we can use caskets with holes in the side so we can hold hands forever."

Lila giggled and replied, "Honey, I'm not talking about some hole-in-the-wall operation."

Slapping her soundly on her rear end, he said, "And you accuse me of being corny. That remark was straight out of Kansas, honey."

Her laughter tinkled out across the open stretch, and they walked, holding hands, over to join the others chatting outside of the church.

Although, through Alex's efforts, Lila had made great progress in reducing the strain induced by Ida's death, and because she was working long hours to keep abreast of Max's flourishing practice, Alex thought that she looked a little more peaked than usual. He felt this way even though her normal gynecological tests had indicated that there didn't seem to be anything abnormal in her physical system.

Marie called Lila and informed her that George had been promoted to vice president of Midwestern operations of the stock brokerage that employed him. She indicated that he would be required to travel periodically to all of the branch offices that he supervised. As a result, they wouldn't be visiting Towson over Thanksgiving, but she might when George got control of his new job.

With his usual concern over Lila's health, and because they wouldn't be seeing Marie over Thanksgiving, Alex decided to surprise Lila with a trip to Walt Disney World in Orlando, Florida. This was going to be his second anniversary gift to her.

Through a friend of his in a travel agency, he learned that Thanksgiving weekend was the single most heavily attended weekend at that resort. He was, however, able to get a reservation at the Contemporary Resort located within the property there. This is the hotel that has the monorail, which is the principal transportation method for the park, traveling directly through its lobby.

When he had all the reservations satisfactorily tacked down, he surprised Lila by showing her the plane tickets and reservation documents.

Lila gasped and squealed with delight. "Oh, honey, I've always wanted to visit that park but the opportunity never presented itself before now. I wonder if we'll run into animated cartoon characters. I wonder if it'll be warm enough to wear shorts."

Alex chuckled and replied, "Well, with your beautiful ass, I'll see if I can influence the weather man. He's also a good friend of mine."

Alex made arrangements for Bear to be boarded at Mrs. Gilmore's. On the Tuesday before Thanksgiving, they drove to Friendship International Airport, the principal air terminal serving Baltimore, where Alex parked in the long-term parking facility, and they flew directly into Orlando, landing at its international terminal, a former SAC military airport.

Alex rented a car, and they drove across the express road, known locally as the Bee Line Highway, to Buena Vista where Disney World is located, and checked into the Contemporary Resort.

During their stay at the Contemporary, they visited the theme park and viewed the many examples of applied genius that are offered at that resort. They visited the Haunted Mansion, the Pirates of the Caribbean, Space Mountain and Epcot Center, that giant metal ball that dominates part of the resort.

They enjoyed eating at The Top of the World, an excellent restaurant on the top floor of the Contemporary. This overlooks the nightly fireworks displays at the theme park. They viewed Cinderella's Castle and walked down Main Street, viewing the daily parade of live persons depicting animated characters.

Alex was delighted to see the layers of stress literally peeling off of Lila, and he heard her delighted giggles of pleasure more that weekend than he had since Ida had passed over. He felt then that every cent that he had spent on making her happy was worth it, since Lila seemed to be coping with her grief and was more like herself than she had been in months.

Alex supposed connection with the weather man failed at the end of their wonderful weekend. An enormous low-pressure weather front was predicted to sweep up the East Coast, containing heavy snowfall. It was supposed to sweep through New England and dissipate itself in the north Atlantic. Airline flights were cancelled, and their flight was the last to be able to land at Friendship, skidding dangerously on the snow-packed runway.

Alex collected their car from the long-term facility, and they had a harrowing, skidding trip that took two and a half hours, when it normally would have taken forty-five minutes.

He retrieved Bear from Mrs. Gilmore, and they were finally settled back home in the Ridgeway.

Afterwards, when they were unpacking, Bear followed them from room to room. He was fearful that they might again desert him and leave with some stranger. When Alex sat down, he would jump up alongside of him and lick his face, hand or any part of him that was uncovered at the moment, deliriously happy to be reunited with his number one best human.

Fortunately, they had foresight to stock a supply of frozen foods before they left, because in Baltimore, the dreaded word S-N-O-W causes many normally sensible persons to rush out and clear the supermarket shelves of bread, milk and toilet tissue, and that storm was a lulu.

On the twenty-sixth floor, they could hear the scrape of snowplows as they struggled to clear the main roads, and could see the streetlights reflecting the falling snow like misty halos. The few persons foolhardy enough to be out walking in that white deluge looked like tiny dolls slogging through foot high or higher snow.

That vicious storm lasted for two days and dumped twenty-eight inches of snow on the Towson region before it raced north through New England into Canada. Five deaths were attributed to the storm. Those were primarily homeless men who weren't able to secure shelter from its wrath.

Like all of Mother Nature's temper tantrums, the storm had mixed blessings. Children, excused from the forced servitude of school, obtained mini vacations, and the huge mounds of snow that were the byproduct of the snowplows' strenuous activity were used as slopes to ride down with their sleds. Those without sleds used sheets of plastic or flattened cardboard boxes which served the same purpose.

To cope with this dangerous activity, several Towson streets with hills were blocked off to serve as sled lanes. Those athletically inclined persons with cross-country skis dusted them off and used them to schuss from place to place.

Courts were closed and all except emergency police and fire services were suspended temporarily.

Lila got three extra days off from work since Max couldn't drive in from Pikesville, a suburb, west of Towson.

Bear's domestication from being a sheepherding dog, in all kinds of weather, to being a well-loved pet, made him forget his heritage, and he absolutely refused the briefest calls of nature if they were made outdoors.

After tugging him and carrying him bodily, Alex gave in and started to take him down to the lowest garage level where the maintenance staff had created a temporary dog comfort station by spreading a layer of sand behind bags of snow-melting compound.

The storm had a unique effect on the owners of the individual condominiums. Normally, residents of large apartment complexes become friendly with their immediate neighbors. As captives of "The Storm," as it now was referred to, neighbors were brought together by blizzard parties and potluck dinners. Normally reticent persons were discovered not to be shy, but really friendly.

After three days, the paralysis that gripped Towson started to loosen. Merchants shoveled off their sidewalks, courts reopened, supermarkets restocked bread, milk and toilet tissue, and Lila was able to return to a backlog of work that had increased exponentially.

Lila and Alex's desire for each other returned, and their normally healthy sex life returned. A mischievous newspaper reporter made an unscientific survey nine months after The Storm and found that the birth rate had increased by twelve percentage points. Potluck dinners weren't all that Towson was engaged in at that horrendous time.

After the Thanksgiving holiday, the traditional start of the joyous Christmas season emerged.

Tempered by Ida's demise, and having just returned from an exciting anniversary weekend at Disney World, their observance of Christmas was somewhat tempered, and all that Alex did to observe it was to erect their small tree and hang a wreath upon their front door.

They cut back on their presents to each other that year, because they realized that their love for each other was not contingent on the size or number of gifts that they presented to each other.

The principal gift that Alex presented to her was a hooded, synthetic-fur-lined winter parka and lined boots for her to wear on the cold days when he couldn't drive her to her office. He also bought her two new charms for her bracelet—a number 3 and a unique gold Mickey Mouse. He filled her stocking with the little odds and ends that she needed but never bought for herself.

She gave him some software that he needed for his work, an authentic Scotch plaid shirt, corduroy slacks and the usual stocking presents.

Bear was the easiest for whom to find presents. His major gift was a giant rawhide chew bone, that even he had difficulty controlling as he gnawed on it.

They both missed the feisty presence of Ida, and her arrival like a minor gale of fresh air, but without mentioning it to each other, both hoped that she was at peace and finally re-united with her one love, Charlie.

They received the usual Christmas party invitations, turning most of them down and accepting the few that they usually accepted. No minor altercations occurred at both parties that they did attend, and for that they were appreciative.

Lila always looked stunning when she dressed for a night out, but she never seemed to realize what a true beauty she really was. It never occurred to her to flaunt her exquisiteness at any time during her life. It was something with which she was born and she just accepted it like a person born with blue eyes. When she fell in love with Alex, and made the decision that he was to be her lifetime mate, no other man ever existed on the face of the earth.

Alex felt the same way about her, and the fantasies that men play in their minds about seducing other women never even entered into his consciousness. Lila was the best wife that he would ever find, and absolutely the best lover that he had ever known, so why concern himself with plain cake when he had a whipped cream cake all to himself?

He had no doubt that Lila would make an outstanding mother, not only because of her gentle nature, but also because the stern teachings that Ida had implanted into her would rub off. Any child to whom she gave she gave birth would benefit from her strong concepts of right and wrong.

Their love of children was one of their greatest emotions. He knew instinctively that having a baby was the final facet to be polished in her personal jewel. Try as hard as they could, it seemed as if the Infinite Jeweler, who created all of the world's beauty, just didn't hear their requests.

Alex offered to her a kitten to allow her to lavish her storming maternal love on. He told her that after a short period the kitten and Bear would settle down and become tolerant of each other, as joint residents of the Baxter household. But she said that she was afraid that Bear would be hurt if they brought in another pet.

"How about a tank full of guppies?" Alex inquired.

She giggled and couldn't resist saying, "Honey, there's something fishy about that statement."

New Year's passed with their laid-back comfort of each other's devotion. Ida's death had sobered them up with the realization of their own mortality. With melting of the winter snow, they both looked forward to the beauty of the Maryland spring.

CHAPTER 16

In late January, Marie called Lila to let her know that they had to put Hercules to sleep, because he had developed a canine condition known as distemper. She said that George was traveling almost continuously to monitor the Midwestern offices that he supervised and indicated that she was lonely. She asked if it would be an imposition if she visited them for a week or so.

Because it as so unusual for Marie to call and complain about loneliness, Lila readily agreed to her visit.

When Marie arrived, Lila noted that she had added girth to her body from the parties and client entertainment that George's new job entailed. She also noted that Marie seemed to be withdrawn, as if she was worried about something. If Lila approached her, Marie quickly changed the subject to something completely unrelated.

Marie did remark that she envied the close affiliation that Lila and Alex enjoyed, and wished that some of it would rub off on George. His new job seemed to be creating a barrier between the two of them. She hinted that George was becoming distanced from her and that she had found a trace of lipstick on one of his shirts while she was preparing the laundry. George was generally out of town several days a week. On those days that he was in Chicago, he worked late, saying that he had to catch upon his backlog. She didn't seem at all pleased with George's new stature within his company, but the economic benefits were fantastic

She stayed a week and seemed to be reluctant to leave. Lila told her that whatever seemed to be bothering her would pass, and if it became too much to cope with, she was welcome to come and stay with Alex and her indefinitely until she sorted out her mental confusion. Lila suspected that George was having a romantic liaison and that Marie knew it, but refused to confront George with her suspicion. That evening in bed, in each other's arms, which is where they held their most important discussions, Lila confessed to Alex that she suspected George to be having an affair.

Alex agreed with her and said, "Honey, the moment that I saw her, I knew that something was wrong, because she's put on so much weight. You Taylor women are one-man women all right, and she doesn't want to make him face her with his cutting out on her. She hopes that she's wrong, and like all women who are facing a crisis related to the man in their lives, she's turning to eating. Some women turn to eating chocolate, some to pastry and some to mashed potatoes. Whatever it is, it generally shows up in their rear end. In Marie's case, her thighs, when she wears slacks, look as packed as sausage. She's a beautiful woman, but she's letting herself go downhill fast.

"Success makes some men who have been working hard pause momentarily and look around. There's always a Painted Woman, as you so aptly call Connie, lurking somewhere, looking for a higher stakes game to play.

"Don't worry, George is just having a mid-life crisis and he'll pull out of it, hopefully in time to save his marriage."

Lila responded, "God, you're observant. I think that if you ever desired another woman, I would shrivel up and die."

Alex laughed and said, "Honey, you're so active in bed that I wouldn't have the strength to take on a paramour. Anyway, I love you too much to even consider the idea, let alone look for a part-time lover. Your can is absolutely the best-looking one in the entire world. I have never seen one that I prefer better."

She giggled and replied, "I'm going to remember that when I'm ready the next time."

He said, "Well, what about right now? You're looking to get pregnant, aren't you?"

"God you're the horniest man that I've ever known."

Max's practice took another upward turn, as his reputation for the remediation of those civil wrongs, known as torts, increased. His ability to win judgements made individuals seek him out as their attorney of record when they needed assistance in righting a wrong.

The result was that Lila, as the only paralegal that he employed, became mired down with work in progress and had to work longer hours to try to stay abreast. Frustrated, she said to Max, "I'm falling so far behind that we're going to miss some hearings if I don't get some help. I'm already working three nights a week, and I'm about ready to keel over from exhaustion."

Max, like all businessmen, was anxious to keep a lid on his overhead and didn't know whether this flurry of new cases was just a temporary blip on his business radar screen. So he contacted a temporary employment agency and hired a contract employee.

The first girl that was sent over could do the work, but she spent more time in the ladies room brushing her hair than she did at her computer terminal. She lasted two days. The next woman was a motherly type, just re-entering the work force. She was anxious to work, but just couldn't master the use of the software being used. She lasted three days. The third girl could do the work but was reserved and cold. Lila and Myra didn't like her either, so they ignored her as well. Eventually, she left and was replaced by another friendlier girl, so peace again returned to that tiny pocket of the world.

Through a friend of his, Max learned of the availability of a paralegal that had just resigned from her job at a prestigious D.C. law firm. She had a boyfriend in Lutherville, a suburb just north of Towson, and wanted to be with him. Max hired her as an independent contractor, which meant that she would have to pay her own personal taxes and FICA.

She really knew her trade and showed Lila many shortcuts. Soon the backlog was eliminated. That plan backfired, though, because one Monday she called in and said that she had broken up with her boyfriend and was returning to her old job in Washington.

Lila was again back at square one, not only with her own caseload, but also with the unfinished work of the contractor. She suddenly had a brilliant idea.

"Max, the college that I went to has a work-study program where it allows seniors to work up to twenty hours a week in their final semester to gain practical on-the-job experience before they graduate. It's a whole lot like a traditional college co-op program. These are real paralegals just about ready to enter the work force. We could hire two to work alternate times of twenty hours a week each. This would be the equivalent of one forty-hour employee. I know the director of placement out there and the last semester has just started. If we're lucky, there may be some seniors still available in the job work-study pool."

Lila made her call to the placement office and found out that there were still several entry-level paralegals available. They interviewed several and hired the two that they felt were the best qualified.

Both apprentice paralegals were eager to put their textbook knowledge to practical use, and with the still unsophisticated sincerity of fresh, new students entering the workforce, were pleasant and eager to be accepted.

The plan worked out so well that Max hired the better of the two at the end of the semester as an assistant to Lila.

Max was so pleased with Lila's idea that she heard him bragging on the telephone to his best friend about the brilliant girl who was his number one paralegal, and how she singlehandedly saved him from losing several judgements with an outstanding idea.

All that Lila wanted to do was to be able to spend more time with her Alex and Bear, so necessity again became the mother of invention.

Marie began to call Lila at least once a week, and finally admitted that George was having an affair with a woman employed at one of the branch offices that he supervised. She said that she was making George sleep in their guest room, and that she was starting on a diet plan with one of the national weight control organizations and that she hoped to lose twenty ponds before she was through. She said that she was very lonely, but still loved George very much and felt that her added weight had caused him to lose his ardor for her. She said that she was going to stay and fight to regain George's love.

Lila asked her if she wanted to visit them again, but she said, no, she was going to stay in Chicago and try to put the pieces of her marriage back together.

After Marie's diet plan was proven to work, and George came back to his senses, they took a Caribbean cruise as a second honeymoon and resumed their marriage as a full-time activity. With George's mid-life crisis behind them, they purchased a new golden retriever to replace Hercules. Marie said that Herk was irreplaceable, as most dog owners feel about their first and best loved dogs. They named the new dog Samson.

On his daily walks with Bear, Alex noticed that he was beginning to have trouble lifting his rear leg to relieve himself, as all male dogs do. He would squat like female dog and did not kick his back legs joyously as he had previously. When it came time to jump back over a curb, he would stand there until Alex picked him and placed him on a sidewalk, and he seemed to no longer be able to climb the stairs.

Alex thought at first that he was just acting like a new puppy and wanted to be cuddled, until one occasion when Bear screamed out in extreme pain.

Alarmed, Alex decided to have his vet check him out physically. He received some disturbing news. Bear was starting through the onset of rear hip displacement.

The vet told Alex that the particular condition that Bear was slipping into was common among the more popular breeds of small dogs, and was probably due to a genetic condition caused by inbreeding of dogs with siblings and closely related litter mates.

Unscrupulous breeders would breed closely related dogs to make a quick buck and any recessive genes present would be perpetuated among the following generations of new dogs.

He also said that Bear would have to be euthanized, or put to sleep, when the condition became so acute that he wouldn't able to control his bowel or bladder functions since that region of Bear's body would become paralyzed.

Alex, who dearly loved his little dog, was completely devastated by the bad news.

The vet told Alex that there was a prosthetic device available that would prolong Bear's life if he could be taught to use the device. It was a sort of cart with two small wheels and an area where the dog's rear legs could be placed together with a harness that strapped around the dog's chest.

Alex ordered one, and when it arrived, Bear was terrified and resisted having his rear legs placed in the cart. Alex was now faced with the terrible decision of having his long-time best friend euthanized.

Bear's condition continued to worsen. Alex was forced to carry him down the elevator and outdoors, and watch him sadly while he dragged his two back legs behind him as he attempted to relieve himself.

Alex was then forced to carry him back on the elevator, and then Bear would lie on a small throw rug that Alex had placed on the carpet beside the favorite place where he sat. Bear's rear legs would twitch, and Alex would reach down and squeeze them tightly until the twitching stopped. Bear would then lick his hand as if to say thank you.

This went on for several months, until one day, while Alex was carrying him down on the elevator, he felt wetness on his body. Bear was dribbling, and the time had finally arrived when he had to be put down out of compassion for his paralyzed condition.

Lila, fully aware of the emotional pain that her Alex was undergoing at facing the worsening condition of his dearest buddy, suggested, "Honey, I know how much Bear means to you, and I know how you are suffering from his physical deterioration. Would you consider getting another corgi when he's finally put down? He's been your dear friend for a long time now, even before we knew that each other existed. I know how much you love him, and it's really sad to see him so crippled. Just think about doing so."

Alex replied, "Honey, I know that you are trying to be kind, but I don't want another corgi after he goes. I'd always be comparing it to Bear and it would always come out second best. I never could love another dog in the way that I love Bear. We had been through some rough times together with Connie. She was always after me to put him down. That brought her cheating on me to a head. I never would have met you, and fallen so hard for you, if it hadn't been for him. He picked me out when I was looking at him and we've been together ever since."

Lila realized that this was one pain she couldn't ease in her beloved Alex and didn't press the matter any further.

Alex reluctantly made an appointment with the vet to have Bear euthanized. He asked the vet, "Will it hurt?"

The vet replied, "No, Mr. Baxter, it'll be just like prepping him for serious surgery. He'll just drift off into a deep sleep and won't ever awake. This is the most humane method of euthanization. It's harder on those whom the animals has lived with than it is on them."

Alex held Bear on his lap while the vet prepared a syringe containing the euthanization agent, and when he injected it into Bear, Alex kissed him on top of the head and said, "Goodbye, old friend. You were the best dog that any man ever had as a companion. I loved you dearly."

Just before he closed his eyes for the last time, Bear licked his hand as if to say, "I loved you too, but it's better this way."

Manly or not, Alex started to sob, because Bear's demise was closely akin to the loss of a dear child.

Lila, who was waiting for Alex outside, entered the room and hugged him tightly until he was able to control his emotions.

Alex had Bear cremated and kept his ashes in the den alongside a picture of him that McGuire had taken in happier times. He added a codicil to his will that Bear was to be interred with him upon his death.

The hardest part of the entire ordeal was the discovery of half-chewed rawhide bones in recesses around their apartment, as well as old squeeze toys, that flooded his memory with the purchase of them, and most of all an old sock of Alex's that Bear and he would play tug of war with when he was in the mood to do so.

Eventually, time, the great healer, dulled the pain that Alex felt. He never bought another dog, but his innate love for them would cause him to stop and scratch a dog being led by an owner, if he were attracted to that animal.

Although Lila now had two apprentice paralegals assisting her, she was still in a training mode with them and was still required to work additional hours to keep abreast of her caseload. The strain of training new employees in the office routine and the rigid rules of court procedure, forms and rules of evidence, which are the routine of every legal practice, started to show in her face and body language, and she again seemed to be losing weight.

Alex, who worshipped her as the other half of his person, was consistently worried about her well-being and urged her frequently to take it a little easier.

On weekends, he would arise quietly, so as not to disturb her sleep, and prepare their breakfast, and afterwards, they would spend Saturday morning relaxing and just reading the morning newspaper. On Saturday afternoons, they would grocery shop at their favorite supermarket.

Glatcher College, a liberal arts, higher education institution was located close to their residence. On one Saturday afternoon, while they were on their way to the supermarket, they stopped at a traffic signal and were waiting for it to turn green. While they were waiting, a small sporty auto, favored by college students, pulled up alongside of them, with two high-spirited young girls in the front seat. They looked at Alex and started to whisper to each other, giggling out loud.

Alex was amused by the high-spirited actions of the two young girls with no responsibility, but Lila was irritated by their obvious attraction to her Alex.

She said, "Honey, that young snip is flirting with you."

Alex laughed and replied, "Sweetheart, that may be true, but someone flirting with me is one thing. The non-existing chance of me flirting with someone else is another thing. There isn't a woman alive who could make stray from the woman that I now have at home. You are the most beautiful woman that I have ever seen. You are the most responsive to my needs, both in and out of bed. You are the wife that any man would kill to possess. I love you more than anything in this idiotic world. So put your mind at ease. If I have my way, you will be the only Mrs. Alex Baxter that there will ever be. The only way that you'll ever get rid of me is if you suddenly find someone who you will be able to love more than me. You're stuck with me, baby."

She leaned over and kissed him on his cheek. "Oh, honey, I was just pretending to be a jealous wife. I know that you love me as much as I love you. There never could be anyone in my life but you, ever. I'm so happy with you my feet haven't touched the ground since we got married."

Alex teased her and replied, "Well, it takes a lot of hot air to float off of the ground for that long."

She giggled musically. "Well, you wondered why I had gas for no apparent reason."

Alex replied, "That's what they call bloated humor."

"Stop it, Joe Miller. You remind me of McGuire the photographer; you're so corny."

"Well, at least I don't have a Brooklyn accent," Alex replied, as they drove into the supermarket parking lot.

In another incident while on their way to the market, they were stopped at a traffic signal, waiting for it to change, when Lila leaned over and started to walk her two fingers up his thigh slowly.

He said, "Stop it. If we wouldn't be arrested for indecent exposure, I'd rape you right here on Fairmount Avenue."

With that, the light turned green and the driver behind them impatiently beeped his horn to get them to move.

Lila giggled and said, "Well, honey, that would give him something to look at while he waited for the light to change."

During their marriage, Lila developed a number of delightful ways of telling him how much she loved him without using words. In addition to sliding her arm around his waist while they were chatting with someone else, while they were shopping and looking at some display, without looking at him, she would reach out and place her hand on his upper arm and slowly slide down the length of it and then pat it gently, telling him without words how much that she loved him. She also used her beautiful hazel eyes to speak to him silently. Alex used to say that she said a thousand things without saying a word.

Their complete comfort with each other was a rare and beautiful union. They didn't often disagree with each other, trusting in each other's judgement in matters of importance. If there were matters of importance that concerned them jointly, they would discuss it in bed, while holding each other tightly. This is where they held their most important discussions. No amount of rancor could ever provoke either of them into a loud tirade with each other.

Their compatibility in bed was also a major contributing factor to the obsession that they felt for each other. Their personal copy of *The Pillow Book* eventually became dog-eared from use, because it offered release to the massive attraction that they felt for each other.

Max, in his fatherly manner towards her, would often comment, "*Bubala,* if we could distill whatever it is that makes you two tick and sell it as an anti-divorce preventative elixir, then my Esther and me could retire to Boca Raton, and you and your Alex could run the world's largest children's shelter. Tax free of course."

Lila would giggle and reply, "That part about tax free wants to make me take it on as a personal research project. You realize that my Alex would have to share in a full one-third of the profits. Then we could be known as the Masters and Johnson of Towson."

Then Max would remark dryly, "Youth is a wonderful thing. It's a shame that it's wasted on the young."

Lila always enjoyed those impromptu homilies from Max, because she felt that they were part of some graduate course in human psychology. She felt that Max, as her surrogate father, was almost as wise as her Alex, who in her estimation was utterly brilliant and observant of human foibles, at least most of the time anyway.

CHAPTER 17

In April of that year they decided to hold a party at the Ridgeway party room, located above the penthouse level of that structure. Alex reserved the room and advanced the refundable security deposit against damage to the room or its contents.

They picked April because that was a time when very few parties were held, in contrast to Christmas week, when one could attend two or three on a single evening. Another reason was that individuals were tired of being confined to their homes during the winter months, had varying stages of cabin fever, wanted to venture out into the increasingly pleasant weather.

Lila engaged a caterer that Mattie Deutsch had recommended as capable and experienced. She arranged for a selection of finger foods, small sandwiches, shrimp rings, miniature pastries, dips and the like. They didn't ask Luigi if he wanted to cater it, because he neither had the staff nor facilities.

She also arranged for an experienced bartender, a garment-checking facility and a disk jockey to play music by which their guests could dance.

Alex purchased what he believed was an adequate supply of liquors and mixers. Since he didn't drink himself, he asked Joe Mooney to suggest popular brands and amounts for a crowd of up to fifty persons. Fifty invitations were sent out, to which thirty-eight responded as attending.

On the Saturday of the party, Lila dressed in the white evening pajama outfit that Alex had given her. This was the outfit made of white brocade, with the pants cut widely, and looked like an evening skirt while she as standing still. It had a long unlined coat of the same material.

She and Alex greeted their guests and circulated among them to keep the party alive and active. As hostess, she was required to dance with any guest who asked her. If she had a dance card to fill out, it would have been crammed with reserved dances. With her stunning appearance—the white brocade against her dark skin brought out her exquisite natural beauty—she glowed with happiness. She fended off numerous propositions from men smitten by her beauty. Her standard answer was, "Thank you, but I'm a one-man woman, and I adore my husband. He's the only man that I would ever let touch me sexually."

Even when she was dancing with Alex, with her head comfortably on his shoulder, he would feel the tap on his shoulder of someone cutting in. After a while, she began to resent the necessary duties of hostess because she wanted to be alone with her beloved Alex.

The party went well and there were no unpleasant confrontations, for which they were grateful.

Alex gave the opened bottles to the maintenance staff, who he paid overtime to clean up the room. He kept a small supply of unopened bottles for guests who might visit their unit in the future.

For the next couple of weeks, Lila received many phone calls from their guests, thanking them for inviting them to such a wonderful affair.

Without Ida to take to church, and Bear to take out and feed, they skipped attendance at the little frame church and slept late. They had a later breakfast at the Diner, where they saw Connie with her latest temporary lover, and were pleased when she didn't acknowledge their presence.

Lila, who was secretly jealous of her Alex, snuck in a comment. "God, she looks haggard. Her late-night activities really show up on her face despite the moisturizing cream that she slathers on. Even her six pounds of makeup don't improve her dissipated looks. I'm so happy that she was so stupid to let you go free."

Alex remarked in his dryly humorous way, "Her lifestyle reminds me of an old hound chasing its tail. She runs in the same boozy circles all the time, and like that old hound, she'll never be able to catch her tail. This times her youthful good looks. In college she had a freshness about her that seemed to be delightful. This masked a witch's cruelty that never ended. Her looks are securely tied to her past. She has no concept of what's important in life."

The only thing that was missing from their wonderful relationship was the presence of little feet happily running around their apartment. They both wanted children and tried all of the conventional methods of getting Lila pregnant. They tried the rhythm method where her fertile and barren days were charted. They tried charting her ovulation, using a thermometer to record her temperature, and stopped short of using fertility drugs because of the possibility of multiple births.

When they saw a happy child at the supermarket or on the concourse of some shopping mall, they would always stop and make a fuss. Almost always, the child would respond to Lila's unique beauty and smile happily at her. Then they would look at each other wistfully and try all over again.

Lila, who enjoyed the physical aspects of marriage, was always eager to try again, and Alex, who enjoyed her body as well, was always eager to resume their search for the key to unlock Lila's door to motherhood.

After one of their more vigorous encounters, Alex remarked, "Honey, if we don't get you pregnant soon, we're both going to develop bedsores."

Lila giggled and responded, "Well, baby, getting pregnant is one of the better aspects of marriage, and, boy, are you a wonderful husband."

After a while, they ceased their charting and temperature taking and let nature take its own normal course, enjoying their vigorous physical relationship.

The beautiful Maryland spring began to burst all around them. The blankets of color created by azaleas and the flowering ornamental trees provided a sort of colorful haze, and the dogwood trees added to the beauty with their beautiful cross-shaped flowers.

They enjoyed walking together holding hands on those weekends when Lila wasn't up to her ears in case preparations. On those walks, Alex would break off a small twig containing flowering cherry and give it to her as a small token of his love. She would smell it and when they got home, place it in a small glass of water. Its presence seemed to brighten their kitchen significantly.

Their happiness at times seemed to be too much in this imperfect world, and they often felt guilty about living in an environment where so much pain and misery existed.

Alex the philosopher felt that everyone in his or her lifetime was entitled to a certain measure of happiness. If they used it up too quickly, their old age would be sad and lonely. He looked to lonely old widows and old men sitting in the malls anxious to speak with anyone who would acknowledge their just being there to support his cockeyed theory.

With the assistance of her two apprentice paralegals, Lila was able to put a significant dent in her case backlog and resume a normal workweek of approximately forty hours.

She decided one day that she would like to have a hobby, and purchased a paperback instruction book, a basic artist's case of paint tubes, and several canvas boards, and began to paint in her free time while keeping Alex company in their den.

Her first attempts were not even worthy of being called art, but with diligence she improved and became a good copyist, but was never able to really develop her own personal style.

She had several of her better efforts framed and hung them in their den, which seemed to becoming a catchall room. She said that even though she was no Rembrandt, painting relaxed her and made her feel good about herself. She enjoyed painting seascapes, especially lighthouses. As she gained experience, her wave construction became very realistic.

This urge to paint lasted several months until she tired of it, and then she only picked up her brushes sporadically, and finally stopped painting completely.

Alex called it her Blue Period, after Pablo Picasso, because it was the tail end of her grieving over the death of Ida, but like all persons who grieve, it filled a void within her, until she was able to cope with her own loss without filling it artificially.

Their life together settled into a comfortable relationship that was happy as any ever was between two mature persons who were completely at peace with each other.

Alex could relate to Lila's grief over Ida's death, because in the relatively short time that he knew her, he had become very fond of the feisty opinionated spinster. She had managed to live a relatively long life. She had been seventy-nine when she passed over. She could have lived longer if her stubborn streak had let her follow Dr. Glass' orders. She had seemed to resign herself to the inevitable after she became certain that Lila and Alex would have a happy, solid marriage. It was almost as if she recognized that her work on earth was completed, and it was now time to stop complaining about her Charlie's loss and to try and find him on the other side of the veil of life.

Because of his strong interest in the game of baseball, Alex often thought in terms of its mechanics. He considered the deaths of two lives with whom he had become closely interwoven, Ida and Bear, in the context of a baseball player at bat in critical game, the game of life as two strikes against him. He was still in the game, but had to be careful of how he swung at the next pitch that life threw at him.

Although he was deeply in love with Lila, to the lifetime exclusion of other women, he did miss the companionship of his old buddy, Bear. He still had flashbacks of the one-man, one-dog relationship with that frisky little bundle of sable and white fur, who could tickle his sense of humor by simply lying on his back with all four legs in the air. He often thought back to the times when Bear delighted in chasing squirrels and how amusing it was to see him running on his stubby legs and no tail after a lively rodent. And how after the squirrel was safely in a tree, listen to the insults that they would level at each other in their own dialects. He remembered how Bear used to love to ride with his head out of the front window into the oncoming rush of air like some comic strip beagle.

He wondered if animals had souls, and remembered a dream he had of Bear on the night after he was forced to have him euthanized. In his dream, Bear suddenly appeared as an odd vision for which Alex could not account, and Alex remembered saying to him, "What are you doing here? You're supposed to be dead."

In his dream, Bear had licked his hand affectionately, as he always had, and then with his rear end fully restored, slowly walked under a sort of overhanging canopy to disappear from view. It was as if his spirit was reluctant to leave his best human and also wanted to see Alex one more time.

These reveries and mind fillings were part of the healing process that both Lila and Alex were slowly undergoing. It was, as Max once said, nature's way of healing the massive wound left in their souls by their personal Shylock death had opened when it cut out important parts of their personal lives.

Alex was asked to become a member of the board of directors that governed the Ridgeway condominiums, and after some hesitation, accepted. He found that the duties were routine and of little importance, and entailed the approval of minor expenditures having to do with routine maintenance matters.

He believed that his time could be better spent with his beloved Lila and resigned from the board shortly thereafter. The common trait of wanting to know what was happening on the inside had little appeal to him, because his writings for the *Eagle* were part of his job of creating such news.

He was once nominated for a national writing award for a series that he had written about man's careless destruction of the ecology of the planet. The nomination never got beyond his name and series being submitted to the awards judges. He was pleased, however, with the recognition of his writing.

After nature's slow healing of their grief, the Baxter household regained its pleasant rhythm again, and the happiness that they derived from their union with each other seemed to magnify.

They continued to attend the Sunday services of the little frame church on Providence Road, and became regular customers at the Diner for Sunday morning breakfast. They frequently saw Connie and her boyfriend of the week. She rarely even acknowledged their presence. Most her attendants were considerably younger than she, and she seemed to delight in showing them off like hunter's trophies that she was going to hang on her wall.

Alex remarked on one occasion, "God, she must have a turnstile in her bedroom."

Lila giggled slyly and replied, "I wonder if they have to pay for the privilege?"

Lila's menstrual period had always been predictable and regular. They had been able to predict its onset with a good degree of accuracy, and the flow was reasonably normal. She experienced pelvic cramping as part of the natural process, so they didn't really get concerned when her monthly cramps increased in intensity. Both assumed that such cramps were part of her normal monthly cycle.

Over a several month time frame, however, her periods became irregular, both in onset time and in the length of time that she was incapacitated. On some monthly cycles, the period occurred early, and the next month it was late, as much as ten days, leading them to hope that she was finally pregnant. Their hopes were always dashed when her flow started.

Their normally active and healthy sex life became spotty and infrequent as Alex, out of consideration for her, refrained from the frequent sexual activity that they usually engaged in.

He urged her to seek medical attention to correct the abnormality, because Lila would almost double over with pain from her normal monthly period. When she felt pain, he seemed to feel it as well.

Lila made an appointment with Dr. McGrath, who examined her and ran a number of blood tests, all of which proved to be negative. He finally recommended that she undergo a D&C procedure, feeling strongly that it would correct her irregularity.

He asked her a number of questions about her family history that seemed unrelated to her problem. Those questions included information about her mother, how old she was when her onset of cancer occurred, other incidents of cancer within her family, and other questions about cancer.

All of her gynecological tests proved to be negative, so with Alex accompanying her, she had the D&C performed at GMMC on an outpatient basis.

It seemed to be successful, and for a time her periodic onset returned to a normal flow.

The new paralegals appeared to be working out satisfactorily and were able to handle the cases that were in-house at the time, so Alex decided to take Lila on a weekend trip to Gettysburg, Pennsylvania, because it was within a short driving time from Towson.

They drove through the pleasant back country roads into that historic town, that has become a tourist center that the Civil War buffs hash and rehash as the turning point of the War of Secession.

They checked into a motel and had dinner in a fast food restaurant. Tired from their drive, they retired early, maintaining the self-imposed sexual activity moratorium with each other.

They slept fitfully until about two a.m., when their massive need for each other overcame the need for celibacy, and they engaged in frantic, fully satisfying sexual activity.

Sleeping late the next morning, they awoke relaxed and refreshed, temporarily purged of the sexually caused tension within them. In their wonderful marriage, their massive desire for each other was so overwhelming that they could restrain themselves only until they couldn't stand it any longer, and then they would frantically seek relief with each other.

After breakfast, they took a bus tour of the battlefield, narrated on tape by a famous Hollywood actor. Later that day, they toured the still working farm of President Dwight D. Eisenhower, who had been supreme commander of the Armed Forces in the European theater of operations.

They learned that the reason the Confederate Army attacked Gettysburg was because it desperately needed shoes. It was still reeling from a bloody battle at Antietam, Maryland. Gettysburg, whose principal industry at that time was shoemaking, seemed ripe for the plucking, and the invasion was met with stiff resistance from General George E. Meade.

They learned of Pickett's Charge, and saw the peaceful meadows that ran red with blood during that high point of the war. It was pointed out to them, when they viewed the numerous statues immortalizing the general officers, often seated on horseback, that a horse with one leg lifted was symbolic of that particular general being wounded in that battle.

Gettysburg is the locale of President Abraham Lincoln's famous Gettysburg address. They visited the cemetery where he delivered that speech and saw some of the electronic maps of the battle as well.

Checking out of their motel, they returned to Towson by another scenic route, fully relaxed and certain of their devotion to each other.

They enjoyed a leisurely Sunday dinner at Luigi's, and Pearl remarked about how relaxed that they both seemed to be.

Lila giggled and said, "Pearl, with a husband like mine, you spend a lot of time in bed."

On Monday, fully rejuvenated, she returned to work to face the sternest tasks that a law practice could generate, and Alex returned to his writing for the *Eagle*.

Their brief mini-vacations always seemed to pep up Lila, and after each of them she would return relaxed for a week or so, but later her vitality seemed to ebb back to the previous exhaustion mode.

Alex couldn't quite figure that phenomenon out. He didn't know whether it was from her throwing herself back into her work, or whether it might be some health-related problems, and that worried him. He loved Lila almost to the point of paranoia, and he had a small fear slowly growing inside of him that something evil was lurking within her and would spring out if she weakened physically.

When he had free time from his writings, he surfed the Internet and downloaded articles on female health, especially cancer. He compiled a folder of those articles, for no special reason except his instinctive fear that his beloved Lila might someday contract that dreaded disease. He, himself, had no fear of contracting cancer, because all of his immediate family had died of heart-related disease, and as far as he could determine, there had never been a recorded case of it in their past history. This included the Broadbanks, the family of which his mother had been a part.

Lila worked hard at Max's law practice and was truly appreciative of his concern for her well-being. Alex attributed some of her continuous fatigue to her strong loyalty to Max, a man who drove himself to the outer edge of endurance before he backed off.

To Alex's knowledge, Max had never taken a vacation since he had started to practice law. The closest thing that could be considered as time off was when The Storm had crippled Towson. He had been forced to take three days off because he couldn't drive from his home in Pikesville. He later made up for that time off by working late every night except Friday, when his religious convictions made him attend Friday night services at his temple. That devotion to the sanctity of the law was another part of the reason of why he was such a good lawyer.

Max had three elements in his life that were of uppermost importance to him. His Esther was one of them, his honesty another, and his complete acceptance of ethics as his way of doing business the third. He couldn't stand lawyers that cut corners in their work. Those individuals he called *shysters* because chiseling and cheap theatrical tricks were completely alien to his way of thinking.

Alex fully believed that his initial meeting with Max had convinced him that Alex was honest, and that was the single most important reason that Max was convinced that Alex was a suitable candidate as a husband for Lila.

In his musings about life, since her tests did not reveal anything malignant, Alex assumed that she was getting cues from Max, pushing herself to the limits of her personal durability. He suppressed his nagging worry until the next time that her peakedness erupted.

CHAPTER 18

One of their favorite pastimes together was the occasional attendance of a movie. With the weather warming to the point that it was comfortable to walk in the early evening, when they wanted an easy night out together, they would stroll over to one of the cinema palaces in Towson and view a good movie. At these outings, Lila would eat most of his popcorn, and with her head comfortably on his shoulder, laugh and cry as the movie's plot unfolded.

Afterwards, they would stop into one of the coffee houses, largely patronized by college students, where Lila would indulge her sweet tooth by eating some calorie-laden pastry, while Alex sipped a cup of coffee and contentedly watched her.

With the warmer weather, they again began to lie on the wrought iron lounge, holding each other tightly, contentedly chatting, and watching the blinking warning beacon in the distance until it was time to go to bed.

Luigi had once told them that theirs was a marriage ordained by a power larger than them.

Their union was not a selfish, closed affair; they frequently visited other friends and had others in for dinner. They just felt comfortable with each other and held no special secrets from each other. It was a relationship like that often shared by twin siblings, who know instinctively what the other is thinking. That affinity towards each other had developed to the point that if one uttered a fragment of a sentence, the other sensed its meaning and often completed the sentence.

Their consideration for each other's personal feelings was also a pillar that their marriage rested upon. Neither ever baited the other, even in fun to get a reaction from the other. If one of them stated something as a fact, the other accepted it as the truth.

Although Lila's gynecological problems were not completely under control, with the arrival of July, her vacation was due to begin.

They decided to spend it in Ocean City, Maryland. This is a popular resort that was once considered to be a haven solely for summer vacations, but with the emergence of the condominium style of living, it has become more of a year-round place in which to live. Retired individuals who had spent pleasant days on its sandy beaches returned to spend their golden years on its turf in the elaborate condo towers that had been constructed densely along the beachfront, residing there year round.

Despite the strong commercial development, it is still very much a family resort, without the slick neon gambling casinos north of it. The city fathers and local residents chose to retain that image, because it kept the lifestyle simpler and law enforcement easier. High rollers just went farther north to get rid of their money.

Alex made a reservation for a week and paid for it in advance at one of the larger motels. They arrived there on a late Saturday afternoon. Tired from the several-hour drive from Towson, they ate a light dinner at the motel coffee shop and returned to their room to unpack.

Stimulated by the recent infrequency of their cohabitation with each other, and as always their normal desire for each other, they frantically engaged in the most vigorous, satisfying lovemaking of their entire marriage, attempting to reach that momentary rush of joy with each other that a successful act of coitus achieves.

Afterwards, gasping for breath, but more than ever in love with each other, they attempted to bring each other back down to reality by engaging in small talk. The secondary effects of such activity, deep sleep overcame both of them, and they drifted off into an almost coma-like slumber. Satisfied and completely relieved of any individual tension, they slept through the night soundly.

Alex had promised himself that he would sleep later that week than his usual seven a.m. wake-up time. His long-established habit, however, had created a sort of internal alarm clock somewhere deep inside of him, and he awoke as usual at that time.

He lay there refreshed from his deep sleep, and contented from their frantic lovemaking, just thinking pleasant thoughts about what they could do that week and how he earnestly hoped that Lila would become rejuvenated during their vacation.

Lila was still asleep alongside of him, so he leaned over and kissed her gently, hoping that he wouldn't awaken her, because she really needed to sleep later than he. She really worked hard for Max, and on this vacation, he was determined that she would get an adequate rest.

Excited as always by her unique beauty, he leaned over and kissed her lips gently, so as not to awaken her. As soon as he did, however, she opened her beautiful hazel eyes and smiled into his with her usual look that said a thousand things without her uttering a word to him. She pulled Alex to her and completed an entirely passionate kiss.

At breakfast that morning, while she was animatedly chatting with Alex, she was thrilled when a middle-aged female vacationer approached their table and interrupted her to tell her that she looked "positively radiant," and she and Alex projected a picture of contented love for each other. After the woman left to re-join her husband, Lila leaned over and whispered to Alex, "Honey, do you think that she believed I'm pregnant? I could be from all that wonderful carrying on that we did last night. It was absolutely wonderful. Do I need a reservation for a repeat session?"

Alex then replied in mock seriousness, "I'll give you the first vacancy on my waiting list, madam."

Later, as she had requested, they rented two bikes and painfully pedaled part of the way up to the Delaware state line, stopping well short of their objective to rest. During that short adventure they looked at the new condos and townhouse communities that seemed to have sprung up overnight along the ocean beachfront.

They then decided to take the boardwalk tram downtown, and slowly strolled up the boardwalk, enjoying the resort activity and peeking into souvenir shops to look at a positive rainbow of colored tee shirts carrying ridiculous messages on them.

They ate lunch at a boardwalk eatery, with several tables set outside like a French café, where Lila had a bowl of crab soup, and Alex had a crab cake sandwich.

Tired from their wild exertions of the previous evening, and the ill-fared bike ride, they decided to return to their room for a nap. After making love again, briefly, they fell asleep in each other's arms.

They awoke from their comfortable nap about five p.m., refreshed and relaxed, and started to dress for a night out at the Pit steakhouse, a newly opened restaurant at which Lila had heard the food was excellent.

Although she had many stylish outfits that she could have worn, Lila chose Alex's favorite dress on her, the black knit cocktail dress that she had worn on their first dress-up date at Luigi's. Since he never tired of seeing her in that dress, she had chosen it as her special occasion dress to bring with her that week. Although the boardwalk was treacherous for wearing high-heeled shoes, she donned a pair of black pumps and sheer black nylons to go with it.

As usual, the dress clung to her in all of the right places and hinted at her magnificent figure that was hidden beneath its black folds. By wearing it, she seemed to enhance the glow of contented beauty of a truly happy woman, which in reality she had become.

Alex dressed in dark slacks, his favorite style of button-down, oxford dress shirt, and wore a blue corded sport coat and no tie, and penny loafers with no socks, which was the style at that time.

They drove down the busy Coastal Highway, parked as close to the Pit as possible, and slowly sauntered in the oceanfront summer evening, down the boardwalk to where it was located.

As usual, the place was crowded. They were forced to sit in the cocktail lounge for thirty minutes, sipping diet drinks, before they could be seated for dinner.

Stray, lonely men, unaccompanied by a female companion and stimulated by Lila's beauty, started to pose into what they considered to be their most masculine modes, fantasizing within themselves about seducing her away from Alex and into their lonely beds for the evening.

As far as Lila was concerned, however, with her chosen mate alongside of her, she never saw them. If she did, it was only as background, like the piano player struggling to entertain the hungry, waiting crowd.

After being seated, they found that the food was as good as it was rumored to be. They selected their steaks from among those bedded in ice, and they both ordered clams casino, baked potatoes with chives and butter, and hearts of lettuce salads to accompany them. Lila finished up with a large slab of Black Forest cheesecake, full of bing cherries, and Alex with his usual black coffee.

Afterwards, to work off their heavy meal, they sauntered back up the boardwalk, tightly holding each other's hand, enjoying the cooling ocean breezes that drifted in from the nearby Atlantic Ocean. They stopped in at a nightspot that featured dancing, but the customers all seemed to be young and single. Feeling out of place, they slowly walked back up the boardwalk with its brightly lit activities and sensory smells and noises to where their car was parked, and returned to the sanctuary of their room.

The next day, Monday, it rained, so they slept late and enjoyed a late breakfast at the coffee shop. Later on, the rain cleared up but left behind a gusty wind that whipped the beach sand into annoying scratchy bursts, and only the most foolhardy tried to sun themselves by creating inefficient barriers with beach towels draped over upturned beach chairs. Even those brave souls surrendered their attempts to obtain a suntan and retired from the beach to pursue other bad weather day activities.

They drove down to the boardwalk and stopped into a boardwalk movie theater that was showing a cheaply rented World War II vintage movie entitled *Father Goose*. They had both seen it several times before, both in movie theaters and on TV.

The plot of this movie had to do with an alcoholic South Seas captain, who is suddenly charged with the evacuation of a girls' school and is weaned off of hard liquor by a spinsterish head mistress. They fall in love and eventually marry during a Japanese kamikaze attack, by short wave radio, using several of the female students as witnesses.

During the movie, Lila leaned her head on Alex's shoulder, and as usual, ate most of his popcorn, crying at the appropriate time and laughing delightedly when she was supposed to.

Afterwards, they played a game of miniature golf. Alex was pleased to see the self-imposed layers of sadness resulting from Ida's death and Lila's overwork being slowly stripped away from her usually vibrant personality.

Her pretended competitiveness with Alex rose to the surface, and he was delighted to see her giggle in her old musical way when she beat him by putting her golf ball into the appropriate cup with a lower score than his.

The rest of their week was spent in typical vacation style. They sunned themselves, with Lila's eye-popping bikini over her dark voluptuousness stirring up the manhood of young and old men who were engaged in the ages-old, delightful, exclusively male sport of beachfront girl watching. The couple also visited some of the many amusement parks featuring thrill rides. On those, Lila would frantically clutch her Alex with real fear until they were deposited onto the safety of the earth.

They ate dinner again at the Pit and enjoyed their food for a second time. They ate Ocean City fast food, which is different than the giant hamburgers served elsewhere and features steamship rounds of beef sandwiches, buckets of freshly killed, non-frozen, Eastern Shore of Maryland fried chicken, and crab cake sandwiches.

Throughout the entire vacation, Lila seemed to glow with an unusual happiness. Her eyes sparkled as if something happy was occurring inside of her, and she slowly returned to the happy, self-contained young woman of their earlier days together, giggling in her unique way as she slowly returned from the barrenness of total emotional desolation that had been brought on by Ida's death.

On Saturday morning, they checked out of the motel and returned to Towson, totally refreshed, and they both agreed that it was the best-damned vacation that they had ever spent together.

Since they arrived home late in the afternoon, they were unable to food shop. They decided to have dinner at Luigi's.

Luigi remarked to Lila, "Lila, your vacation seems to have done wonders for you. I have never seen you so happily glowing in all the time that I have known you."

She giggled and responded, "Luigi, Alex just went out if his way to please me. He got me to relax in more ways than I ever dreamed were possible. To quote his favorite expression, 'Wow, it was great.'"

Luigi smiled knowingly, but tactfully refrained from any further comments, knowing full well to what she was referring. He led them to a banquette and laid down two menus.

Pearl, however, was more matter of fact. She told Lila, " Mrs. Baxter, there's a special glow about you. Your eyes sparkle with a special glint. You both must have had a super-marvelous time together. The air around you both has resumed that special crackle that it had when you first started to date each other. I envy your magnificent love for each other."

They attended the service at the little frame church and Mattie Deutsch remarked, "Lila, you always look truly beautiful when I see you, but there's just some special beauty about you today that I just can't put my finger on. You look positively fulfilled."

Lila giggled and said, "Mattie, I've never been happier in my entire life. I believed that I could never love my Alex more than I did before we left. How wrong I was. If I were a physicist, I'd say that my love for him has made a quantum leap over what it was. How lucky I was to meet him when I did. I love him so much. He is the finest man that I have ever known and the anchor that has kept me from being swept away."

Alex, upon hearing that conversation, became embarrassed, and in his usually shy manner when being praised, kissed her on the cheek, to the delighted laughter of Mattie and her husband.

They were both delighted to be back home in Towson and securely within the community comfort of the little frame church congregation once again. They greeted their friends as if they had been gone for a year.

Even seeing Connie at the Diner when they had breakfast didn't cramp Lila's happiness, and she chattered like a child whose parents had just taken her to see the circus.

Lila returned to work on Monday morning, happily contented. She gave the saltwater taffy to the other girls, and the carved wooden statue of the grizzled old sea captain to Max.

Max appreciated her gift and placed it on his desk until he could find an appropriate spot in his cluttered office.

Myra amusedly remarked, "The first time that I saw Alex, I asked him why he wasn't wearing a big S on the front of his shirt and a cape over his shoulders. Maybe I changed my mind too quickly, and he really can leap over buildings in a single bound, because he seems to have been able to perform miracles with you. You look absolutely, divinely happy, and after all that you've been through, it's about time."

Lila continued to glow with some internal personal fulfillment that had been brought about by their happy vacation in Ocean City. She returned performing the little loving things that she had previously. She would lay out Alex clean clothes for the day before she left for the office. If she saw a new novel by his favorite author, she would enter the store and purchase it for him.

When the urge entered into her mind, she would suddenly lean over and kiss him soundly. This last gesture sometimes pleasantly startled Alex, who might be typing at his PC, but he was always absolutely delighted that she seemed to rapidly veering back into the wonderful Lila whom he loved so well.

About six weeks after they returned from Ocean City, she called him and said, "Honey, can we go to Luigi's tonight? I feel like getting out."

Even though he was working against a deadline, Alex replied, "Sure, honey, I'll make a reservation."

That evening, while they were dressing, she giggled and said, "Honey, I believe that I'm putting on weight. This dress seems to be getting tight."

That broad hint made no impression on Alex, whose mind was on the article that he was writing, and the deadline by which he had to have it completed.

Luigi greeted them with his usual enthusiasm. "Lila, you just seem to glow internally from a happy fulfillment. With you as a customer, I can save a fortune by turning off all the lights in here and allowing you to provide the illumination for the entire restaurant."

Pearl, in her usual down-to-earth bluntness, said, "Mrs. Baxter, the glistening in your eyes is a dead giveaway. I believe that I know the reason for your great happiness tonight."

After they gave Pearl their food orders, a puzzled Alex asked Lila, "Sweetheart, how about letting your husband in on the secret that everybody seems to know about but me."

She giggled happily in the delightful manner that Alex loved so well and replied, "Well, Father Goose, you finally hit the jackpot. You're going to be a daddy. I visited Dr. McGrath today, and he examined me. He tells me that I'm about six weeks pregnant. In April, our bedroom will have to double as a nursery. That wild carrying on that we did in Ocean City did the trick. The rabbit finally died."

It took a few seconds for the realization to register in Alex's mind, but when it did, he whooped out loud and yelled at Luigi, "Luigi, I'm going to be a father. Finally, I'm going to be a father!"

Luigi laughed heartily and replied, "Alex, I've known that for weeks. That's the way my wife looks when she gets pregnant. Congratulations, I'm really happy for you both."

All of the other diners broke into applause at Alex's confession. He reddened with embarrassment, although Lila's statement was closely akin in his mind to finally finding the Holy Grail.

When the dinner rush tapered off, Luigi sat down at their table and started to pleasantly tease them about the coming blessed event. "Well, you've gone and done it. That child will be the best-loved baby in Towson. I'm sure that it will have an IQ of 200, belong to MENSA, win the Nobel Prize and be drafted a President, despite its political affiliation. I felt the same way about my first child until I had to get out of a warm bed at three a.m. to change a dirty diaper and feed it, so that my wife could get some badly needed rest.

"There's something about the smell of a dirty diaper, after you've just gotten home at midnight, that seems to magnify its unpleasantness. But within hours, your heart will do flip-flops when you see it cooing happily and smelling clean after a warm bath. When you hold it against you, it'll feel like no other baby in the universe. And when you rock it to sleep, you'll experience the greatest happiness that you have ever known. A baby is God's greatest gift to you. All children are beautiful, but that one will be yours and will be the most beautiful baby ever conceived. Then you'll see it blossom into a perfect flower, and you'll realize, that with all of man's knowledge, a baby is the most important thing that a happy marriage can produce. You both are a truly magnificent couple. Congratulations, again."

Max was ecstatic when he heard the news. He said, "No more overtime for you, my *bubala*. Make sure that you get eight or nine hours of sleep every night. Drink lots of milk, it's got calcium and is good for the baby's bones. Chicken soup is also very good. When my Esther was pregnant, she used to eat a big bowl every day. She calls it her Jewish penicillin."

Alex's reaction to Lila's pregnancy was amazed pleasure that they were finally going to be parents. If he saw her picking up a heavy object, he would immediately rush over and take it from her. He made her place her feet on a hassock and generally treated her as a delicate, easily cracked eggshell.

She enjoyed the attention for a while, and the reason it was being lavished on her. Her own sense of independence eventually took over, though, and she told Alex, "Honey, I'm just pregnant, not an invalid. Women have been expecting for thousands of years, and they've always been treated as if they're totally incapacitated. Somehow the human species has survived the father-treat-mother-to-be-as-an-invalid syndrome. I know my limits, and I won't exceed them. I love you for your concern, but I can take care of myself."

Alex replied, "Well, baby, just take care of yourself. You're one and a half people now." He laughed as a sudden thought developed within him. "Sweetheart, they often measure beauty on a scale of one to ten. Do you know how they measure an expectant mother on that scale?"

Lila replied, "No, but I know that I'm going to learn."

He laughed again and replied, "Ten and a half when you count the wonderful gift that you're carrying."

Lila groaned and placed her hands on her belly. She said in mock severity, "Did you hear that, baby Baxter? Your daddy in going into his burlesque routine again. I'm covering your ears so that you won't know that he's really a corn farmer."

As with all women that are happily expecting, Lila would sit for hours, while they were watching TV or visiting some friends, holding her belly and giggling at Alex's corny humor. His jokes were designed to make her laugh, because he felt that happiness in an expectant mother affected the chemistry within her. He felt that a happy mother would have a happy baby and pre-partum happiness had a positive effect on the baby's personality. In any case, his humor kept her mind away from the discomforts of early pregnancy.

CHAPTER 19

In the early stages of her pregnancy, Lila was afflicted with a particularly vicious form of morning sickness. Until it ran its normal course, the very thought of food in any form completely nauseated her. If she saw someone happily munching on a large hamburger, she would make a mad dash for the nearest ladies' room and regurgitate whatever food that she had recently eaten. For a long time, all she could retain within her body were saltines, toast and cola syrup, which had been prescribed for her by Dr. McGrath.

She developed strange cravings, as do many expectant mothers, for odd food combinations. Dill pickles slathered with mustard, bread covered with chocolate sauce, mustard on top of her breakfast eggs, and a massive yearn for fruit jelly on most everything.

As her normal clothes became too tight for her to wear, she slowly started dressing in early forms of maternity clothing. Mattie Deutsch told her that she looked like a professional model hired by some baby magazine for a special promotion. She had a special affinity for maternity dresses with large soft bows at the neck and solid colors that enhanced her beautiful dark complexion. She was often told that she looked even more beautiful while she was expecting than she had before the blessed event occurred.

She began to eat like a longshoreman after a hard day's work. Double helpings of mashed potatoes, large servings of Alex's famous stew, and four or five slices of bread with her dinner were common parts of her diet. If there was any food left over, she would eye it hungrily before she ate it all up.

Dr. McGrath cautioned her to maintain some semblance of weight control. He indicated that most of the weight that she would add to her figure while she was expecting would be from water retention in her body, and that it would easier in the delivery if her body didn't develop the enormous rolls of flesh that would make it difficult to access the baby's delivery channel.

She glowed with the fulfillment of all women who are happy when they are pregnant. Although women's rights have been a long-fought-over ideal, ever since the biblical story of Eve's creation from Adam's rib, all species of life that require a male and female gender to procreate; the process of having a nestling is the purpose why the two sexes were created. "Perpetuate the species" is the term most commonly used to describe the function of procreation. No matter how it is described, it is the greatest gift that God can bestow.

Lila spoke to Marie often by telephone. Since her reconciliation with George, after his mid-life crisis—when young curvaceous girls look most attractive and a man's candle appears to briefly flicker brightly—they were getting along well together.

Marie didn't want any children. She said that they both wanted to enjoy the economic benefits of George's promotion to vice president, and that they were content with Hercules' replacement, Samson.

Lila's pregnancy seemed to make her more physically fatigued than usual. The new assistant paralegal that Max had selected had developed enough skills to handle all except the most complicated cases, so she worked out a schedule with Max of ten a.m. until three p.m., plus being on call for consultation if the need arose.

Alex always made Lila take a short nap when she arrived home from work.

She would giggle delightedly, while holding her rapidly expanding front with her two hands, as she viewed herself in her mirror, and began to call herself "Mrs. Basketball Belly."

Her main concern became that of the developing life that she was carrying inside of her. Alex, out of concern for her well-being, refrained from having sexual relations with her, and she appeared to appreciate his gesture enormously.

She developed a strong need to be held tenderly, and often fell asleep in her comfortable way, with her head on his shoulder and both hands holding her belly. If there ever was a child that was as strongly desired as the one inside of her body, it was certainly very rare.

Curious as to its sex, they had a sonogram taken and learned that it was going to be a boy. Alex was delighted to learn what gender their child was to become, but Lila was secretly disappointed, since she would have preferred a little girl whom she could dress in the beautiful outfits available in the children's shops. In any case, however, any healthy child was acceptable to both of them.

Although their child was still in an early formative stage, when they learned that it was going to be a boy, they eagerly started to think of names by which they could call it. Like many expectant mothers, she purchased a book of names, with their meanings and a general history of each.

After trying out numerous names, they finally settled on calling him Alexander William Baxter, after Lila's father, William Taylor, and Alex. Her father, although he had literally drunk himself to death, had always been a kind and generous parent with his two beautiful daughters. Lila thought that the name that they had chosen was a dignified name for a future President of the United States of America.

They began to stroll slowly through malls, holding hands, looking at nursery furniture displays in specialty and department stores. Lila would giggle when she looked at displays of toys and devices meant to train and keep little ones occupied.

As her condition started to show, she became more enveloped in the love that was part of what made the little frame church so unique. The mothers of that little church had all become members of a very exclusive sorority. Most women have a secret desire to become part of that group, but it takes hours of labor to qualify for membership.

Lila continued to glow in the beauty of impending motherhood. She took on a very protective attitude regarding the baby's welfare. During the onset of maternity, no mother lion ever protected the oncoming birth of her cubs more devotedly than did Lila. A famous doctor's book on childcare became her bible and source of information for attending to her maternal needs. She followed Dr. McGrath's guidelines completely, and for a while it seemed that the birth was going to be routine and uneventful.

Three months into her pregnancy, she suddenly started to feel painful contractions in her pelvic region. This concerned Dr. McGrath, who urged her to take long-term bed rest to contain the potential onset of a miscarriage. He took samples of her amniotic fluid to determine if there were any potential birth defects that were apparent that could not be accounted for. Apparently there didn't seem to be any, but he looked grim every time that he did examine her.

To assist her in her weakened condition, Alex took over the heavy housecleaning chores in order to maintain the cleanliness of their apartment. As with all men, his idea of cleaning was to place the old newspapers in a different pile, place the dirtied dishes into the dishwasher, run the vacuum cleaner when the dust started to make him sneeze, and take the trash down to hall to the garbage chute.

Lila was suddenly terrified that she was going to lose her baby. Frantic with fear, she fervently prayed that she would be allowed to carry her baby to the full term. She followed Dr. McGrath's instructions religiously, and with longer bed rest, the contractions eased to the point where she only felt them occasionally. She would still wince and clutch her belly when one suddenly grabbed her.

Her attendance at work became very spotty and her assistant often brought new cases to the Baxter residence so that Lila could outline a procedure to get her started in her research to prepare for a new hearing. This included where to look for precedents, what forms to file with the clerk's office, how to guarantee service to the litigants and other vital services.

Myra called her frequently to check on her well-being. Mattie Deutsch and Kitty Mooney would occasionally stop by and bring with them some sugary pastry to satisfy her sweet tooth. During those visits, her emotions would be lifted, and with the temporary sugar fix, her energy level would become very positive, and she would chat animatedly with them until they left.

Marie was concerned that there might be some underlying physical condition for the discomfort that Lila was feeling. She would sometimes call twice a day to check her welfare, and often told Alex privately that she as worried about Lila and feared that she would lose the baby.

Lila's health, which was never robust, seemed to be deteriorating rapidly. Alex was frantic with worry over the sudden reversal of Lila's health. He would hold her to him fervently as they watched a rented video. When they played their favorite board game, he would sometimes let her win the game that they were playing, just to hear her old musical giggle.

Even Max, her surrogate father, often called her to check on her health. He often asked Alex if he needed any money for immediate purposes. Alex never needed any financial assistance, and if he had ever had, would never dream of accepting it from him. Max was a workaholic that drove himself beyond the norm to complete the task in which he was currently involved. He expected his staff to follow his leadership, and he always rewarded them with cash bonuses. He was a hard-driving and generous employer.

Lila's painful false labor contractions never completely stopped their random appearance in Lila's body. One evening, while sleeping closely cuddled up to her Alex, she awoke from a sound sleep, feeling wetness about her lower body.

Sleepily, she reached down to see what was causing the wetness, and when she withdrew her hand, she discovered that it was covered with a red wetness that could only be one thing—blood.

She gasped and threw the blanket back from her body to discover that the bed sheets were deeply stained from a large pool of blood. She was hemorrhaging. She was having a miscarriage and going to lose the most important thing that she and Alex had ever wanted—their first child.

She frantically shook Alex into wakefulness and started to sob uncontrollably. Crying out desperately, she said, "Oh God, I'm hemorrhaging, having a miscarriage. I'm going to lose the baby."

Alex, jarred into wakefulness by her desperate cries, reached over and grabbed her cell phone and dialed 911. He then called Dr. McGrath's answering service and identified himself. He told them that his wife was hemorrhaging and having a miscarriage, that he had called 911 and was having her taken to St. Matthew's emergency room.

He quickly dressed in the clothing that he had worn the previous day, wrapped Lila in a light blanket, and carried her out into the living room to await the emergency medical technicians of 911.

They arrived quickly, accompanied by the building manager, examined Lila and packed her with gauze to slow down the massive blood flow slowly draining her of her vital life fluid.

Placing her on a gurney, they rapidly wheeled her down the hall, with Alex holding her hand tightly, onto the waiting elevator, which they had locked into a reserved, waiting position, through the lobby and into the lighted, steel interior of their ambulance.

Alex rode with her, holding her hand, unable to stem the cries of deep emotional pain that were being forced out of her by the ordeal. They drove, with siren blaring loudly, the short distance to St. Matthew's emergency room.

Alex accompanied the gurney into the examining cubicle, and was gently, but firmly forced out, while they attempted to treat Lila and stem the massive bleeding that she was having.

A ward clerk approached Alex with a clipboard and started to take down the necessary insurance information from him. Irritated by the late hour, and from overwork, she was not very polite to Alex and abruptly told him that his coverage did not cover certain procedures and that he would be required to pay for the difference.

Alex, frantic with worry over Lila, suddenly yelled at her, "Dammit, girl, back off! I have money in the bank to pay the difference and I will. I want my wife to have the best care possible while she's here. Do I make myself clear?"

The rude ward clerk, enraged at his response, abruptly walked away from Alex.

Alex called Marie in Chicago, using Lila's cell phone, and told her of Lila's condition. Marie indicated that she would be in later that day and to get her a hotel reservation. She said that George was in the middle of negotiations with a large Midwestern corporation for a new stock issue and couldn't accompany her.

Then Alex called Reverend Busch and told him the news. The gentle reverend asked what he could do to assist Alex and told him that he would remember Lila in his prayers.

Dr. McGrath arrived, looking sleepy and grim, and entered the examination room while Alex sat in the general waiting room area, a lonely figure. He would alternately hold his head in his hands and periodically pace back and forth like some hopelessly caged animal in a zoo, with no emotional escape from the reality of Lila's emergency.

Finally, Dr. McGrath emerged from the cubicle. "Come with me, Alex."

He led Alex to an empty office close by and sat down facing him. "Alex, we lost the baby. We did all we could to save it, but it was really hopeless. Lila's body completely rejected the fetus entirely. It was what is called a spontaneous miscarriage, caused by some underlying medical condition. I have strong suspicion regarding the root cause, and with your permission, I would like to keep Lila here for several days to run a series of tests on her to confirm my diagnosis. I plan to order a CAT scan, a magnetic resonance imaging, which is also called an MRI, and a complete battery of blood tests. When these tests are completed, I will have more reliable data on which to base my decision. After the tests are completed, I'll sit down with you and discuss the alternatives in language that you will understand."

Alex replied, "Dr. McGrath, you didn't need to ask my permission on something as important as that. The answer is positively yes. When can I see her?"

He replied, "Well, she's highly sedated right now because the loss of your child was a cruel blow to her emotions. She'll remain asleep for a period of time. The nurses are cleaning her up now, and she'll be taken to a room when one is located for her. You can accompany the gurney to her room and you may stay as long as you choose. She'll be somewhat disoriented when she awakes, but that's normal in cases like hers. I'll be in later this morning to check on her, when I make my morning rounds. I promise you that when an accurate diagnosis is developed, I will sit down with you and thoroughly discuss her situation." He stood up and placed his hand on Alex's shoulder in a gesture of sympathy, then left the room.

Alex sat in deep emotional pain for a while, trying to make sense out of this total collapse of his wonderful life with Lila. He had previously felt that Ida's death and Bear's subsequent euthanization were two strikes against him in the game of life. Now Lila's illness and the loss of their son was the third and most critical strike against him of all. He was out, but still in the ball game, because she was still alive.

When two orderlies wheeled the gurney stretcher to an elevator, with Lila's inert body on it, Alex accompanied it to a room several floors above the ER. He sat there praying to the God that he had thought was merciful, that he would be kind to his beautiful creation, Lila, and grant her a degree of peace from the deep emotional pain that she had long endured.

About six a.m., with Lila still asleep from the heavy sedation and tranquilizers, he decided to return to the Ridgeway and change his bloodstained clothing. He took along the badly stained blanket that he had wrapped around Lila. The hospital staff had placed it in a large plastic bag, and he dropped it down the garbage chute into the lower level garbage dumpster.

After a quick shower, he shaved and donned fresh clothing. Physically he felt clean and refreshed, although tired from lack of sleep. His mind, however, was a mass of emotional incisions. The pain that he felt for his beloved Lila was so acute that he unconsciously blocked it out of his mind.

He had lost all desire to eat, but forced himself to boil two eggs, made a couple of slices of toast, and washed the whole thing down with very strong black coffee. After he ate, he did feel somewhat better.

On his way back to the hospital, he stopped at his florist and purchased a dozen American beauty, long-stem, red roses. These were Lila's favorite flowers.

Lila was awake, but drifting in and out of sleep, as the effects of her sedation slowly wore off. Her emotions were rubbed raw from her trauma and were still largely buffered by the Valium that was still within her system. She was full of the realization that only a female could feel over a miscarriage, but did not yet realize that she might be seriously ill.

Looking weak from her blood loss, and with a sort of pallor under her olive skin, she took a rose from the bouquet, placed it to her nose to inhale its perfume and fell back to sleep, dropping the rose onto the front of her white hospital gown. It lay there, with its brilliant red color, looking strangely like a drop of blood on freshly fallen snow.

Alex leaned over and kissed her with all his pent-up love and fear for her safety.

He picked up the rose and returned it to the vase that the floor nurse had provided, and sat down alongside of her to await her full awakeness.

She awoke about a half an hour later and gestured to Alex to lean over and kiss her.

He said, "Hi, sweetie, you really had a rough night."

Her beautiful hazel eyes slowly filled with tears and she replied, "Well, we lost him. I wanted that baby so badly, honey. I thought that the bad luck witch, who has my name engraved on her forehead, had finally given up, and I was going to have some good luck. That nasty bitch must have been on vacation when I met you or else she would have found some way to screw us up. Max has said that my guardian angel was sitting on my shoulder on the day that I met you. Maybe my angel was on vacation yesterday, and she sneaked in when he wasn't looking."

Overcome with compassion for her, Alex quickly reached down and grabbed her hand. "We can still keep trying, sweetheart. There's no great rush. Dr. McGrath wants to keep you here for a couple of days to run some routine tests on you to see if he can find out what caused the miscarriage. He just wants to see if he can prevent the damned thing from reoccurring. The important thing is for you to recover and come home. I love you with all of my being.

"I called Marie, and she's probably on an airplane, somewhere between here and Chicago, right now. She said to tell you that maybe the four of us can take a West Indies cruise next spring to let off steam."

Marie got into Towson about eleven a.m., and after renting a car at the airport, drove directly to the hospital before she checked into her hotel. She bustled into the hospital, full of good cheer for her ill sister, and the two of them casually chatted abut gossip that was related to them.

Lila was still not completed free of the sedation and mostly nodded vaguely at Marie's cheerful statements.

Afterwards, while they were having a cup of coffee at the first floor cafeteria, while Lila was taking a nap, Marie told Alex, "Our mother was about Lila's age when she was diagnosed with stage IV ovarian cancer. I suspect that her gynecologist is aware of that and wants to explore her insides to see if that filthy beast is lurking in some hidden corner of her, waiting for a chance to sneak out and secretly take her life."

Alex, who had been suspecting the same thing, agreed with her.

Marie said, "Lila is a smart girl, and it won't be too long before she will put all of the pieces together and come up with the same conclusion. She saw the symptoms that Mom endured and probably suspects her condition right now."

Max arrived later that afternoon, while Marie was off checking into her hotel. The first thing that Max said to Alex was, "Do you need any money? If you need any help, just tell me the amount, and I'll transfer it to your account. I do business with the same bank that you use."

Alex replied, "No, Max, we're in pretty good shape financially. I don't believe that she will be here more than a couple of days. The excellent hospital insurance that you provide for your people will cover all but a few of her charges here."

Max looked down at the sleeping Lila. The skilled lawyer, who could reduce a witness to a sodden wreck in record time, started to get tears in his eyes. He said, "She looks so helpless. Like a little girl who was just put to bed by her mother. Until she met you, those two *schmucks*, Bobby and later that *gonif*, Lupinsky, did nothing but take advantage of her gentle nature.

"When she met you, it looked like her luck had changed. She often told me about her Alex and what a wonderful man and great husband that you are. I never saw her happier in all of the years that I have known her. When she learned that she was pregnant, her joy was as great as if she had won an Oscar. My Esther and me love her like another daughter. Alex Baxter, you're a damned *mensch*.

"When she gets home, I'll call you and see if it's OK for my Esther and me to come for a visit. We'll wait a while so that you won't be bothered by us. I know that the two of you are absolutely crazy over each other, so we'll call ahead to make arrangements so that we won't interrupt anything important."

Alex replied, "Now listen here, Max. She has always said that you are her surrogate father. I want you to know that you can come for a visit when you please, stay as long as you please and leave when you're damned well ready to leave. I suspect that they'll discharge her soon, and I'll call you when she's home. You and Esther are always welcome. Both she and I think of you both as close relatives."

"Alex," Max replied, "I feel so hopeless seeing her like this. She was completely fulfilled when she learned that she was going to have a baby. When I look at her now, she seems to be such a little girl, not even old enough to have reached her puberty. Did the doctor tell you what it is that he suspects is the cause of her miscarriage?"

"No," Alex replied. "But her sister suspects that it may be ovarian cancer, because that's what their mother died of."

Max replied, "God forbid that it is. If it is, she'll suffer such pain. A beauty like her should be pampered and not medicated. I'll pray for her every day. Maybe the Great Jehovah will grant her peace. Please let me know first if you ever need any money."

Alex replied, "No, Max, my income from writing is pretty good., and we don't spend it like a sailor on shore leave. Thanks for asking. If anyone is a *mensch*, it's you. If I ever find that I need money, I'll let you know."

"I have to go now," Max replied. "I have a client coming in at three. Please let us know when she'll be home."

"I will," replied Alex. "Tell Myra about Lila's condition. They're such good friends that I'm sure she would like to know. I'll call you when I get her home. I'm positive that she will want to see Esther and you."

CHAPTER 20

The next day, Alex left for the hospital early because he wanted to spend more time with his Lila.

He took the elevator up to the floor on which her room was located and walked down the hall to her room. There, he found Lila asleep on a gurney, with two orderlies and a nurse ready to wheel her out.

The nurse said, "We're just taking Mrs. Baxter down to the MRI Room for a scan that Dr. McGrath has ordered. You can wait here for her, but it'll be over an hour before we have her back. There's a waiting area at the end of the hall with a TV, and the chapel is on the right if you care to meditate. The cafeteria is open on the first floor if you feel the need for a snack. When we are finished with the MRI, she'll be returned to this room, but as I said, it'll be upwards of an hour."

Alex then realized that, in his rush to visit Lila, he had neglected to eat breakfast. He informed the nurse at the nurses' station that he was going down to the cafeteria, and took the elevator back to the first floor.

He purchased a copy of the *Sun* at the gift stand and entered the cafeteria. There, he ordered a Danish sweet roll and a container of coffee. He left the Danish largely untouched, but began to sip on his coffee as he scanned the newspaper.

He was desperate with worry over his Lila's condition and hadn't been able to sleep except in brief stretches since her miscarriage. He had no appetite for food and just wanted to be with his lovely wife.

Marie, who had stopped by the nurses' station, joined him shortly thereafter. She sat down at the little table where he was sitting. Alex asked her if she had had any breakfast and she replied, "No, but I'm not really hungry. Some coffee would be very welcome though."

He purchased a plastic container for her and they sat together discussing Lila and why they thought that Dr. McGrath had ordered the MRI and so many tests.

Marie said, "Mom was just about Lila's age when it was discovered that she had stage IV ovarian cancer. At that stage, it is so advanced that it is virtually untreatable. All that they can do is to try to shrink the tumors with chemo or radiation. That is unless they haven't metastasized too widely. I suspect that Lila has the same type of cancer, because the gene that promotes it is probably present in her system as it is in mine as well."

Alex, who had secretly suspected the same thing, was reluctantly forced to agree with her. They sat there discussing their limited knowledge of cancer treatment and then decided to return to Lila's room.

They found Lila looking weak and groggy from the sedative that had been administered to prepare her for the confinement within the enclosed MRI chamber. Her duty nurse was re-hooking her to her vital signs monitors.

She looked weak and helpless, so Alex leaned over and kissed her soundly. "Honey, are you feeling any better today?"

Lila was disoriented by the tranquilizing effect of the drug inside of her and didn't immediately answer, only drifting in and out of sleep until it cleared up several hours later.

Dr. McGrath stopped by on his morning rounds and told Alex that he had the results of most of the tests that he had ordered, with the exception of the MRI, which he expected later that morning. He wondered if a meeting at eleven a.m. could be arranged to discuss the results.

Alex introduced him to Marie and wanted to know if she could sit in on the briefing because she was Lila's only living blood relative.

Dr. McGrath agreed, and they arranged to meet them at his hospital office.

They located his office, on the second floor of the hospital, and sat down to wait for him to appear, or as Alex phrased it, "Wait for the other shoe to drop."

When Dr. McGrath did appear, dressed in his white lab coat with his stethoscope draped around his neck, he looked harried and pressed for time. He glanced at his wristwatch briefly and sat opposite them in the small cluttered office and slowly began to speak. "I know how concerned you both are about Lila and her health condition. Hold any questions that you may have until I'm through with my dissertation because I may answer them as we go along.

"I am often asked, what is cancer? My answer to that question is that it is a group of related diseases that the root cause of has yet to be discovered.

"The onset of all cancers begins at a single place within the human body's cells. The cells are the basic building blocks that make up all of the tissues that exist within the body. The tissues, in turn, are the basis of all of the organs within the body, and the organs, in turn, govern the body's vital functions.

"Normally, cells die off and a process of division creates replacement cells in a normal manner. This is a continuing and normal process for as long as you are alive. When the old cells outlive their usefulness they die, and new cells are created from the existing cells to take their place.

"Sometimes, in this orderly fission process, something goes awry and new cells are created when the body doesn't need them. These cells form an abnormal mass or lump that is called a tumor.

"Those masses or tumors can be either malignant or benign. This means that they are either cancerous or non-cancerous. Benign tumors do not metastasize or spread into other vital organs. Malignant or cancerous tumors do spread into other vital organs and frequently are life threatening. That process is called metastisization.

"The onset of cancer is not selective. It can occur anywhere within the body. The original malignant tumor is the source of all other malignancies, and is called the primary tumor. It is named for the part of the body in which it is created. If in the lungs, lung cancer. If in the stomach, stomach cancer. On the skin, skin cancer and so on.

"When a cancer spreads, some of its cells break off and enter the blood stream or lymph nodes of the body. This is the principal method by which a cancer is spread within the human body.

"If it spreads into the lymph nodes or nearby organs, the original tumor is called a regional disease. If it spreads into vital organs far from its primary mass it is called a metatastic cancer.

"Metatastic cancer cells are like those abnormal cells of the mass from which they originate, and are still known by the cells from which they have originated. This is because under a microscope, when viewed by a pathologist examining a biopsy, or sample of the tumor, the abnormal cells look like those of the cells in which it originated.

"Metastatic cancers always originate at one place, anywhere within the body. Sometimes, cancer can be discovered only after the metatastic cancer has found its way into other parts of the body, such as prostate cancer spreading into the bones.

"The efforts to locate a cancer may involve tests, radiography or x-rays, CAT scans, MRIs, as well as other procedures. Its treatment is through chemotherapy, radiation, surgery or any combination of techniques available at the time, depending on the age of the patient, the health, size of the tumors and their location within the body."

He then paused and inquired, "Do you understand what I have said so far?"

Alex and Marie both nodded their heads.

"Ovarian cancer is known as the silent killer because in most cases there are no specific major symptoms of its presence until it has progressed into advanced stages—stages III and IV.

"Its early symptoms are generally mild and well hidden, even from gynecological tests that are given to women. Early symptoms may include feelings of fullness or discomfort in the pelvic area, indigestion or bloating that is not relieved by over-the-counter antacids, abnormal periodic bleeding, and swelling and pain in the abdominal region."

At that point, Alex suddenly remembered the indigestion and gas that Lila had suffered from during the past year and her remarking to him, "How could gas be connected to anything gynecological?" He also remembered her abnormal periods, their unpredictability, and length of their flow, before Dr. McGrath had ordered a D&C procedure at GMMC. If only they had had the foresight to have her tested for ovarian cancer, they wouldn't be in this emergency. Her mother had died from the dreaded disease.

Dr. McGrath continued, "Early detection of ovarian cancer increases its curability up to 90%. If it is left untreated, this silent killer frequently spreads into the abdomen and most of those cases die within a five-year period. It is the most common malignancy that causes mortality among women. Up to 25,000 new cases are diagnosed each year. Thousands of women die from it each year, and its prognosis of cure depends on the stage at which it is discovered. Early physical indications are uncommon at its onset. While the precise cause of its onset is still yet not fully understood, factors such as reproduction, genetics and heredity play a big part in its beginning. Family history plays a large part in determining a woman's risk in contracting this silent form of cancer. Where there is a prior history of its onset, a woman's risk is dramatically increased."

Looking at Marie, Dr. McGrath asked, "Your mother died of it, didn't she?" Marie nodded in assent to his question.

He continued, "There are four stages that develop after its onset. Stage I, where the malignant tumor growth is limited to the ovaries; stage II, where it has spread into the pelvic area; stage III, where it has spread into both ovaries and may involve the liver. Stage IV involves distant metastasis, where it has formed tumors in vital organs not close to its primary location.

"As I indicated previously, treatment is by use of chemotherapy, radiation, and surgery. Surgery is not a recommended procedure when it is determined that a woman has Stage IV of the disease.

"The onset of ovarian cancer in women younger than age forty years of age is rare. If I am wrong, please correct me, but I believe that Lila turned forty some time last year, didn't she, Alex?"

Alex nodded his head.

"The only sure way of present determination that a woman will not eventually contract ovarian cancer is the surgical removal of both of her ovaries.

"When Lila first came to me for health maintenance several years ago, I rapidly determined that her mother had died of ovarian cancer and that her father had succumbed to another form of it as well. This led me to suspect that there might be a genetic link within her that would make her prone to contracting cancer.

"At that time, she expressed a fear of contracting ovarian cancer, and I casually suggested that the only way of being certain that she would not contract it was the surgical removal of her ovaries.

"Later on, after you two were married, she expressed a fear again, and I again suggested surgery. She indicated that you both wanted to have children and the surgical removal would effectively sterilize her. I could find no reason to doubt her logic as long as she was aware of the risks involved with her contracting that disease.

"There were certain anomalies in her physical condition that have always worried me, but all of her gynecological tests always proved to be negative. The irregularity and length of her periods for instance have always concerned me. Her pelvic pain during her monthly periods was also suspicious. She stubbornly refused to have her ovaries removed despite my many suggestions."

Alex then commented, "Stubbornness is a common trait among the Taylor women. Her Aunt Ida personified that trait."

Dr. McGrath was rapidly coming to the focal point of his discussion and said, "That, in brief, with many gaps, is an overview of cancer in general and ovarian cancer specifically. I have just covered the high points to familiarize you with the elements of what cancer is, how to treat it, and the relative prognoses of women who might be prone to its onset.

"There are many excellent articles available in libraries, through the several societies that specialize in the area of ovarian cancer, and also through the Internet. My nurse can provide you with a list of society names and titles of publications if you want to research into that topic further. Those articles go into detail about where and how such tumors form and the various aspects of its onset, prognoses, and life expectancy after its onset.

"Now, regarding Lila, she has the onset of stage IV ovarian cancer. A CAT scan, MRI and needle biopsies have all confirmed that she has masses throughout her body. The primary tumor is located within her left ovary, but the cancer has metastasized into her stomach and liver, and there is a smaller mass attached to her right lung.

"As someone who has stage IV, because of its widespread incidence in her system, it will be difficult or almost impossible to effectively treat her condition. We want to treat her with chemotherapy to try to reduce the size of her tumors, since they are too widespread to be operable.

"It is our plan to use platinum compounds, such as paclitaxel. Those will be used, along with Cisplatin and carboplatin, in a three-cycle therapy. Those agents are the approved therapy for initial treatment of ovarian cancer. Those compounds seem to be the most effective regimes, as we presently are aware of the state of the art. Their effectiveness is generally dependent on the degree of metastisization.

"The chemo will make her very nauseous and she will lose much of her hair. The hair will eventually grow back. You may seek another opinion if you so choose."

Alex sat back, stunned by the confirmation of his suspicions and the negativity of Dr. McGrath's diagnosis. His last hope for a return to the enchanted life that he had enjoyed since he and Lila first met had been smashed like a glass jar dropped on a concrete sidewalk. "How long does she have to live?"

"Six months to a year," Dr. McGrath replied.

Alex's emotions started to churn inside of him as he realized that, in terms of baseball, the game was over. He had lost to the beast, Death.

Marie was also stunned. "When I get home to Chicago, the first thing that

I am going to investigate is the surgical removal of my ovaries."

Dr. McGrath again glanced at his wristwatch and said, "Dr. Raj Patel, who is a gynecological oncologist, will assume the role of primary care specialist. He is very capable and abreast of the current state of the art in such cases. He is familiar with all of the aspects of Lila's condition, as I know them. I will act in a consultative role and will always be available to you if you need me."

Glancing at his wristwatch again, he said, "If you have no more questions, I have other patients who urgently need my attention. I also have office hours this afternoon. I'm sorry that I had to be the one to deliver this news, but unfortunately, that's one of the negative aspects of practicing medicine. Try to make her as comfortable as possible, because she is facing the complete destruction of her chosen lifestyle, and even more, moving over to the other side of life." With that comment, he placed his hand on Alex's shoulder in sympathetic empathy and left the room.

Alex and Marie just sat there for a while, too stunned to even speak.

Finally, they arose and returned to Lila's room, shaken, but determined to make Lila's last days as comfortable as they could.

Back in Lila's room, they found that she was now awake and had reluctantly accepted the hard cold fact that she had lost her firstborn son, but was yet unaware of the critical nature of her underlying illness.

Marie said, "Honey, when you defeat this lousy son-of-a-bitch illness, and you're back on your feet, let's the four of us take a Caribbean cruise this spring. There are some really quaint ports that those cruise ships stop at, and the climate will take any frost right out of your bones."

Lila wasn't fooled by Marie's attempts to make her feel better. "Marie, Mom had the same symptoms as I do now. I won't be here to take that cruise."

Alex was overcome with emotion and sat on her bed. He hugged her tightly to him. "Lila Baxter, I absolutely adore you. You are the half of me that will always be important. I love you with all my heart."

Lila began to cry softly, and he pressed her to him tightly and slowly began to rock her back and forth to try to calm down her fears of the unknown. Finally, she drifted back into a deep sedated sleep while he was still holding her close.

Marie said, "Alex, I have to return to Chicago. My flight leaves at 8:22. I'll keep in touch. How do you plan on taking care of her?"

Alex replied, "I think that I'll call Keisha Paddington to find out if she's available. She is one of the best things that ever came into Ida's life while she was here. If she isn't on a case, maybe she'll agree to come back. She and Lila always got along together. She's an LPN and is licensed to administer the strong pain relievers that Lila will need down the road."

Marie kissed the sleeping Lila goodbye, kissed Alex on the cheek, and left to check out of her hotel, leaving a desolate Alex behind with his only true love.

After she left, Alex sat desolately for a long time, drinking in the beauty of his precious Lila. He found that he was unable to think clearly. All that he could think of was that he was going to lose her. She was the very center of his world, and the only person that he would ever love. He felt like he wanted to cry, but the strain worrying about her illness had conditioned him into a numbness that prevented him from feeling real emotion.

Finally realizing that Lila desperately needed help, he placed a call to Keisha Paddington to determine if she was available and could take Lila's case.

She was shocked at the news and said, "Oh, Mr. Alex, I'm so sorry. I know how much the two of you love each other. I just started a new case about three weeks ago, and it would be unethical for me to leave right now. If you had called me three weeks ago, I could have started immediately. I'm genuinely sorry because she's so beautiful, but also because she has real compassion, and was very nice to me when I worked for her Aunt Ida.

"My sister, Nikita, is also an LPN and is available at the moment. I've told her about Mrs. Baxter many times, about how beautiful she is, and how uniquely happy you both are with each other. If you would like, I can have her call you and outline her experience to you. I'm sure that she would care for Mrs. Baxter as if it were her own daughter."

Alex replied, "Keisha, if you recommend her, that's all the reference that I'll need. Just ask her if she can start immediately."

Nikita did call that evening and was well versed on Lila. She related her credentials to Alex and indicated that both Alex and Lila had been very kind to her sister during the period of Ida's illness.

After establishing her daily hourly rate and normal hours, she agreed to start at seven a.m. on the following Monday, but indicated that the length of her daily shift really meant nothing to her, since she was used to working the twelve-hour shifts that are common in health care. She had her own transportation and had no unusual problems at home since her family was all grown and living apart from her.

CHAPTER 21

On the Saturday morning before Nikita was due to start, the insurance restrictions that were part of Lila's group plan required Alex to have Lila discharged from St. Matthew's.

Since it was close to lunchtime when he got her home, he thought that a bowl of soup might be appetizing to her and set up a TV table in front of her as she was sitting in an easy chair. He poured some soup into a bowl and set it in front of her.

She took one spoonful of the soup and cried out, "Take it away, honey, I'm going to be sick," and started to throw up all over herself, her clothing and the carpet.

Then her body began to shake with uncontrollable sobs at her inability to adequately control her ingestion of the food.

Alex stripped the soiled clothing off of her and placed it in the washer, and re-dressed her in her favorite old sweatpants and one of his tee shirts. He picked her up physically and sat on the sofa with her on his lap. She leaned her head on his shoulder and suddenly his composure failed him and he began to cry along with her.

"Oh, Lila, how I love you, and how it hurts me to see you this way. If it were physically possible, I would substitute myself in your place to give you the peace that you deserve. Don't worry about that accident, I'll clean it up in a short while. Those things happen all the time.

"I have a nurse starting on Monday morning to take care of you. She's the sister of Keisha, who took such good care of Ida when she was so ill. I've never seen her, but Keisha recommended her highly."

At 6:55, the night desk clerk called on the intercom phone connection and said, "Mr. Baxter, there's a Nikita Brown who is Mrs. Baxter's nurse on her way up to your unit."

A few minutes later, the doorbell rang and Nikita Brown turned out to be a stout, pleasant-faced woman in her late fifties, dressed in a white nurse's uniform. She held out her hand and said, "Good morning, Mr. Baxter. I'm Nikita. My sister tells me that your wife is the most beautiful woman that she has ever seen."

Alex said, "Come on back to the bedroom and let me introduce her to you."

Nikita immediately started the job of taking care of Lila. She said, "The first thing that we're going to do is to prettify you up for that handsome husband of yours, who is obviously so crazy in love with you. Then we're going to see if you would like some boiled eggs, toast and tea to give you some nourishment to keep you beautiful.

"I hear that you think that you're the world's best board game player. Where I come from, I've beaten the pants off of some of the best players in Baltimore City, and I'm always looking to add another scalp to my collection. But first things first, let's get you cleaned up, because you always feel good when you're feeling fresh."

She drew a pan of warm water and sponged off Lila, then dressed her in slacks with a matching blouse and a light sweater across her shoulders. When she was finished, she walked Lila into the den, where Alex was working on an *Eagle* assignment and said, "Don't she look beautiful, Mr. Alex?"

Alex replied, "Nikita, the first time I saw her, I thought that she was the most beautiful woman whom I had ever seen. I never have changed my mind about that. I love her madly, more than anything in this world."

Lila smiled weakly and said, "Love in this house is a two-way street. I love him just as much."

Nikita said, "Honey pot, let's get some nourishment into you."

Nikita prepared two boiled eggs and spread margarine and marmalade on two slices of toast, and prepared a cup of tea for Lila, who managed to eat most of it. But more importantly, she managed to retain it in her body and not regurgitate it.

When Nikita showed up, she seemed to bring with the sunshine, even on the grayest of days. When Lila became nauseous, either from the chemotherapy or from the strong medication to which she was prescribed, Nikita would hold her on her lap and rock her back and forth until Lila fell asleep.

On those times she would say, "Hush, honey pot, when you're sick there ain't nothing you can do about it. Try to get some sleep, because it's real important that you keep up your strength."

As her disease progressed, Lila lost more weight and her pain magnified, requiring the use of stronger pain alleviation agents. She no longer was mobile, so Alex rented a wheelchair for her to get around the apartment and to visit Dr. Patel on her regular appointments.

Her magnificent face became etched with the pain that she tried to silently endure. It seemed to shrink around her skull like some plastic shrinkwrap. Her beautiful hazel eyes seemed to bulge from her face and seemed to reflect the hopelessness that she was enduring. Her voluptuous body wasted away, until she seemed to be just a skeleton covered with skin. Her hair, which had previously been her only vanity, became dull and lifeless, and when Nikita brushed it, it would separate from her head in clumps.

Her two best friends from the little frame church, Kitty and Mattie, visited her several times a week, bringing with them some outrageously sweet pastry, at which Lila would pick at to be polite. During those visits she seemed to momentarily forget her impending doom, and she even, on occasion, would join in the exchange of female gossip. Alex always appreciated those visits, because they momentarily dimmed her fear of the unknown that she was bravely facing.

On their anniversary, Luigi sent them two complete dinners—veal scaloppini for Lila and bragiole for Alex. He also sent a spumoni for her dessert. Lila just couldn't eat any of it, so Alex asked Nikita to join him.

Normally, at Christmas, her little girl quality peeked out of her and she would jump in with both feet to enjoy the beautiful but temporary season of celebration and goodwill, and giggle delightedly at her gifts.

That year, when Alex erected their little tree, she didn't seem to notice the bright lights and ornaments. It was as if her strong fighting spirit had given up, and she had surrendered to the beast.

Max and Esther were frequent visitors. And Esther always brought with her a mason jar filled to the brim with her famous Jewish penicillin—her chicken soup that was guaranteed to cure any ailment that afflicted man.

Max was often overcome with grief, and when he couldn't stand it any longer, he would rise and walk into the den and cry silently. Then he would walk back into their bedroom and try to banter with Lila, who could only smile weakly and thank him for his concern.

Nikita still hovered over her like a Southern nanny, protective but gentle, trying to protect her like some child that had grown up under her care. Her presence with Lila always chased the gloom away.

Her pain had now magnified to the point where the strongest pain elimination medicines were now prescribed. As a result, she slept longer and had more brief periods in between.

In January, Dr. Patel, after noticing her debilitated physical condition, suggested that, even though Nikita was an LPN, re-admitting Lila to St. Matthew's Hospice Center. They could give her greater comfort and pain control than she could receive at home.

Alex asked Nikita if she would remain as her special duty nurse, because she was the link to Alex and the one that Lila had grown to love.

At that point, Alex felt that he should make the final arrangements for Lila's funeral. He stopped by the funeral home that they had used for Ida's interment, pre-paid the funeral costs, and selected a casket for Lila. He felt very ghoulish doing it with Lila still alive, but he'd been told that her end was near, and he wanted to have her buried with dignity.

Alex, now emotionally drained and feeling great compassion for her, sensing that the end was near, spent more time with her, taking only enough time to complete his *Eagle* assignments. Before his visits to her, he always stopped into the small chapel and prayed to his compassionate God that he would grant Lila some relief from the terrible pain that she was enduring.

He felt that the agony that she was enduring was the purging of all the earthly wrongs that she might have committed in her lifetime, and that she would automatically be assured of a place in some pleasant hereafter. That was the only rationale that he could find for her physical pain.

During her lucid moments, she would hold up the medallion that Alex had given her and motion for him to lean over and kiss her. He never knew if that kiss was going to be his last one, so he always obliged her.

Nikita, who was watching for the telltale signs, finally said one day to Alex, "You won't be needing me any longer, Mr. Alex, it's time."

That evening, Lila briefly shuddered and opened her beautiful eyes for the last time, grabbed her medallion and motioned for Alex to lean over and kiss her. She said, "Honey, I'll meet you at the end of the tunnel," and closed her eyes for the last time, passing through the veil of life.

Alex, numbed from the emotional trauma associated with Lila's slow descent into oblivion, sat there for a while, mesmerized. He seemed to be watching somebody's bad dream. He finally fully realized that he would never see his beloved Lila again, at least on this side of the veil of life.

If the primal scream that welled up inside of him could have been magnified, it would have echoed into every corner of the world. When his beloved Lila died, he died with her as well. He had believed that he was emotionally conditioned for Lila's death, but when it did occur, his emotions completely fell apart. Unlike his general unemotionality when he had put Bear to sleep, he sobbed bitterly at his loss.

He sat there in a sort of trance while the nurses performed the necessary post-mortem job of preparing Lila's body for burial. Finally, he roused himself from his lethargy and called Marie to inform her that it had finally happened.

Marie said, "I'm so sorry, Alex. You've lost your greatest treasure, and I've lost my only sister. She suffered so much from the pain that in a way it's a blessing. She has now passed over threshold of pain that she was able to cope with. Comfort yourself with the fact that you were the only man in the world for her. She loved you more than her own life. George and I will be in as soon as we can book a flight into Baltimore. Hold on, George wants to talk to you."

George entered the conversation and said, "Hang on, Alex, we're here to lean on. The love that you two had for each other was so strong that it will carry over into the hereafter. She's waiting for you there, and you will be reunited again one day. We'll be in as soon as possible."

Then Alex made two more calls that took every bit of courage that he could muster up. He called the funeral director that he had selected and requested that they pick up Lila's body. Then he called Tom Deutsch, the trustee in charge of the little frame church's cemetery, to open up Lila's grave for interment.

He called Reverend Busch to let him know and to ask him if he would select six members of the congregation to act as pallbearers. Kitty Mooney asked if she could deliver a eulogy at the funeral service, because she dearly loved Lila.

The last call that he made was to Max, who had assumed the role of protector to Lila before Alex and she became a couple. He had made this the last call deliberately, because he knew that Max's strong paternal love for Lila would make him feel a strong sense of loss over Lila's demise.

When he received the call, Max said, "Oy vey, Alex, such a loss. Such a beautiful woman. I loved her like she was from my own blood, like a third daughter. I'll recite the *kodish*, the prayers for the dead. She suffered bravely, and I know that she finally has peace within her soul. She had so much pain and trauma in her life, with her parents dying and the treatment that she received from those *schmucks*, Bobby and Lupinsky, and also the physical pain from her cancer. She loved you madly. You gave her four years of great happiness. If anyone deserves a place in Paradise, it's my Lila. Thank you for letting me know. Please let me know when the viewing is and also the funeral services. You're a good man. Do you need any money?"

Alex said, "No, Max, I'm really OK financially. Emotionally, I'm all shook up, but I have to cope with it. She really was the only woman that I have ever truly loved in my entire life. She gave me so much happiness that I was almost scared to accept it. We could be completely happy sitting together looking at the aircraft beacons and just talking. I'll have more memories of her to sustain me until I join her. Without her, I'm just a lost soul. I'm like those lonely people that sit in the malls all day hoping that someone will just say hello."

Alex reached down and pulled off Lila's engagement and wedding rings. He also pulled the medallion that he had given to her, which she had vowed that she would never remove from her neck as long as she lived. He placed them on the chain that held the matching medallion that Lila had given him. In doing so he felt that it would provide some last link to his Lila.

When her body was transferred to the hospital's morgue, he returned to the Ridgeway to shower and change clothes.

He had never felt so alone in his entire life. His beautiful Lila was dead. He had lost his best canine friend. His parents were dead and so was Ida. Their once happy home was the loneliest place that he had ever been in. All of the indications of Lila's presence were there, as if she would come bustling in from the office at any minute.

He sat down with the picture of her that McGuire had shot, and the full realization of her death finally struck him like a strong jab into his solar plexus.

Finally, the wall holding back the emotional well within him broke, and he started to sob over his loss. Mother Nature had finally allowed him to release the emotional valve of grief that was suffocating him.

Afterwards, he felt better, but the loneliness of their condo, without his Lila, seemed to make it difficult for him to breathe. He could almost feel the presence of her spirit close to him. He remembered an article that had read somewhere, that some cultures believed that a person's spirit lingered at the place where it had been the most comfortable for as long as three days before it finally passed over to the other side of life. It was an eerie feeling that was difficult to overcome, but he believed that Lila was so reluctant to leave him that she refused to go.

Marie and George arrived later that day. When Marie saw Alex, she hugged him tightly and burst into tears. Alex patted her shoulder, while George, in typical male fashion, stood helplessly by, unable to cope with her sobs.

After a while, Marie got control of herself and said to Alex, "She's at peace, finally. Her exquisite beauty was her worst enemy. Until you came into her life, men would always attempt to take advantage of her gentle nature. Boys in high school who considered themselves to be studs would always try to score with her. That son of bitch, Bobby, conned her into marrying him, while all the time he was playing house with anyone who would let him pull up her skirt, and that slimeball Jeff Lupinsky, I can't think of a name low enough to call him.

"On the Saturday that she finally met you, she called me and told me that she had met the man that she was going to spend her life with. She hoped that you were decent, but she had fallen head over heels in love with you, and win or lose you were going to be her mate for life.

"It turned out that you were a decent man, and you gave her the four happiest years of her entire life. She loved children and always wanted to be a mother. Even when we were small girls, she always pretended to be my mother. When she became pregnant, that seemed to be her destiny, but then that beast within her and I surfaced, after waiting for some weakness to develop within her, and she was doomed. I had my ovaries removed six weeks ago. It won't catch me in its chilly grip, you can bet on that."

Alex asked them to stay with him while they were in town, not only because he was so devastated emotionally, but also because he wanted to discuss Lila's last wishes with them.

Marie had slimmed down, and Lila's clothes now fit her comfortably. Alex told her that she could take whatever of Lila's outfits that she wanted. She selected the three-piece white brocade evening pajama outfit, Alex's favorite black knit cocktail dress and several other high-style dresses. The remainder, Alex was going to give to a battered women's shelter that Reverend Busch had recommended. He said that the women living at that facility didn't normally have enough food, let alone high-style clothes, and that such a gift would improve their lifestyle tremendously.

Alex gave Marie one of Lila's most treasured items, their mother's string of pearls. He told George that he was relinquishing whatever rights he had inherited in Lila's trust fund, and if George would send him the proper documents, he would immediately sign them and return them to George.

Lila's last will had left all of her assets to Alex, but as he felt when Lila had offered him the opportunity to see the balance in her trust account, he felt the trust money was now Marie's exclusively and totally belonged to her.

He asked them if there was anything else that they wanted.

Marie said, "No, Alex, you are being very generous, and there is nothing else that we want."

CHAPTER 22

With his normal sense of hospitality, Alex insisted that Marie and George use his bed while they were in Towson. He, in turn, decided to use the convertible sofa in the den.

Normally he slept in his underwear, but since he had guests, he elected to use pajamas and closed the door to give them a degree of privacy.

He slept fitfully, and only in brief stretches, because he kept getting flashbacks of his happiness with Lila. He tossed and turned uncomfortably, not only because he was unused to the uncomfortable sleep sofa, but also his grief over Lila's loss was now compounding itself within him like a bad bruise to his soul.

Finally, he decided to make himself a cup of tea, hoping that it would assist him to relax enough to sleep. He hadn't slept more than four or five hours at a stretch during Lila's illness, and was so keyed that he felt as disoriented as a zombie. H didn't yet realize it, but he was now operating on nervous energy. His mental processes were reacting to his sleep deprivation, and he found himself sometimes unable to choose the right word to complete a sentence that was thinking.

He arose and opened the door to the den, discovering Marie sitting by herself, quietly crying.

He sat down alongside of her and put arm around her fondly. "Are you able to cope with the loss of Lila?"

"Yes, now that George has come to his senses, I can lean on him for support again like I used to. I was just sitting here thinking of your beautiful Lila, and how much you loved each other, to the permanent exclusion of all others. She was so beautiful, and she loved you so much. She once told me that she always knew that you would come into her life someday. The moment she first saw you when you were walking with your dog, she said she knew that you were the one. From that day, she was trying find a way to meet you without you believing that she had her hooks out for you. Your love for each other was a textbook case, because you both instinctively knew that you were meant for each other."

Alex said, "I was just going out to the kitchen to make myself a cup of tea, hoping that it would relax me enough to sleep. I'm exhausted, but I'm too keyed up to sleep. Can I make you a cup?"

She said, "I would really like that, thank you."

"How do you like your tea?" Alex asked.

"With two sugars."

He placed the teakettle on the range, and when it started to whistle, he poured hot water over two teabags that he had placed in mugs, added sugar, and carried them into the living room and sat down alongside of her. They continued to talk, mostly relating anecdotes about Lila, until dawn poked its head over the fringes of Towson.

Afterwards, since no one felt like cooking, they had breakfast at the Diner.

There were two viewings at Lila's wake. The first one was scheduled to be observed in the afternoon, from one until four, then in the evening from seven until ten.

Alex had requested in her obituary that flowers be omitted, and that in lieu of that, contributions could be made to the American Cancer Society. He himself had arranged for four dozen red roses be delivered, because they were Lila's favorite flower, representing the four years that they had been together. They were to be placed at the head of her bier.

Alex had decided to have her interred in one of her favorite outfits, the light green pants outfit that he had given her for Christmas, and they took that along with them.

After they just picked at their breakfasts, they left for the funeral home to deliver the clothing and sat in an adjoining room while her bier was being prepared.

The afternoon viewing was well attended, with friends from the little frame church, her office building, Max and Esther, Kitty and Mattie, and many others who had learned of her death from the published obituary.

Luigi and Pearl stopped by, and when Pearl saw Lila, she started to cry uncontrollably. "Oh, Mr. Baxter, how sorry I am that you lost your beautiful wife. When I saw the two of you together, it was always the best part of my day. You loved each other so much."

Reverend Busch stopped by with the list of six church members who had agreed to act as pallbearers. He asked Alex how he was holding up under the strain.

Alex replied, "Right now, I'm just coping. Reality hasn't yet set in, and I'm operating on nervous energy generated by adrenaline."

Reverend Busch said, "I'm available to comfort you, Alex, at any time day or night."

When he left, Alex was standing at the head of Lila's casket, lost in some reverie about his and Lila's happy years together, when he felt the presence of someone standing beside him. He looked up to see Jeff Lupinsky standing there with tears in his eyes.

He said, "Hello, Jeff. Thank you for coming."

Jeff, who had been a flamboyant dresser, looked exceedingly seedy. He badly needed a haircut, and he was wearing a suit jacket that didn't match his pants. He said, "I hope that you don't mind my paying my last respects to her, Alex, but when I learned that she had passed on, I just had to see her one more time. I really loved her Alex, and if she had loved me as much as she loved you, I could have changed. She was the most beautiful and gentle woman that I ever knew. When she first saw you with your dog, she said that you seemed to be such a strong decent man and the most handsome man that she had ever seen. When she kept referring to you, I knew that you were going to be trouble. When I saw you leaving her building that night, I knew that I had lost her to you. I did all those crazy things hoping to win her back. I bought that fancy car believing that if she realized how financially successful I was, she would want to share it. I guess that I was damned fool. She lost so much weight. She looks like she must have suffered terribly."

"What are you doing now, Jeff?"

"I'm personal consultant to an investor who has holdings in book stores and entertainment. I advise him of his legal rights when he has legal problems related to his businesses."

When he told Alex the name of the individual who employed him, Alex was shocked. That man was reputed to have strong mob connections and fronted as the owner of a chain of porno book stores and peep shows that were always being raided for showing hard pornography. Max had been right when he remarked that, "A leopard never changes its spots and a *gonif* is always a *gonif*." Jeff hadn't changed; he was still his old greedy unethical self.

Jeff asked Alex, "Would you mind if I took one of these roses to remember her by? Red roses were always her favorite flower."

Alex reached into the vase, extracted one, and gave it to him.

Jeff then asked, "Would you mind if I attended the funeral?"

Alex replied, "No, Jeff, I personally would have no objection, but Max Weiner will be there, and I'm sure that you're aware how he feels about you. I wouldn't want to have bad scene there."

Jeff replied, "I'll sit in the back and leave before any one else." Jeff then signed the remembrance book and left.

Marie, who had been watching the interplay between Alex and Jeff, approached Alex and asked, "Wasn't that Jeff Lupinsky? Wasn't he disbarred? He looks like he's just one step away from skid row."

Alex relied, "Well, when you walk down a crooked path, you find yourself walking in a circle, and you eventually end up catching up to yourself. He was captain of his own ship, and he ran it onto the rocks of life. He'll never change because he believes that he can con anybody in life. Ida used to say that life was a four-letter word, depending on your mood. In his case, the four-letter word is one that isn't used in polite company."

Marie then said, "My God, how lucky Lila was to have met you when she did. Can you imagine what her life would have been if she had ended up with him?"

The evening viewing was equally well attended. Keisha and Nikita both attended and indicated that they planned to attend the funeral. Max and Esther attended again. Max showed evidence of crying and stood by Lila's bier wearing his *yarmalka*. In observance of the long-discontinued Jewish custom of rending their garments upon the death of loved one, they both had pieces of ribbon pinned to their clothes that had been partially severed by scissors.

Many of their friends from the little frame church on Providence Road came to pay their last respects and shook Alex's hand sadly. It was almost like the feeling of a community losing a valued treasure.

When the final viewing was over, Alex, Marie and George drove back to the Ridgeway, exhausted by the ordeal of keeping up a solid front while hemorrhaging emotionally on the inside.

Although no one felt the desire for food, they hadn't eaten anything since picking at their breakfasts. Alex ordered a pizza to fill the gap between meals. Nobody was able to finish his or her individual slices, so Alex ended up grinding it in the garbage disposal.

They all tried to make small talk, but the strain on them made it difficult. About eleven p.m., Marie yawned and said, "I can't keep my eyes open any longer, I'm going to go to bed."

George and Marie retired to the bedroom, leaving Alex alone with his thoughts of Lila.

Keyed up so tightly by his tragic event, Alex couldn't sleep, so he took one of the sleeping capsules that Dr. McGrath had prescribed for him. He did finally drop off to sleep, but he slept fitfully and had a recurring dream of being lost in a forbidding, strange town composed of massive fortress-like, stone buildings, with no other person in sight, trying to find Lila. He never was able to find her, and he woke up gasping for breath and perspiring freely. His momentous grief had started to manifest itself within him, and he silently sobbed alone for his lost Lila.

Everyone arose early, showered and dressed in their sober-colored funeral attire. Alex wore his best navy blue suit, Marie dressed in a black dress, and George in appropriate clothing for the funeral.

Although no one had eaten anything substantial for several days, no one was interested in eating any food. Nobody said much to anybody, each one dreading the finality of the occasion.

Since the church and its adjoining cemetery were just a short distance from the funeral home, and Lila was to be interred in the plot that she had given to Alex, Alex did not engage one of the limousines that were available. He had arranged for Lila's casket to be transported by hearse and set up in the little church.

They found that it was already in place and sitting upon a folding, wheeled platform in front of the altar.

The weather forecast had indicated that there was a chance of snow later that day, or early that evening, so a sort of tent was erected over the yawning grave to attempt to provide some shelter for the mourners if necessary. Several folding chairs were placed alongside as well.

Alex, Marie and George took seats in the first pew. When Max and Esther arrived, they were ushered to seats alongside of them. Kitty Mooney and Mattie Deutsch, who were to deliver eulogies, sat with their husbands in the second row of pews. The pallbearers sat alongside the altar where the small choir generally sat. The small church was filled almost to capacity by members who had grown fond of Lila in the short time that they had known her. Alex caught a glimpse of Jeff, who entered just before the service started and was trying hard to be inconspicuous. He felt a brief twinge of pity for Jeff because he still felt a strong love for Lila, even after she had bluntly severed their relations.

Reverend Busch began the service by reciting the well-loved Psalm that began, "The Lord is my shepherd, I shall not want…." Then everyone sang several of Lila's favorite hymns, including, "How Great Thou Art," "Oh For a Thousand Tongues to Sing," and several others.

Kitty and Mattie both delivered stirring eulogies that described Lila's beauty, not only physically but also how gentle and kind she was inside. They both referred to the great love that she and Alex had enjoyed, and that if there ever had been a marriage made in heaven, it was theirs.

Reverend Busch invited all that were in attendance to a farewell luncheon in the educational building, which also doubled as a social hall.

The six volunteers assembled at the entrance and escorted the casket to the edge of the grass, then lifted it and carried it to the gravesite and placed it on several broad canvas straps stretched across the open grave.

Alex, Marie, George, Max and Esther took seats alongside the casket, and Reverend Busch started to deliver the final words that were part of the burial ritual, and at last, it was over.

When the service was completed, anyone that cared to was invited to attend a light luncheon catered by the same people that had catered their successful party at the Ridgeway.

Marie and George were scheduled to return to Chicago the next day, so Alex, Marie and George returned to Alex's condominium. There they reminisced about Lila and her unique beauty, and how she had adored her Alex.

After a while, George said, "Boy, I could sure use a strong belt."

Alex remembered that he had saved several unopened bottles of liquor from their party and opened a bottle of Scotch whiskey. He poured stiff drinks for Marie and George, and even though he did not drink, he made himself a weak drink, because he thought that it would help him to relax.

They toasted to Lila and clinked glasses.

Alex took one sip and became violently ill. He made a mad dash for the bathroom to throw up, and afterwards said to George, "God, I'm the world's worst drinker. "

George laughed and said, "Alex, you're better off without it."

They decided to have dinner at Luigi's that night, and the need for food finally overcame them.

Alex introduced Marie and George, and Luigi briefly sat at their table. He spoke in glowing terms about the magnificent love that had existed between Lila and Alex.

Pearl grew emotional and started to cry when she saw Alex. A Roman Catholic, she said, "Mr. Baxter, would you mind if I had a mass said for the repose of the soul of Mrs. Baxter?"

Alex replied, "Thank you, Pearl. All of our prayers are funneled eventually to the one God. He doesn't care if you're Catholic, Protestant, Jewish or Muslim. Everybody prays to him in his or her own way. He hears everybody. I'm sure because of your special intention that he'll give your petition special attention. You are a dear soul."

Finally hungry, they ate well, and returned to Alex's.

CHAPTER 23

That evening, it snowed briefly, enough to cover the surface of the ground.

Marie and George, anxious to get home with the weather closing in, decided to leave for the airport earlier than they had originally anticipated. They hoped to get an earlier flight to O'Hare. The three of them had an early breakfast at the Diner.

As they sat there drinking their second cups of coffee, both Marie and George urged Alex to keep in touch and to try to visit them in Chicago. Marie remarked that she wondered if Samson would react in the same way and follow Alex all around like Hercules had on Alex's previous visit.

That innocent remark brought a momentary flash of pain to Alex, as he remembered the happiness that he and Lila had enjoyed on that delayed wedding trip.

After they reluctantly parted outside of the restaurant, and Marie and Gorge drove away, Alex felt the same pang of loneliness that he had felt when he heard Lila's car drive away from their complex on the first weekend that they had fallen so madly in love. Now he was totally alone in life, without even Bear to provide him with companionship.

He dreaded returning to his now lonely apartment, made barren by Lila's lack of presence. No longer would he ever hear her tinkling giggles, or delightful teasing, or the little acts of love, like her laying out his clean clothes for the day before she left for the office.

He had a sudden urge to visit her grave and talk to her. Stopping at his favorite florist, he purchased his usual long-stemmed rose and drove over to the little frame church.

The snow that had fallen had covered the earthen gash in the grass where Lila was buried, and the cemetery was quiet and peaceful.

He placed the rose on the snow that covered her grave, and it seemed to stand out like a drop of red blood against the pure whiteness of the snow. It appeared to symbolize his broken heart over Lila's early death.

That little act of love became a weekly habit for as long as he lived. Every Sunday that he attended services at the little frame church, he would lay a red rose on her grave—snow, rain, summer and winter. That was his special way of remembering her and their eternal love.

He stood there, a lonely figure in the quiet burial ground, and silently talked to her, telling her how much he loved her and how he missed her, and about the tinkling giggles that always made him feel good, no matter what problem he was facing in life. He told her that he hoped she was happy where she was, and that one day he hoped to join her and meet her at the end of the tunnel, wherever that was.

Finally, purged of his loneliness, he felt an exhaustion overtake him, and suddenly felt an urgent need to take a nap.

He returned to his now lonely Ridgeway apartment, and lay down across the bed that he and Lila had shared so gloriously and fell into a dreamless sleep for two hours.

Awakening refreshed, he began to pack Lila's clothing into boxes for donation. While he was cleaning out her closet, he discovered a box labeled MY ALEX.

For a long while, he was reluctant to open it because he felt that might be invading her privacy by looking at things as personal as writings in a diary. He finally realized that she no longer could care, so he carefully opened it.

Inside of it, he discovered a treasure trove of little mementos of their lives together that she had valued enough to keep as precious treasures.

He discovered the blue velvet presentation box that her engagement ring had come in; a fast food label on which was written "Deep Creek" and the date; a book of matches from the Pit steakhouse in Ocean City; stubs from *The Nutcracker* ballet that they had attended and loved for its music and orientation toward children; movie ticket stubs; pictures of him laughing at the beach and at the theme park that they had visited in Orlando; and other small items which might normally be disposed of, but to her, were valuable enough to retain as valuables.

All of a sudden, he realized the true depth of her mighty love for him. While he had been attempting to perpetuate his love for her with golden baubles on a wrist bracelet, she had been secretly collecting the simple but truer mementos of their short life together.

Sitting alone and lonely amid the packing boxes he was going to use to dispose of some of the lingering memories of her, his emotions spilled over, and he began to sob with all of the fervor that only a lonely person can muster up. He wondered then how he would ever get along without her love. He remembered Max's comments about a personal Shylock who cut away a pound of flesh from the soul, leaving a gaping and painful wound behind.

Shortly after Lila's funeral, he began to receive telephone calls from widows and single women who attended the services at the little frame church. They always began with expressions of regret over his loss of Lila. They always ended up with an invitation to come to their homes for a decent homecooked meal. Others would tell him about some female friend of theirs, who was always very beautiful, and who had recently lost their husband and always had so much in common with him. They believed he and she would really hit it off. The women had often seen Alex in church and were always impressed with his appearance.

Still others somehow always managed to bump into him at the supermarket or bank, and after chatting with him for a while, thought that it would be nice for him to forget his loss for a while and join them in pleasant dinner that they would prepare, with an optional dessert.

He always declined such curious invitations on the first time. When they called the second time, his answer was always that his love for his Lila had not diminished in any way, and he was not at present, and would never, be interested in developing a relationship with another woman.

His ex-wife Connie, whom Lila had labeled "The Painted Woman," called him several times and asked him if he would escort her to several black tie dinner dances. His bitter memories of her vile treatment of him and her blatant disrespect for their marriage vows by cheating on him with other men still rankled him, and he found that it was difficult for him to be even civil to her. Her habit of collecting young lovers-of-the-week finally forced him to be blunt with her and tell her that he could never, ever become re-interested in her, even if she were the only woman ever left living in the entire civilized world. He told her bluntly to stop bothering him and to stick to her young studs as long as she was able to.

Those invitations got to be so annoying that he almost stopped attending the Sunday services. Only his deep affection for the little church and his love for what he considered to be his own personal God kept him in attendance. That, plus his continuing desire to place a rose on Lila's grave, was what made his mind up to still attend.

He felt that the relentless pressure on him to seek another relationship so soon after Lila's tragic death was like a pack of wolves pursuing a lost sheep, smelling a weakness that really didn't exist.

Those frantic efforts to snag him into the clutches of lonely widows continued for several months after Lila's death, and finally, all but the most persistent gave up and sought easier prey. Even Connie, with her thick skin that fended off insults like water running off of a pitched roof, finally gave up and stopped bothering him When she saw him at the Diner after that, she didn't even bother to acknowledge that he was there.

To ease his feelings of grief, he worked harder on his writing assignments and met his deadlines more readily. This, in turn, was like a double-edged sword, because it allowed him more time to brood over his loss and didn't really compensate his emotional being.

His emotional health seemed to be in a holding pattern and he felt numb in his personal feelings. He still admired a full female figure, with his heterosexual feelings, but the desire to possess such a female had ceased to exist, like a water spigot that had been shut off after long use. He literally had died when Lila had, and ate, slept and worked mechanically like some kind of robot.

Like many that mourn, he turned to snacking on high-calorie and saturated-fat foods. Without Lila to restrain him, he developed a strong preference for the added butterfat ice cream that Ida had long preferred. When he shopped for groceries, he would always purchase three or four pints of it and store them in his freezer.

With his now sedentary lifestyle, and family history of heart-related health problems, this became a dangerous habit to have. He would often consume as much as a pint at a sitting, while watching some innocuous, shallow sitcom on TV. Such programs, he wouldn't even have turned on while Lila was alive, but they filled in his numbed feelings and helped him get through an evening without continuing to brood over his tragic loss.

At his regular physicals, the tests would reveal that his blood pressure was high, in the range of 190 over 90, and his bad cholesterol was close to 200, while his good cholesterol was less than 40. He was a walking time bomb, waiting for a heart attack or a stroke to happen.

His personal physician would always urge him to get more exercise, watch what he ate, and stick to a low-fat, low-salt diet to lower his very dangerous vital signs.

Alex would always promise that he would do what the doctor wanted him to do, but never did, until one afternoon when the elevators at the Ridgeway were down for some maintenance problem and he had to slowly trudge up the twenty-six flights of stairs to his floor. He felt strong palpitations in his heart and couldn't catch his breath for a long time. His sedentary lifestyle and couch potatoitis had weakened his physical stamina to such a level that he was becoming unable to consider himself as being an active person.

He then purchased a stationary exercycle and began to pedal it, eventually working up to the equivalent of three miles a day. He purchased two five-pound dumbbells and developed his own version of an exercise program, working up to one hundred individual sets of each exercise.

With that exercise program, his lipids level descended to safe level, briefly, but his regular diet continued to contain high levels of saturated fats.

Cooking for one person had now become a real chore to him, so when his appetite returned, he started to eat at Luigi's several times a week. At dinner there, he chose whatever appealed to him at that moment, and those choices were generally the high-fat, heavily salted foods that are served in restaurants. In reality, in ingesting such food, he became a prime candidate for a heart attack.

He continued his exercise program religiously, but after a while, when he felt better, he reduced the bike riding to four times a week, then three, and finally stopped pedaling completely.

His weightlifting regime took the same direction, slowing down and finally stopping completely.

He then turned to walking as an alternative and started to walk several miles a day around the pleasant streets of Towson. With fatigue and sore legs, he lowered his ambitious walking to one mile and finally stopped completely

With Lila's death, his interests became very restricted. He no longer enjoyed the activities that he had enjoyed. Long weekends alone without her company were no longer any fun. Visiting friends without her became something that he no longer enjoyed, because his friends feeling compassion for his lonely singleness would often have some attractive female sitting alongside of him at dinner, and he just was no longer an eligible bachelor-once removed. Like Lila, he had become a one-woman man, and she wasn't there any longer.

One of the few major pleasures that he still enjoyed were his once or twice a month lunches with Reverend Busch and Joe Mooney. They would pick out some nice restaurant and discuss everything but politics, since his views of the political scene were radically different from Joe's and he valued Joe's friendship completely.

Another of the privileges that he allowed himself to have was the added butterfat ice cream that he had learned to enjoy thoroughly.

Because he had become reasonably well known from his writing for the *Eagle*, he was asked to be a guest lecturer for a creative writing class at the local university.

At that lecture he spoke about the importance of reality and creation of vivid descriptions in writing. His lecture was well received, and he was invited to become an adjunct professor by the head of that department. After weighing the responsibilities of maintaining a discipline of keeping a class schedule, even as infrequently as with such an un-tenured position, he turned down the offer but guest lectured several times a semester.

He was just as no longer interested in fame and fortune and was happy completing his writing assignments from Rick Kelly.

He was now financially secure from being beneficiary to Lila's insurance policies. He had disavowed any dower rights that he might have inherited in Lila's trust fund as her husband and had signed and returned the proper forms to George shortly after the funeral. He no longer had any responsibility for anyone other than himself.

After he had lost his most valuable treasure, Lila, he no longer felt any need to generate a large income or seek fame, nationally, as a good writer. Lila's insurance had left with more than enough money to adequately support him.

He revised his will because Lila was no longer there to be his beneficiary. He had no idea as to the value, if any, that his writings might have, but left them to the local university, where he guest lectured, to do what they chose with them.

Because of Lila's having died with cancer, he bequeathed $10,000 dollars as a memorial gift in her name to the American Cancer Society, and also a gift of $10,000 to the American Heart Association.

He named Joe Mooney as executor of his estate and endowed him with another $10,000 to compensate him for the time and trouble that he might have in finally settling Alex's estate. Since he had no close relatives, he left the rest of his estate to the little frame church. This included the equity in his condo, his car, jewelry, and whatever items had any value.

He reluctantly sold Lila's valuable jewelry back to Morey, including her diamond pendant, engagement ring and her charm bracelet along with several other items that belonged to her. He was satisfied with the amount of money that Morey finally offered him, and deposited it in his checking account. Since he had no other person to make final arrangements for him, he pre-paid the funeral establishment for his own funeral and selected a casket in which to be buried.

He told Joe Mooney, his best friend and wedding best man, where he kept his will and important papers, and gave him a key to his apartment. He showed him how to disarm the apartment's security system and gave him a power of attorney, in case he became incapacitated, telling him that he was endowing him with $10,000 to compensate him for his time and trouble as his will's executor.

Max allowed him to continue under his group insurance plan as a 100% contributor, which saved him the hassle of going out and obtaining a personal plan that would cost him more and provide him with lesser benefit. He always paid the premium at least six months in advance and felt that if he ever became ill, that he would be cared for, and with the pre-paid funeral he would be buried with dignity.

As he wound down his affairs, he found that he was having difficulty meeting the *Eagle*'s publication deadlines. This was a side effect of Lila's death. He frankly just didn't care anymore. His ambition to be a writer of national prominence was no longer a driving force in his life. It had died and been buried along with his beloved Lila. He was still suffering the pangs of deep grief and was still out of step with his own sense of responsibility.

After Lila's death, he began to call Marie and George on a weekly basis. At first, those calls were warmly welcomed. After a while, he sensed that they were not too eagerly accepted, because they always seemed to be on their way out of the door and could only talk for a minute or two. He ended up that practice and only called them on major holidays, if then, to wish them a happy holiday. They now seemed to be caught up in the new lifestyle that went with George's promotion to vice president.

To fill his lonely hours, he still read all of the novels if his favorite techno-thriller author. He found that he was no longer thrilled by the deeds of the novels' heroes as they moved through the pages filled with espionage and crime.

Some skilled analyst might say that he was suffering from a deep depression or melancholy. The truth of the matter was that he had surrendered his ambition and turned in his life's union card, just treading water in his daily activities. He was just waiting to re-join his Lila.

On his weekly attendance of the services at the little frame church, he still left a red rose on top of her grave. He would stand there silently, telling her how much he still loved her and how he missed her in his now-barren life. He would tell her that he hoped that he would see her and enjoy her tinkling giggles once again. And when he left her grave to enter the church for the start of the service, he would mentally kiss the image that he visualized of her and tell her goodbye until next week.

All but a few of the single women who attended church regularly had now given up hope on trying to back him into a corner and measure him for a nose ring. Although he might still be considered to be an eligible bachelor, he always refused the offers for a nice home-cooked meal. He just was no longer interested in the optional dessert that such offers included, because his interest in such desserts had died when Lila had died.

His brown shaggy hair became a mixture of what some call salt and pepper, and eventually the streaks of gray in it made him seem even more attractive to the females seeking the male companionship of a man around the house.

His once healthy sex drive that he had joyfully expressed with his beloved Lila had been shut completely, and he had become an emotional eunuch, as had his appetite for food. Now he just ate when he was hungry and didn't pay too much attention to what he did eat.

He now ate most of his principal daily meals at Luigi's. When things were slow, Luigi would sit with him for a short time while he ate. Their conversation always seemed to eventually settle into a discussion about Lila, her beauty, and her one-man-for-life attitude. Luigi confessed that he had had a secret crush on Lila, but would never, ever pursue it because he was married with three children. More importantly, he felt Lila made no pretense that she was a one-man woman and that Alex was the only man that she would ever be interested in.

Alex was now pretty much a hermit, seeming to mechanically perform the tasks for which he had been programmed before Lila's demise. His barren life continued until one evening while he was eating his nightly snack of a pint of added butterfat ice cream and watching some drivel on TV. He developed what seemed to be an enormous attack of indigestion. He started to perspire heavily and strong pain radiated down the length of his left arm. Suddenly, he developed an excruciating pain in the center of his chest. He knew enough about heart problems from his mother to realize that he was having a massive heart attack.

Using the cell phone that he had procured for Lila's convenience, he called 911 and gave them directions on how to locate him. He then called the desk clerk in the lobby to alert him that the Baltimore County EMTs were on their way and to let the building manager know so that he could be let into Alex's apartment.

Now gasping for breath and with a terrible chest pain, Alex's last conscious impression before he blacked out was the building manager accompanied by two emergency medical technicians wheeling a gurney stretcher into his living room. Then he slipped into the blessed oblivion of total darkness.

He was taken to St. Matthew's emergency room, stripped of his clothes and dressed in a loose, shapeless hospital gown, and attached to life support monitors and a slowly dripping IV solution.

From the information in his wallet, it was determined what health care insurance he was a member of, his identity, and an in-emergency-please-call card that listed either Joe Mooney or Reverend Busch as the persons to call.

Calls were made to them both, and they were referred to Max Weiner who confirmed that Alex was a member of his group plan. Joe Mooney told them that he had Alex's power of attorney and would be responsible for whatever charges that might not be covered by his hospitalization.

Alex never recovered consciousness and remained in a coma for three days. At that time, he passed through the veil of life, hopefully to join his beloved Lila for all eternity.

Joe Mooney determined from the documents in the chest drawer, where Alex had indicated that he kept his important papers, that Alex had pre-paid for his funeral expenses. As executor of Alex's estate, he arranged the funeral services at the little frame church.

Alex was interred finally alongside his beloved Lila. His final wish was that the only flower to be placed on their graves was to be a single red rose.

Alex's last will and testament had a codicil added to it that Bear's ashes were to be interred with Alex upon his death. It was learned that this might be against the church's national canon law, so just be safe, Bear's ashes were mixed in among the soil that covered his grave, so in a sense all three of them were finally perpetually united.

Joe Mooney, when giving Alex's eulogy, remarked, "There will never be any more roses on the snow again...."

EPILOGUE

The moment that Alex died, he found himself standing in a cold, dank, dark area clad in the last earthly garment that he had worn on the other side of life, a shapeless hospital gown with no back.

Weak and confused, he stood there shivering in the dank chill, trying to learn where he was and what he was supposed to do after he did find out.

He looked around to see what he could discover. To his right, in the far distance, there was a faint pinpoint of light that seemed to be the exit from this forbidding, strange place. To his left, he saw a misty figure of some kind, behind what appeared to be a whitish box, busily leafing through what appeared to be a large ledger of some kind. The figure, whom Alex could not quite make out the details of, appeared to be a sentinel or guard at some hidden entrance to strange place.

He stood there for a while, chilly in his light hospital gown, totally ignored by the misty figure. Finally, it snapped the ledger shut.

Alex said, "What do I do now?"

Without speaking, the figure pointed with what seemed to an arm toward the pinpoint of light, showing the far distance, and re-opened the enormous ledger again to scan its entries, as if checking upon some other soul entering into this void.

Alex turned and began to painfully trudge toward that far exit. As soon as he began to slowly walk, some strong force grasped his being, and he found himself being rapidly propelled toward the ever-growing light, until he found himself deposited at the entrance to the greenest, most lush landscape that he had ever seen

Through some miracle, his shapeless hospital gown had now been transformed, and he now found himself clad in white chino trousers, a white polo shirt and white docksider shoes. This was the clothing that he had normally worn on the other side, except that it was white.

Amazed at the beauty of the green landscape, Alex stood there in quiet awe, drinking in the beautiful greenery.

Where he was now standing seemed to be the entrance into the most beautiful garden that he had ever seen. Its green landscape looked as fresh as if it had recently been planted. There was no evidence of dead branches or wilted flowers anywhere that he could see.

It was pleasantly lighted, but the light did not seem to be supplied by any sun or other satellite. Its temperature was delightfully pleasant, especially after the chill of the long dark tunnel.

Pools of water were scattered about the area, as if they had been placed there by some master landscape architect, and the pleasant sound of water trickling over stones, somewhere, echoed. It was soothing to his listening ears.

He caught a glimpse of himself, reflected from one of pools of water, and found that he looked as young and vibrant as he had on the day that he had met and fallen so deeply in love with his Lila. He wondered how that had occurred. His hair had reversed its appearance was now no longer streaked with gray, but was its former brown shade.

Directly in front of him, at the tunnel entrance, was an immaculate, well-tended path leading down a hill and around a curve toward brilliant, almost blinding light in the near distance. Birds in trees were singing a symphony of happiness, and the overall effect of the beautiful scene was so breathtaking that it was difficult to adequately describe. The joyful singing of the birds, the fresh smell of the plants and the perfume from the flowers filled the air delightfully.

He sat down on a boulder alongside of the tunnel entrance to try and sort out the myriad of sensory impressions that crowded his consciousness. As he did, he saw an antelope chasing a lion, as if they were in play, running rapidly, and quickly disappearing over the brow of a hill.

Alex thought to himself, *Isn't that strange? Antelopes are considered to be food for lions and are themselves ruthlessly stalked.* This seemed to be an odd place, indeed.

As he sat on the boulder, trying to make some sense out of what he was seeing, he heard a familiar, well-loved voice speaking to him.

"Oh, honey, how I've missed you. I've waited so long to see you again. I've never stopped loving you for even one minute, and when I heard that you were finally coming, I dropped everything and rushed up here to be the first one to welcome you. I promised you that I would meet you at the end of the tunnel, and here I am."

Startled, he looked up to see his long-departed lifetime love, Lila, standing in front of him with her arms extended, ready to again embrace him. The wasting effects of her long illness had been completely reversed, and she looked as beautiful as she had when he had first seen her emerge from under the trunk lid of that old car that she had driven.

Her figure was again filled out to the female beauty that it had before the onset of her wasting disease, her long hair had been restored to its former shining beauty, and her beautiful, velvety olive complexion was glowing with pleasure. Her magnificent hazel eyes gleamed with the happiness of seeing the only man that she had ever loved.

She was dressed in a white mini skirt, white tee shirt, and was wearing white flat shoes. White seemed to be the preferred color of this odd, yet-to-be-defined place.

He quickly arose from his seat on the boulder and grasped her to him so tightly that he thought that he might be hurting her, feeling the old rush of pleasure of her self against him. He kissed her frantically, over and over, and again smelled the familiar faint perfume of her body.

He said, "Oh my God, honey, how I've missed you. I never knew for certain that I would ever see you again. You look absolutely wonderful, just as beautiful as you did on the first day that I fell so madly in love with you. How have you been? Now that we're together again, nothing will ever separate us from each other again."

She replied, "I've kept track of you since we parted. After I passed over, I lingered with you as long as I was able, trying store up seeing you until we met again here. Finally, I had to leave you behind, and I've waited for you ever since.

"I felt your pain of my leaving you constantly, and there were times when I hoped that you would find someone to comfort you. Then I would selfishly hope that you would keep your memories of me alive, because even now, I love you with all my soul."

They both sat down on the boulder, holding each other happily, and for a few moments, not saying anything, enjoying this moment of reunification.

Finally, Alex said, "This is absolutely the best and most wonderful surprise that I have ever experienced. There is just one more small thing that would complete my total happiness. If only I could see Bear again."

Lila giggled in the old familiar way that Alex had missed so much. "Sweetheart, there's someone here that is impatiently waiting to also welcome you."

Alex heard a series of barks and looked down to see his old friend Bear, with his rear end completely restored, prancing eagerly around his legs.

He stooped down to pet him, and his face was immediately covered with wet kisses and whines of joy from Bear at being reunited with his best human once again. When he stood up, Bear made wild leaps, trying to keep on kissing Alex.

Alex sat down on the boulder again and put his arm around her shoulders. Bear flopped down in front of them in his old familiar pose of his head between his front paws.

Lila then said, "He kept me company all of the time that I was waiting for you, and he kept me from being utterly lonely for you."

All three of them sat there quietly for a few moments. Finally, Alex asked, "Honey, is this heaven?"

She replied, "It's been called many things over the short span of man's total existence. It's been called heaven, Valhalla, Paradise, Eden, Olympus, the hereafter, and many other names down through the centuries. It's all of those, plus more. It's a place that has no limits. It stretches through infinity, and its beauty is endless. Each new part that you discover seems more magnificent than the one that you had previously visited.

"Although there are many billions of us here, we only see and relate to those who we knew and loved on the other side. We see them as we were used to seeing them, at their best when we knew them. I see you as the handsome man that I fell head over heels in love with, and you see me as I was before I became ill. We will both see Aunt Ida as the feisty old spinster that we knew and loved, but to her Charlie, with whom she now united, she looks like the young beautiful girl that he left behind when he went off to fight a war. It's a place of great miracles. If you wish for something, it is instantly made available to you.

"There are a great number of animals here also, because animals also have souls. The animals that were slaughtered for food now graze contentedly on the tenderest new grass that is never ending. The hunters are now stripped of their need to hunt, and now walk among their former prey and play with them like the youngsters of their breed. Pets wait for their best friends and romp with each other while they wait.

"It's place of great contentment, also, and although certain of us are eligible to be born again into the mortal world, few of us ever do seek that, because almost everybody is waiting for someone special, and doesn't want to miss them when they do finally arrive here."

Alex, now completely comfortable being re-united with his Lila and Bear, asked, "Honey, is there any sort of social order here?"

Lila replied, "There are five levels here, and four of them are uniquely beautiful. The first level is known as the Level of the Blessed. I've never seen it, but I am told that its beauty is positively breathtaking. That's where The Godhead resides, along with all those who are related to him. He's been known by many names since he created the universe—God, Jehovah, Yahweh, Allah, and many others, and as the father and supreme being ever since the beginning of time. He is the creator of all things and the focal point where all things come together.

"The second level is known as the Level of the Chosen. That is where the individuals that we knew as saints reside. It is also where the martyrs or people who have died while performing his good works are located. It is also supposed to be an exquisitely beautiful area as well.

"We're on the third level. It is known as the Level of the Accepted. This, apparently, is the most populous level of all. It is a place of great contentment. It is populated with decent, ordinary people who have accepted some form of theology, not necessarily interrelated or mainstream, but one that they found to be comfortable. For the most part these are individuals who were law-abiding, decent souls who lived according to the tenets of the theologies that they accepted, raised their families and believed in some sort of religion. The previously wealthy individuals here are those who acquired their wealth legitimately, shared some of it with others as was needed, and who also accepted a form of religion. They were known as philanthropists.

"The fourth level is known as the Level of the Pending. It is populated by individuals who passed over with some small forgivable stain still on them. In some theologies, this is called purgatory. After a period of cleansing, those individuals become eligible to reside on this level. They are eligible to be able to return to the other side to accelerate their cleansing process, and some do return to take advantage of a second chance for acceptance. Those individuals have committed minor wrongs, such as believing themselves superior because of wealth, and were not forgiven at the time they passed.

"The fifth level is the most horrible place in the entire cosmos. It is known as the Level of the Damned. That is where the dictators who ruled areas of the other side by ruthless force and murder reside. Also there are the serial murderers, and those individuals who have committed vile and horrible crimes in their lifetimes. Those individuals relegated there walk through the tunnel for centuries and even longer trying to find an exit. When they do discover one and step out of the tunnel, they are subjected to the same crimes that they committed against others, over and over, for all eternity. At some point in your early orientation, you will be forced to look at those punishments, and you will never forget the horror that you will see. You will recognize many who are listed in history books."

She continued, "Your mother and father are here, and I've met them. I really like them. My mother and father are also here, and I've told them all about you, and what a wonderful man and fine husband that you are. They're waiting to meet you and welcome you as a son. Aunt Ida has gathered all our friends and relatives for a welcome home party, so come along, sweetheart, and let's get you checked in and join the others."

Alex asked, "Just one more question, honey, do they have sex here?"

Her laughter tinkled musically across the garden and she said, "I really don't know honey. I've never wanted to try it with anyone but you. I suspect that they do, because I've seen couples who were married for a long time act as newlyweds after their first time of being alone together. We can find out together when were alone. I imagine that you want to find out as well, after such a long time."

Alex laughed and replied, "Sweetheart, you still have the best-looking rear end in the universe."

So with Lila's arm around his waist in the old comfortable way, and with Alex's arm around her shoulders, and with the fully restored Bear leading the way, lifting his leg to leave his calling card for the legions of celestial dogs that would follow (it has said that all dogs go to heaven), they happily strolled down the path toward the brilliant light in the near distance, the three of them united joyously forever.

AUTHOR'S NOTE

The written part of the gentle love story about Lila, Alex and Bear, as told to me by Joe Mooney and Reverend Busch, is winding down. Their undying love for each other, however, is just beginning. If you were a member of the little frame church while they attended, and can recognize their voices, you might listen some Sunday and faintly detect them in song, as they sing the old familiar hymns that they loved so well. Afterwards, if you have the ability, you might see them with Lila's arm around Alex's waist, standing and smiling as their friends chat in the long-accepted custom of that church. Bear is always with them, lying in front of them with his head between his front paws. That is, unless they're all off somewhere exploring some new and more beautiful part of their eternal abode. Oh, by the way, they do have sex there, and without the necessity of birth control measures. Why do you think they call it Paradise?

Printed in the United States
28495LVS00004B/334